The lady's maid meets her match..

Wenna Chenoweth's future is secure, until dashing Devon Courtney's illicit flirtation gets her dismissed from her job as a lady's maid. With nowhere to turn, Wenna is forced to accept Devon's bold proposal: To be his bride. To enter society on the handsome aristocrat's arm. To give him the heir he requires. It's a foolproof plan. Except Wenna finds herself falling hard for a man who can never love her for who she is....

Wenna is passionate, mysterious, and ill-suited to the idle life of a society wife. She's also exactly the kind of woman who could endanger Devon's hopes to build his own future far from his family's influence. For the spirited beauty has embarked on an unthinkable plan of her own—one that could lead him to surrender his resolve, and sacrifice everything he believes he holds dear....

Yet amid the wondrous landscape of colonial South Australia, anything is possible. Perhaps even love between two people the boundaries of society would keep apart....

Books by Virginia Taylor

South Landers Series
Starling
Ella
Charlotte
Wenna

Published by Kensington Publishing Corporation

Wenna

A South Landers Novel

Virginia Taylor

LYRICAL PRESS
Kensington Publishing Corp.
www.kensingtonbooks.com

Lyrical Press books are published by
Kensington Publishing Corp. 119 West 40th Street New York, NY 10018

All Kensington titles, imprints, and distributed lines are available at special quantity discounts for bulk purchases for sales promotion, premiums, fund-raising, and educational or institutional use.

Special book excerpts or customized printings can also be created to fit specific needs. For details, write or phone the office of the Kensington Special Sales Manager:
Kensington Publishing Corp.
119 West 40th Street
New York, NY 10018
Attn. Special Sales Department. Phone: 1-800-221-2647.

Kensington and the K logo Reg. U.S. Pat. & TM Off.
Lyrical Press and the L logo are trademarks of Kensington Publishing Corp.

First Electronic Edition: January 2017
eISBN-13: 978-1-5161-0010-1
eISBN-10: 1-5161-0010-7

First Print Edition: January 2017
ISBN-13: 978-1-61650-928-6
ISBN-10: 1-61650-928-7

Printed in the United States of America

Author's Foreword

Years ago when I was a newbie writer, via online groups I met a best selling romance writer named Deborah Smith. Deborah is a woman with a wild sense of humor and a personality larger than life. This incredibly talented woman helped all us newbies with our queries about writing. Not only did she reveal 'the secret' of writing a best seller that every newbie writer thinks exists, but she did one thing for me that still puts a lump in my throat. I told her I had never read a book she had written. We didn't have any in the book shops in Australia. We also didn't have Amazon in those days. Not long after that, a huge box of books arrived for me, all signed by her. She had even found books that were out of publication and bought them to send to me. I was then and still am stunned by her generosity.

So, thank you Deborah Smith for being Deborah Smith.

Chapter 1

South Australia, January, 1865

A warm, yeasty aroma wafted from the bread resting on the kitchen window ledge, making this the only compensation for being in the hottest room of the house. Garbed in the cook's second-best calico apron, Wenna Chenoweth sliced knobs of butter into a big white mixing bowl. Although a lady's maid wouldn't normally help the other servants, Wenna's employers kept their country house half-staffed during the summer sojourn into the Adelaide hills, and with a houseguest to cater for as well, Wenna had offered to make an almond cake.

Elsie, the scullery maid, glanced up shyly as she heaved a bag of sugar onto the table beside Wenna. "You've seen Miss Patricia's beau, Miss Chenoweth. What does he look like?"

Wenna used a cup to scoop and pour the sugar onto the butter. "I've only seen him from a distance, mind, but my impression of him is that he is very handsome. He dresses well."

"Rich, too, I suppose?" The trim gray-haired cook, Mrs. Green, dumped a load of washed vegetables onto the table.

Wenna considered her answer while she whipped her mixture of sugar and butter with a long wooden spoon. "Would that matter to the Brooks? What they want for Miss Patricia is *class,* and he is connected to our former governor, which makes him an English gentleman, or so Mrs. Brook said. I expect her father's money would be his lure."

"You're a one, you are." Mrs. Green laughed. Her gnarled fingers efficiently peeled the potato in an endless, almost transparent, length.

"You don't want Miss Patricia to hear you talking like that, not when she's already got it in for you."

"She thinks finding fault is indispensable to a lady, but a real lady treats her servants with respect." Or so Wenna's mother had said, and she had been employed as the personal maid to a countess back in the old country, Cornwall, that she had taught Wenna to call home.

"I don't know why she treats you like dirt under her heel. You've gotta be one of the hardest workers I've met. Not too many lady's maids would take on all the extras you do."

"It's the extras that make my job interesting." The extras made Wenna's job bearable. She had risen to the top of her profession because she could read, match hairstyles to hats, gowns to jewelry, cook, run a household, and shut her mouth when need be. Her parents had never expected her to end up in service, but her parents had also not expected to die young.

"I s'pose you're right. Doesn't do a body no good to be too specialized, not if a body is planning to marry one day." The cook winked at her.

"When I find the right man, Mrs. Green." Wenna cracked two eggs into her bowl.

The cook stared at her, her bright brown eyes twinkling with humor. "Shouldn't be too hard. Just look around you. There's more men than women in this colony, and any man would snap up a smart woman like you."

Wenna smiled, hoping she looked flattered, but only in her dreams would a woman with skin that blotched like a bullfrog's in the sun, and shocking, bright red, frizzy hair attract the sort of man she would accept—a man with brains and ability, one who would work alongside her to better himself.

Light momentarily flooded the room as the back door opened. "Miss Chenoweth?" One of the men hired locally to help in the garden stood staring hopefully at Wenna. "Mrs. Brook sent me for you. Something about Miss Patricia's hat."

"What about her hat?" Wenna beat her egg-and-butter mixture into a frenzy while she frowned at the man.

"Dunno. S'pose she wants you to fix it."

She glanced at the almonds and flour on the table. "I wonder if she would rather have a readjustment to a hat, or cake for afternoon tea?"

The man laughed. "Reckon she'll get both."

"For the price of one." Sighing, Wenna wiped her hands and removed her apron. "I won't be long," she told the cook with a helpless shrug. "I'll be back in time to finish the cake, clean the house, sew a new gown, and repair the roof." She checked that she had the comb and the sewing kit in the little leather pouch she kept buckled around her waist, never knowing when she might be called.

"Likely you could do just that."

Wenna left the cook laughing, which pleased her. If she could learn to relax more often, people would grow to like her. Not too many in the household did because she was "uppity."

Her father had been a mine manager in Cornwall when he had married her mother, an educated lady's maid. He'd always said Wenna was just like her mother. He'd meant "ambitious" like her mother. In looks, Wenna didn't compare.

Her beautiful Mumma had convinced Da they would be better off in the south land, Terra Australis, where thick copper lodes had been discovered. "A better life to bring up our children," she'd said, but she'd only produced one girl, much to Da's disappointment. Nevertheless, he had insisted Wenna have the education he would have provided a full house of sons.

In this new land, each man was as good as his work, and Wenna's work was superb. She'd made each of her mistresses into the stepping-stones of her ambition. Now twenty-six years old, and at the peak of her profession, she could only better herself by working for herself, which she planned to do as soon as she found a few more potential clients. She had an idea that might make her enough money to achieve her aim, which was to go back to Cornwall wealthy enough to be of use to her elderly grandparents.

She followed the gardener through the sun-dappled orchard to the scythed open grassland behind, where gentlemen in white stood dotted in various positions while playing their cricket match. The beautifully clad ladies sat in grouped chairs along the sidelines, guarding picnic baskets and stone bottles of ginger beer. In the paddocks beyond, tall gums stirred lazily in the heat.

The hollow knock of the ball sounded as the fair gentleman, the house-guest meant for Miss Patricia, swung his bat high. He ran, and even the leg pads he wore couldn't make him look clumsy. His effortless strides took him to the other wicket and back again before the ball was returned to the bowler by another gentleman. Wenna would have liked to stay and watch, but Miss Patricia was making hastening movements with her arm.

"My hat was dislodged, and now my hair is a mess," she said as Wenna reached her side. But for her pouting discontented mouth, she would have been very pretty, endowed as she was with thick brown hair and large brown eyes. "Don't dawdle. You've wasted enough time."

"Don't be ungracious, darling," Mrs. Brook, Wenna's mistress, said to her daughter. "It's unbecoming."

Since birth, Miss Patricia had been indulged with every luxury, her father having made his fortune in the colony's first building boom. With a flick of her head, she ignored her mother and dragged Wenna by the arm to a chair at the end of the row.

"Would you like me to fix your hat back on your head, or fix your hair?"

"Both, you stupid creature."

Miss Daphne Grace, a pretty young lady who invariably dressed in too many frills and flounces, turned, apparently surprised by Miss Patricia's words. Miss Patricia batted her lashes, and Miss Grace redirected her attention to her friend, an understated, dark-haired beauty. Most of the young ladies in the colony knew each other and attended the same functions. Wenna doubted that any would recall who she was, but she always remembered the names of the well-connected. In her profession, politeness and a scrupulous reputation were essential.

"Carefully, Chenoweth. Stand in front of me. I don't want the gentlemen to see my hair on end."

Dutifully, Wenna moved in front. While on holidays in the country, she "did for" the daughter as well as the mother. "I brought my comb. I'll have this fixed in no time." She removed the hastily placed hatpins from Miss Patricia's smart blue hat and put the creation on the lady's lap.

Miss Patricia tapped her foot while Wenna combed sections of the lady's enviable hair, re-pinning the loose curls. Satisfied, she stood back and placed the young lady's hat precisely. "Now you look perfect again," she said with a pleasant nod.

"You're so slow today." Miss Patricia checked her hair with her hand. "I'm sure you dawdle around just to annoy me. I hope you didn't do anything too fussy. My hair is my crowning glory."

"You're very lucky, Miss Patricia. If I could do my own as simply, I would be the happiest woman in the colony."

Miss Patricia cast disdainful eyes over Wenna's lace cap, which hid most of her tightly braided, densely packed hair. "The way you wear yours completely out of sight is suited to your position. It doesn't do for the maid to imitate the mistress."

Wenna nodded, hoping the fair young giant didn't need Miss Patricia's money. She was, without a doubt, a very unpleasant young woman.

"If you've finished with my hair, check the fall of my gown, would you?" Miss Patricia said in her loud, over-privileged voice. She stood.

With a critical eye, Wenna rearranged the loops at the back of the pink crinoline so that when Miss Patricia sat, the skirts would fan around her.

"You've done well, Chenoweth. You may go."

Wenna inclined her head and turned, only to be stopped by Mrs. Brook at the other end of the row of chairs.

"Thank you," her elegant mistress said in a low voice. Under Wenna's tutelage, Mrs. Brook had become one of the most stylish ladies in the colony. "Daphne Grace tried to help her, but she couldn't do a thing with her hair, and then Patricia starting making such a fuss that I thought she might not be showing herself to her best advantage. You have an efficient way, Chenoweth, of smoothing out situations."

Wenna smiled. "Or at least smoothing out hair. I'm glad I could help."

Unfortunately, her mistress' gratitude didn't abate Wenna's irritation about being told that she was only a maid, when she was a *lady's* maid, and her position didn't call for her to hide her ugly hair. If she chose, she could leave off her silly frill of a cap. She glanced one last time at the fair cricketer who was standing with his bat waiting for the bowler to run up, knowing handsome young gentlemen would never be part of her world. Her cake awaited.

Already pulling off her cap, which she decided she would never wear again, she reached the slatted gate of the orchard. With her tight arrangement now disturbed, some of her pins had loosened, and the long plait of her hair unfurled down her back. Using her fingers as a comb, she loosened the braiding and shook out the frizz of her hair in defiance. Behind, she heard the shout of male voices yelling, "Out, out," and she glanced back.

The young gentleman walked to the closest wicket, trailing his bat along the grass, a big smile on his handsome face. "Thank you, Worthing," he called as he walked. "I'll bowl *you* out when your turn comes."

The auburn-haired man holding the ball laughed. The guest passed his bat to another man, fixed his gaze on Wenna, and starting walking in her direction. She stood transfixed, not knowing what he might want of her. Her first thought was to pretend she hadn't noticed and go on her way, but he was staring straight at her and coming closer with each step.

"Do you need me for anything, sir?" she asked before he got too close. His cricket whites and light hair contrasted with his golden tan.

"I'm parched. Could you lead me to a gallon of cool water?"

The color of his hair reminded her of Da's, and her heart constricted. Her father, the big, blond Cornishman, had been crushed during a mine cave-in. Always frail, her mother had died soon after, leaving Wenna to fend for herself from the age of thirteen. But fend she had. In the thirteen years since, Wenna had worked her way from being a kitchen helper in the mining town of Clare, to being a lady's maid in a wealthy urban household.

In two paces, he stood beside her. She glanced up at him, watching his gaze travel over the untamed outlines of her hair. His expression said that he, unlike everyone else, didn't find a frizzed mass of bright red appalling. He lifted a hand, wound a spiral around one finger, and smiled down at her.

She stepped back, jerking her head away, her cheeks heating. He wasn't her father, but a stranger taking liberties, as gentlemen liked to do, though not usually with prickly Wenna. "Water. Yes. In the kitchen."

A flock of lorikeets swooped into the orchard, their bright red-and-green plumage blending into the leaves, which trembled as they searched for ripening pears.

"Lead on."

Wenna stiffened her spine. The man was a golden god with a straight nose and a perfectly chiseled jaw, and he strolled beside her as if it were the most natural thing in the world for a handsome young gentleman to accompany a spinsterish tongue-tied maid through an orchard.

"I'm Devon Courtney," he said in a cultured voice, staring at her with a question in his eyes. He had the thickest brown eyelashes she'd ever seen, and stark clear blue eyes. His hair shone dappled white in the orchard.

Her pulse quickened, and she lost the thread of her voice. "I'm Mrs. Brook's maid."

"Is that Cornwall I hear in your accent?"

"Is it? I don't know."

"It sounds like Cornwall." He rolled his words with a lilt like Da's. "Do you have a name? I can't call you 'maid.'"

"Wenna." She should have said "Miss Chenoweth." She should have kept her hair confined.

"Wenna. Definitely Cornwall."

"My parents came from Cornwall. I might have picked up their speech."

"No doubt about it, lass." He stood, blocking her way, glancing from her hair to her mouth. If he wasn't trying a line with her, she didn't know the ways of the gentry.

Her insides tickled in reaction to his scrutiny. No young man before had shown such blatant interest, but no sensible maid would be foolish enough to be flattered by his attention. His sort would see a working-class woman as a mere diversion, a quick tumble to be forgotten in a second. "You said you wanted water."

"Indeed, I do need cooling off," he said with a mischievous smile as he stepped aside.

She slowly let out her breath and marched on, not about to let him see her confused reaction.

He followed her into the kitchen, compounding her acute embarrassment. "This is Mr. Courtney," she said to the cook, breaking the thick silence of the servants in the room. "He wants a cool drink of water."

"If it's not too much trouble." He smiled at Mrs. Green. "If it is, just direct me to the pump, for I'm sure I need to wet my head as well to completely cool down."

Mrs. Green finally closed her jaw. "Just out from the old country, are you, sir? Takes some time to get used to the heat."

He laughed. "I'm not a very new chum. I've been here two years now. You must take into account I've been playing a very strenuous game of cricket and make allowances for that." He flashed a wide complicit smile at Wenna.

She didn't know if he was a natural-born flirt, or if he was looking for an easy conquest. However, he had charmed Mrs. Green and impressed the scullery maid, and his resemblance to Wenna's father had almost torn her heart from her chest. If he meant to charm her, too, he would have quite a road to go, making a wasted trip, for he would not take a lady's maid in marriage. Anything else she would not consider.

She crossed her arms while she watched him gulp down a pint of water, wipe his sleeve across his mouth, and smile at a room full of new admirers. He nodded at her, then left through the back door.

"You're right. Miss Patricia will be lucky to get that one," Mrs. Green said after the door had closed. "My, did you see those shoulders?" She glanced at Wenna.

"He talked, Mrs. Green. I barely glanced at him." Wenna realized she'd been holding her breath. Yes, she had seen those shoulders and she had seen those eyes. She could allow herself a moment of envy of Miss Patricia, whose papa could buy her almost any husband she wanted.

Wenna squared her shoulders and took up her basin and wooden spoon. She couldn't buy a husband, but she wouldn't want one she could buy. She made cakes as well as she styled hair. Taking into account her spotless reputation, she would always have well-paid employment. She didn't need a husband. She could support herself.

* * * *

Devon Courtney duly took his opportunity to bowl out all his friends, some of whom had lost their competitive edge. Devon hadn't lost his yet, nor the interest of parents with daughters. He'd accepted Waldo Brook's invitation to the country cricket match and the weekend stay, although aware that Waldo had an eye to marrying off his only child. The fortune that came with Patricia Brook would endear her to Devon's father, but she was a vain nineteen-year-old who didn't have a word to say that wasn't about her.

At this stage of his life, Devon wanted little more from a woman than an enthusiastic tumble. He should have politely fobbed off the invitation, but his friend Anthony Hawthorn had recently married and decided to entertain his new bride elsewhere, which left Devon's accommodation open to change. Keen on the game of cricket and, unlike the others, happy to make up the numbers on either team, Devon therefore accepted the first invitation he received—that of Waldo Brook.

He dropped his dinner suit onto a bed dressed like a maiden aunt's long-collected trousseau and began removing his sweaty cricket shirt. The moment he'd seen the redheaded maid's bright, unconfined hair, he'd wanted to snatch her up and race her back to town, assuming she'd be as bold as she looked. In bed she would be a treat—uncontrolled, laughing, biting, scratching, and giving him kiss for kiss. Thinking about her made him hard. He imagined her hair spread across his pillow, her eyes shining with love, and her mouth soft with wanting, his Jenny—no, not Jenny. "Wenna," she had said.

For a moment, he smiled regretfully. The maid was a guarded, graceful woman who no doubt had rebuffed hopeful advances many times. The juiciest fruit always seemed to be the most difficult to reach. Tomorrow he would be back in Adelaide and too busy to think about tupping anyone.

Before the water in his rose-painted bowl cooled, he washed and changed. An evening of dancing was planned by the Graces, an eminent colonial family, in their large country retreat a mile or two away. The Brooks planned to attend. Devon, who had met Hubert Grace at Cambridge a few years back, would go, too. He shrugged into his evening jacket, wondering why he wouldn't want Patricia in his bed even for a large fortune, but he would take the redhead in a shot. He didn't know the woman, who seemed wary, if not tense. In that way, she was nothing like the woman she resembled: laughing, joyous Jenny, the woman who had caused him to be banished here to the end of the earth.

He wanted to live at the end of the earth for the rest of his days. He loved this land. He loved the opportunities. From the moment he'd stepped onto the sunlit sands of this vast colony, he'd been accepted on merit and now, so far away from home, he relished being his own man. He completed the bow of his tie, stepped out of his room and, "Oof!"

A body smacked into his, and a soft fabric hid his view. He pushed the material aside and stared at Wenna, the delectable lady's maid who had occupied his thoughts for the last few minutes. The redhead dropped her hold on the dark blue satin-and-lace gown she'd been carrying, leaving the fabric hanging from his shoulder and covering past his knees.

He laughed. "It's an interesting idea, but I don't normally wear a gown in the evening."

She stared, her face tensing with embarrassment. "I was in a hurry to Mrs. Brook's room, and I didn't want the hem of her gown to trail on the floor."

"Of course not," he said. He tried to sound sympathetic, but considering what he'd been thinking, he could only see providence in their collision. "Does the color suit me?"

"It looks better on Mrs. Brook," she said, her chin raised. "With respect." Evading his gaze, she scooped one hand around the bodice of the gown at his chest height and the other under the fullness of the skirts. The top of the gown dropped onto her arm, but the bottom didn't move. She tugged.

He might have not have noticed the lace had caught beneath the placket of his fly buttons had she not given an almighty jerk, which almost pulled him forward. Strangely, his voice came out husky. "You're gripping my fly. I don't mind, of course, but if you leave your fingers there, I'm liable to think far too kindly of you."

She reared back, only to be stopped by the skirts again. "Can you—oh dear Lord—untangle the lace from yourself?"

He glanced down, trying not to laugh again. "I'll likely need to unbutton my trousers."

"Better you than me," she said, staring at his fly with exasperation.

"I don't want to damage the gown. You'll be quicker."

"Stand still." She worked the fingers of one hand into the material, apparently trying to feel her way to the right button.

"That's good," he said encouragingly. "A little lower."

She lifted her head. "I'm not doing this for your amusement."

"I'm not as amused as I was. Now I'm downright interested, which you will feel if you keep groping blindly in that area. You can either get down on your knees to see what you are doing, which will maintain my interest, or we can go into my bedroom, where I can fiddle around with my trousers without an audience."

"Well, there's a choice," she said, sounding frazzled.

Her fingers moved faster, his cock twitched for attention, and suddenly the material came free.

"Chenoweth!" He turned his head and saw Patricia standing at the end of the passage, her eyes narrowed and her mouth tight.

From where she stood, she would see him and Wenna standing close enough to kiss. If he turned, she would see his blatantly incriminating thoughts—so he stood, exactly where he was, his gaze on Wenna's.

"Serves you right," she mumbled under her breath.

"Your fault," he muttered back. "Distract her."

"You distract her."

"Good evening, Patricia. I expect Wenna will be with you soon. I think she might be waiting for the proposal I may be forced to give now we've been caught in the act together."

Wenna's green eyes iced with fury. She flapped the skirts of the gown like a flag of surrender. "Mrs. Brook's gown. Mr. Courtney got caught in it. No harm done."

She moved out from behind him and walked on.

He subsided, discreetly rearranged himself beneath his trousers, and turned.

Hands on her hips, Patricia watched Wenna enter the first bedroom on the right, Mrs. Brook's room. "I hope she wasn't bothering you," she said as she walked toward him.

"Not at all," he said, though Wenna certainly did bother him. As a servant, she was untouchable, of course, and yet he wanted to do more than touch her. In his mind, he'd had her twice, but in the real world he would likely never have her.

"Poor thing. I ought to feel sorry for her." Patricia exaggerated a shudder. "Old and ugly, and with that frightful red hair. I suppose that's why she's so desperate for attention. I don't know why Mama keeps her on, truly. She sets such a bad example to the younger maids."

He hid his surprise. Old and ugly? Wenna was slender, graceful, and unafraid, her most attractive trait after her glorious red hair. "I expect your mama keeps her on because she is highly efficient."

"She didn't look particularly efficient while she was detaining you in the passage. She was wasting time."

He considered Patricia's tight-lipped annoyance and decided he'd said enough. Any more, and Wenna might suffer from the humorless young lady's tongue.

Later that evening, he scrupulously performed his duty dance with Patricia Brook and spent the rest of his time in the Graces' sprawling comfortable house with his cronies. Finding common ground with a rich, spoilt nineteen-year-old didn't appeal to him as much as discussing the day's cricket match, or the various political shenanigans. Before he left, he arranged to borrow a gig from James, Anthony Hawthorn's younger brother, for an early departure in the morning.

In the carriage on the way back to the Brooks' country residence, he sighed with relief. He didn't know why he had agreed to stay with the couple. He couldn't possibly offer for Patricia Brook. No amount of money would make the daughter of a builder acceptable to his family.

Chapter 2

Wenna awoke early the next morning, having slept badly. She didn't trust Miss Patricia to keep her mouth closed about Mr. Courtney's appalling comment the night before. Clearly, the young lady hadn't found time to complain about Wenna to Mrs. Brook before the family left for the evening's entertainment. However, with the wariness of the once-bitten, Wenna arose earlier than usual.

Too nervous to eat her own breakfast, she waited until Mr. Brook appeared for his in the dining room. With some trepidation, she scooted upstairs and knocked on Mrs. Brook's door. Normally her mistress ate her morning bread and butter in bed.

Asked to enter, she walked into a modest-sized bedroom, expensively wallpapered with pink blossoms on a white background. The aquamarine bedcover had been kicked to the foot of the bed, exposing the snowy white linen sheets and Mr. Brook's crumpled nightshirt. Mrs. Brook, encased in a pink velvet robe, sat on the dressing stool, staring at her smooth face in the dressing table mirror. Most of the furniture in the room, shunted off from the city house when the newer furniture had arrived from England, was roughly carved out of the inferior local pine, or so Mrs. Brook said. Wenna loved the rich red sheen.

"Good morning, Mrs. Brook."

Mrs. Brook heaved a sigh and frowned at Wenna. "I have a megrim. Don't say a word. Just help me with my gown. The yellow cotton, I think."

Her breath heavy, Wenna took the bodice and the skirts from the chest. Usually, she had quite a conversation with Mrs. Brook in the morning, and if Miss Patricia had complained about her, she would like a chance to explain. Nevertheless, she did as told and dressed her mistress, who then sat in front of her mirror waiting for her long brown hair to be brushed. This gave Wenna an opportunity to meet Mrs. Brook's gaze in the mirror, but Mrs. Brook avoided this by staring at her fingernails.

"Permission to speak?"

"When you've finished my hair."

Wenna scooped Mrs. Brook's hair to the back of her head and tied a braid of cotton around the mass at the nape. Next, she clipped one long hair pad from ear to ear, making the base for the smooth roll she pinned at the nape of Mrs. Brook's neck. When done, she said, "I had a small problem with your guest last night."

"Why didn't you tell me last night?" Mrs. Brook massaged her forehead.

"Because I thought Miss Patricia would."

"She didn't. She told her father, who then told me." Mrs. Brook's gaze finally met Wenna's in the mirror. "I'm sure you didn't have your hand in his trousers, Chenoweth, because you are not a silly woman. You wouldn't do that in the hallway. However, the description Patricia gave her father sounded as if you did."

Wenna swallowed, utterly aghast. "My hand in his—trousers? What sort of mind would invent such a wicked thing to say?"

"I hope you're not criticizing my daughter," Mrs. Brook said in a severe tone. "Of course she didn't use those words. That was Mr. Brook's interpretation."

Wenna had to force herself to breathe. "I was walking with your blue lace gown, ma'am, the one you wore last night, holding it above my head so the skirts wouldn't drag. Mr. Courtney came out of his room, and I walked into him. The lace got caught on his buttons."

"Buttons?"

"Trouser buttons, ma'am. He wanted me to work the fabric off. He thought it was amusing. If Miss Patricia heard him laughing, that was why. I don't know why he said what he said, but I'm sure he thought that was amusing, too."

Mrs. Brook heaved a sigh. "The thing is that he hasn't made a proposal to Patricia, which doesn't suit her father, who also wants to see you in the drawing room at ten. It's just past ten now."

Wenna *wasn't* a silly woman. She knew she would be dismissed as well as she knew Mrs. Brook had made sure she had her hair done before Wenna went into the sulks. Pressing her lips together, Wenna turned and marched down the hallway to the drawing room at the front of the house.

She rapped smartly on the door.

"Come in," Mr. Brook called. He sat on the piano stool, idly toying with the keys. The room was only slightly larger than the other rooms in the house—six all told, with a hall running down the middle, the kitchen and bathroom on the back. Mr. Brook had plans for a larger extension in a bid to keep up with his neighbors, and had begun with a long room where the servants slept. Since the family had only brought Wenna, Mrs. Green, and two maids, they weren't too cramped.

"You wanted to see me, sir?" She stood just inside the door, her hands clasped together in front of her, trying to ease her shoulders. The room smelled of stale cigar smoke.

"We can't have the maids servicing the guests," Mr. Brook said in a righteous voice. "Especially when they haven't serviced the master." His mouth turned down. But for the amount of food he ate and the port he drank, he could have been a good-looking man, but his belly strained at his waistcoat buttons and his eyes had a puffy rim.

She drew a breath deep enough to expand her chest. "Bearing in the mind the second, you must believe that the first isn't true," she said, clasping her icy cold hands.

"Do you say it isn't true?"

"I do. I'm sure Mr. Courtney would say the same."

"I'm sure he would, too." One half of a cynical smile appeared. He sighed. "However, last night he told my daughter he'd been caught in the act with you."

"He was joking. Ask him."

"I would hardly order a guest into my drawing room to interview him about his dealings with my wife's maid."

"I'll happily fetch him."

"That would give you a chance to get him to confirm your story. And no." He held up one beefy palm. "I won't either fetch him or confront him. Patricia said he kissed her and gave her the idea that he was interested in her. He is leaving this morning. She expected him to stay an extra day and says he won't because you embarrassed him. She wants me to dismiss you. I would be happy to send you off now, but my wife suggests I allow you to remain until we arrive back in town."

"That's very kind of you both," she said, her mouth stretched into a straight line and her face hot with anger. "But I didn't ask to leave your service. You have dismissed me, for no other reason than your daughter wants me gone. I'll leave right now, sir, after you pay me my wages."

He crossed his arms over his belly. "You will leave when I say you will leave."

"I will leave with the money I have earned." Her chin firmed.

"If you walk out now, nothing."

"I don't work for noth..." She stopped speaking when she heard footsteps.

Mr. Courtney ranged beside her. He wore a light suit and tan gloves, and he held a wide brimmed felt hat and a leather valise. "Good morning, Wenna. Do you mind if I have a word with Mr. Brook?"

"Not at all. I was about to go."

"You will not leave, Chenoweth, until I say so," Mr. Brook said tightly. "I'll be but a moment, Courtney."

Mr. Courtney's gaze left Wenna and flitted over to Mr. Brook. "No need to hurry your conversation along for me. I simply wanted to thank you for your generous hospitality. No doubt I'll see you and your family in town."

"No doubt," Mr. Brook said, his tone one decibel above a growl. "Well, please take your redheaded *doxy* with you, or my daughter will have my head."

"He means me. I'm the *doxy*. Do you have transport?" Wenna glanced at Mr. Courtney's face, which she couldn't read. Surprised, was he, or trying not to laugh? Oh, Lord, she wanted to shove him into next year, the blackguard.

"Almost," he said, and as if cued, wheels crunched over gravel outside, and stopped. "I have the loan of James Hawthorn's gig—looks as though he's brought it over himself." He stepped back to squint through the pane of etched glass in the front door.

"Well, make room for me, because it's your fault that I've lost my job."

"My fault?" He glanced back to Mr. Brook.

Wenna didn't care what they said to each other. She was too mad to think. Grabbing at her skirts, she ran up the hallway and through the kitchen to the servants' quarters, where she snatched up her other black gown, her spare collars and cuffs, her underwear, and her nightgown, and roughly shoved them into her bag. She pushed her plain black hat onto her head.

As she ran back through the kitchen, she said to the maid and the cook, "I've been dismissed, and I'm leaving with Mr. Courtney." Deathly silence followed her. She didn't care. No one accused Wenna Chenoweth of luring gentlemen, or called her a *doxy*. She rushed out the front door, terrified that Mr. Courtney would leave without her. The trip back to town on foot was possible and done by the Silesian women of Hahndorf weekly, yoked up like oxen to take their goods to market. But Wenna was an indoor servant and not a leathery country woman.

However, Mr. Courtney stood beside the two-seater gig in the pleasant sunshine, watching young Mr. Hawthorn swing over a paddock fence and disappear into the scrub before turning to her. "Bearing in mind that I'm taking a passenger to Adelaide, James has decided to walk back to his brother's house. It's only a mile or two as the crow flies, and the exercise will do him good."

"I'm *so* glad to hear he won't be too much put out," Wenna said between her teeth. "And this is from a woman who won't get two months' pay, a reference, or another job because young gentlemen *don't* like being put out."

Mr. Courtney took her bag from her. "We'll have time to discuss my failings on the way down to town. Brook told me what happened; I accept that it's my fault, and I can't talk him into taking you back. Therefore, I'll give you a ride into town and see what I can do for you. Please alight and quarrel with me elsewhere." He tossed her bag into the back of the high-sprung gig, which likely cost more than a house. "Do I need to hand you in?"

She took a look at the high step and disdained his help. With a lurch, she heaved herself onto the front seat, wishing he had a carriage with a shady hood. The horses had apparently been expecting to leave, and began to prance. The vehicle lurched and the wheels creaked. Mr. Courtney leaped in front of her, took up the reins and sat, easing off the brake. The gig jerked into movement, beginning the journey Wenna dreaded—the journey to beginning again. She tied on her hat.

"Brook said you're all mine. Apparently, he doesn't like someone else playing with his toys," Mr. Courtney said in a conversational tone. "I decided not to put him straight, and I hope you don't mind, but you didn't lure me on, and I objected to his estimation of my character."

"*Your* character? Do you honestly think I would let a man like him touch me? Oh, he would like to, and he certainly gave me enough hints, but I didn't once let him think I heard him. Not once."

"I'm glad to know that, because I gave you a hint or two, and you didn't let me think you heard me either. If I can't be better than he is, I don't want to be worse in your estimation."

She clutched her bag tightly on her knee, already feeling the sweat collecting under her hat and trickling down behind her ears. "Don't worry about my estimation. I don't like either of you, and I'm going to burn to a cinder in this sun. I don't suppose you have a parasol?" She hoped she sounded more polite than at the end of her tether.

"Feel under the seat. I don't know what James has here, and I rarely use parasols myself, unless wedged under with a pretty flirt."

"You are a man of no discrimination."

"So I've heard. Or, have you met my father?"

"Of course I haven't met your father."

"No. He's never been out of England. We're about to pass the Graces' soon. I'll drop by and ask to borrow a parasol. With four or five women in the house, they're bound to have at least one."

Wenna sat with her lips clamped, annoyed by his confidence. This over-privileged man was never at a loss. He couldn't be embarrassed or made to feel guilty no matter what she said.

Sure enough, he took the gig off the main road and along a shady lane until he reached pair of imposing, rendered gateposts, one marked "The Graces." He drove in and pulled up in front of a single story stone-built house.

Lady Grace, a pretty little woman who had visited Mrs. Brook a number of times with her look-alike daughter, came out of the front door. "A parasol?" she said, after Mr. Courtney made his request. She looked up at Wenna with concern. "Of course you can borrow a parasol. You shouldn't be out in the hot sun. I'll go inside and get the big white one. That ought to reflect the heat best. Haven't we met before?" She waited for Wenna to answer.

"No, ma'am. I'm Mrs. Brook's maid. You might have seen me."

"Of course," Lady Grace said, smiling. "Yesterday. You made Patricia's hair neat again. And now you're off to the city with Mr. Courtney." Apparently, she hoped Wenna would say why, but Wenna simply nodded.

The parasol was found and presented. Mr. Courtney promised to return it to Lady Grace as soon as possible, and he drove off. Wenna shaded her face. "A lady. A real lady."

Mr. Courtney nodded. "In more ways than one. If she put you off, you can bet she would have sent you away with shade and your wages. You're far better off out of the Brooks' service."

"I would have preferred to leave when I was ready, with money and a reference." At the moment, she seemed to have little control over her tongue. She could see her time wasting away while she fought to earn back the money she had lost. "I was a lady's maid for a year before Mrs. Brook offered to double my wage if I came to her. She was a credit to me. Other ladies were beginning to notice I had a way with hair, but I didn't plan to stay with her. No. I was on my way up. Before she employed me,

I could save no more than a few pounds a year. Now, because of you, I'm going to have to start all over again."

"You're a smart woman. You'll get another job."

"Without a reference, I'll be lucky to get a job as a housemaid. Do you think I can say to my next employer that I was Mrs. Brook's personal maid but she sent me off without a penny because a gentleman accosted me? Not a person in the world, looking at me, would believe that."

His brow wrinkled. "I could back up your story." He turned slightly to look at her, and his broad shoulder brushed hers.

Her insides tightened each time he accidentally touched her. "Don't be ridiculous. A word from you, and I'll be seen as the *doxy* the Brooks say I am. In the meantime, I don't have anything but my savings to live on. And I don't want to live on them, which is why I have savings." The gig hit a rock, and the handle of the parasol whacked the side of her head, making her eyes water.

He glanced at her but stayed silent. The track began to wind down the hill, through the spindly scrub. The occasional sheep wandered in and out of the trees. A kangaroo zigzagged ahead, stopped abruptly and stared, scratching under his arm as they drove past.

The sun grew hotter. Wenna's face dripped sweat, her mouth dried, and her arm ached from holding the parasol. The area around looked interesting enough, but she had no tie with this land. In Cornwall, she would find pretty fishing villages and ancient stately houses, beauty made more authentic by the history of the country. Here, no one told exciting tales of smugglers. No one spoke of anything but making money or exploring the harsh empty land.

"What are you saving for?" Mr. Courtney asked eventually.

Jaw tight, she glanced at him. "I made Mumma a promise to take care of her parents. I've been sending money to them for years, but I want to see them."

He raised his eyebrows, staring sideways at her. "Not all families want to be together. I suppose that's very worthy of you, though. Presumably, they still live in Cornwall?"

"They do."

"It's a pretty place," he said with what sounded like reluctance. "Warm, sometimes, but the winters are wild."

"Do you know Cornwall?"

"My family also lives there." He shrugged. "I'm expected back this year. Needless to say, I don't want to return."

"Don't want to return?" She gave a bitter laugh. "That's the way of the gentry, isn't it? My dream is to go to Cornwall, and just a few thoughtless words from you ended that—and you don't want to return."

Angry with him all over again, she stared straight ahead over the gray-blue forested hills to the flat of the settlement, the spreading township of Adelaide. The colony slowly but surely pushed ahead. New roads had been clearly marked, and even at a distance she could see how the place was built in pockets, with large holdings for the rich sitting side by side with smaller allotments built on for those who would provide the household labor.

"I can make up the wages you've lost."

"I won't touch a penny of your money."

"You're being bloody-minded. If you need the money, I will give it to you. How much are you owed?"

"Two pounds." Her lost wages almost equaled a man's pay, taking into consideration the free board. She elevated her chin, sneaking a glance at him.

"And I'll take you to the labor exchange."

She flicked a dusty leaf from her black gown. "If you don't mind, I would rather you took me to the Brooks' town house so that I can collect all my belongings."

"I'll do that, too." Although he looked unconcerned, his mouth curved into a rueful smile. Likely he'd never had a worry in his life. Now that she'd been forced into proximity with him, she was all too aware of his maleness. She glanced at his hard muscled thighs and wished she hadn't. She wanted to see him as an irresponsible dilettante rather than an attractive male.

They reached the tollgate at bottom of the hill, and he stopped to water the horses. "Do you want to stretch your legs?" He tied the reins to the brake and stepped down, holding out one large gloved hand to her.

Touching his hand was too intimate; the firm grip, the steady balance as she climbed down from the gig. All this care from the man whose thoughtless words had lost her a stable job and a solid wage. She wobbled slightly when her feet touched the ground. "I didn't realize how cramped I was."

"How tense you were. Walk around and ease your shoulders. The trip is quite safe now, and the roads are better down here. I'll let the horses rest for a while before we go across town to the Brooks' place." He led the horses to the trough by the guardhouse and took a drink from under the pump.

She followed, mainly to get out of the way of a mob of sheep. The shepherd lifted his hat to her and paid the toll, while his dog kept the group in a huddle. Soon enough, the doomed beasts continued down Glen Osmond Road, on the way to the market on East Terrace.

After turning right at the tollgate and clipping along the ring road to Walkerville, the rest of the journey passed quickly enough. Sweaty and travel-stained, Wenna collected her poise and walked through the back door of the Brooks' double-storied town residence. A group of servants sat around the big kitchen table, drinking lemonade and eating frosted wedges of cake. In a trice, shame-faced, each rose to his or her feet.

Wenna smiled. "Even Mrs. Green wouldn't fault you for taking a break while the master and mistress are away. Sit, please. I'm here to collect my things. I'm no longer employed by Mrs. Brook."

"What happened?" The outdoors man sounded worried. He'd always been very respectful of her.

"Miss Patricia believed her swain was more interested in me." She stood, earning the hurtful reaction she expected—laughter. "And so I'm running off with him."

"You're a one," said the youngest housemaid, wiping away tears of mirth. "What really happened?"

"While I'm packing my belongings, glance discreetly out of the front window and see the man sitting on the gig. *He* was Miss Patricia's swain." And because she hadn't spoken an untrue word, chin up, she left for the servants' quarters behind the house and collected her belongings.

She might have been dismissed, but she certainly hadn't lost face.

Chapter 3

Devon, or Dev as he was starting to think of himself in this less formal country, hoped he wouldn't have to keep the horses standing too long in the heat. Most of the shady native trees had been removed from North Adelaide, and the new plantings of the more popular oaks and elms from the old country hadn't yet grown tall enough to provide good cover. Fortunately, after no more than ten minutes, Wenna walked back through the squeaky side gate of the two-story, bluestone mansion, holding three bulky cloth-tied bundles. She wore a plain navy blue cotton gown with a flat straw hat. The blue of her gown and the white of her skin contrasted with the bright red hair she wore closely knotted at her neck.

He leaped down from the gig to take up her bundles, which—should they contain all her worldly goods—showed she had few. "Good Lord. Not only are you the fastest packer on both sides of the ocean, you've had time to change and freshen yourself. I hope my travel dustiness doesn't put you to shame."

She glanced at him in disbelief. "I'm applying for jobs. Of course I've freshened up. And it doesn't matter how *you* look."

He blinked. "You're right." Nevertheless, he'd been properly put in his box yet again by this forthright female.

She made him want to laugh. Shorter by half a head, slender, jobless, and, according to her, penniless, she would try to punish him for his transgression until her last breath, if she could.

"We can pretend I'm your driver. I'll only need to hunch over and button my jacket tightly and no one will ever know I'm not."

She aimed her green-gold pitying eyes at him. "Even if you only wore a fig leaf, you would still look like the lord of all you surveyed." Her cheeks turned a hot shade of pink.

"Ah, you noticed my poise." He enjoyed her self-embarrassment, and he imagined her sitting on his lap in the gig with her skirts up around her waist, and her knees under his arms. He groaned and breathed through his reprehensible moment.

Last night he'd dreamed of Jenny again. In his dream, he'd held her, and she'd laughed and kissed him; undressed him; caressed him. She'd been insatiable, and he'd taken her again and again. He'd had to ease himself, half awake, wondering where she was until he remembered.

This redhead was no substitute. Wenna was feisty. If a spirited woman such as she loved him, she wouldn't let herself be torn from him. She wouldn't quietly agree to marry a local farmer. She would fight for him until the bitter end. Or would she simply fight him? Doubtless, he would never find out, for she was just a passing fantasy who would find herself a good job, more than likely without his help. She had competence and confidence written all over her. She was nothing like gentle Jenny.

"Well, dear lady, take your seat and we'll be off."

Wenna swung up into the gig beside him.

When he reached the city, he drove along King William Street at a slow pace. Unlike the other colonies, which had simply grown, Adelaide had been planned. The city streets were wide and set in a grid-like formation as a shelter from the hot north winds. A *bullock dray* passed in the other direction on the way to the port. Whips cracked and men shouted. The carriage in front rumbled to a halt, and he needed to pass carefully. Dust swirled and settled, leaving the taste of grit in his mouth.

The sun sat high in the sky. He couldn't leave James's weary horses standing outside the labor exchange in the searing summer heat. Instead, he pulled up in the center of the road. "I'll leave you here and be back in about an hour."

Wenna narrowed her eyes at him. "Then you'll hand me my things out of the gig."

"You can't wander around with that load. You'd be smothered under the weight."

"Better that than losing the lot."

He lifted his eyebrows. "What use would I have for ladies' clothing?"

She didn't stir. A wagon laden with sawn wood pulled up behind them, and the driver shouted for him to move along.

"I can't afford to trust you," she said, her expression mutinous.

"You can take my fob as surety. It's solid gold."

She stared at him as if he were a lunatic. He worked the fob off the chain, pulled off his carved emerald signet ring, and placed both in her palm.

"That's the greater part of my worldly possessions. I'll be back to claim them in an hour."

Shaking her head, she stepped off the gig and, without a backward glance, headed toward the tall Georgian building clearly marked "Labor Exchange." Business thrived in this colony, and hard workers were as well rewarded as those who had money to buy land. Already the colony exported a wealth of minerals along with the golden wheat.

With an hour to waste, Dev headed down Flinders Street, as requested, to drop off the gig. James Hawthorn owned a carriage-building business, and he'd said one of his staff would deliver the equipage to the grand mansion where he lived with his newly married older brother.

Wenna's belongings caused a slight problem, resolved by the generous offer to have an idling employee of Hawthorn's drive him back to his lodgings with the load. Duly dropped off with Wenna's three cloth bags and his own leather valise, he strolled into his rooms, needing to match her with a change of clothes and a wash.

First, he swigged a pint or two of water. Next, he found himself an orange and a fresh shirt. Energized, he strode back to the Labor Exchange a city block away. When he walked into the cavernous entry hall, he saw Wenna sitting on a long wooden bench, dwarfed by the height of the walls, knees together, hands neatly clasped. She gave him an unreadable glance and stood. Her cheeks looked fever red, but her mouth was etched in gray. She took a step toward him and began a slow crumple. He made a dive forward and grabbed her before she hit the ground.

He stood with his hands under her armpits, looking for a place to put her until she recovered from her swoon. Scooping an arm under her legs, he lifted her back onto the bench. The other occupants stood to give her space to lie down.

"Faint, did she? It's 'ot in 'ere. Wouldn't mind a little faint mesself." A stout middle-aged woman peered out from under a faded blue bonnet. "Someone get water."

Someone did. Wenna's eyelids fluttered as he trickled the liquid onto her lips, and she struggled to sit. Dev kept the cup at her mouth. Water dribbled down her chin and darkened the neck of her gown, but she began to sip. He belatedly realized she hadn't had a drink all day, unless she'd taken one in the Brooks' house, and was no doubt dehydrated. When she stared at him, he could see dark rings of exhaustion under her eyes, and he mentally cursed himself.

"I'm a brute," he said, blotting her face with his handkerchief. "You need a meal and a rest. I'm taking you home."

"Your lady wife, is she?" the stout woman asked, her lips pursed. "She shouldn't be out lookin' for work in her condition. Expectin', aren't you, lovey?"

Dev nodded rather than explain she'd been driven in the heat all the way from Stirling in the hills without a drop to drink. "Could someone find me a cab? We live a block away, but I don't think I can carry her so far."

Wenna looked dazed. "I can walk." She stood. Her face turned pale green.

"Sit, rest, drink another cup of water, and I'll find some way of reuniting you with your possessions."

"You won't find a cab around here, mate," the man who had supplied the cup of water said. "If you live close, I'll bring me wagon to the front and take you home."

"Is Rundle Street close enough for you?"

"I'm goin' there anyway. Give me a few minutes and I'll see you outside."

* * * *

Mr. Courtney gave the wagon driver a few coins for his trouble while Wenna stood on the main business street in Adelaide, too woozy to argue. Perhaps the combination of not eating and travelling had caused the faintness. Normally she wasn't at all frail, but normally she had a good job and somewhere to live.

"Now, let me show you my humble abode." Mr. Courtney placed a hand on her elbow and opened a gate connected by a short paling fence to the nearby shop front. Paving stones along the side of the building led to a black door paned with glass at eye height, which he opened into a tiny foyer. A narrow stairway stood between two green painted doors. "Did you find a job?"

"Everyone wanted maids. Maids, maids, maids," she muttered wearily. "Young, live in, and paid a pittance." With his hand lightly guiding her, she trudged to the top of the stairs, where she spotted her unpacked bags.

He indicated the doorway on the left, and she proceeded into a smallish musty-smelling room containing a fireplace, two worn armchairs, a small desk and chair, a side-table, and a magazine rack. Old newspapers occupied a section of the dusty floor, and a pile of books sat in one corner. The stiff lace curtains didn't hide the dirty set of windows, which showed a smeary view of the hotel fronting the other side of the main street. "I could have taken a job as a housemaid, a scullery maid, a laundry maid, or a general all-purpose maid, but not a lady's maid. Upper servants are normally hired by word of mouth. I have good references, but not from anyone who employed me as a lady's maid." Her eyes met his. "The first wouldn't give me one, of course, because I left her for the second."

"And the second didn't bother because of my ill-considered words."

She needed to sit again. Her head throbbed.

"And you are faint because of my unconsidered *actions*. At least let me put that right. Tidy yourself, and I'll take you to the pastry shop for a good meal."

"I could have been a governess. I can read and write. But I'm too old," she said with disgust from the depths of the saggy armchair. Even her bones ached. "The position was for a younger woman."

"We will worry about that later. First we need to eat." His gaze wandered over her hair. "But your hat is hanging over one ear, and you might like to freshen up. I have a mirror and a basin in my bedroom."

She leaned her head back and narrowed her eyes. "You're not luring me into your bedroom."

"Dash it." He grinned. The man had an amazing ability to look guileless while he behaved badly, and a weaker woman might smile.

Not about to succumb to a charmer who clearly knew his own worth, she checked her wayward hat with her hand and found she'd lost a long, beaded pin. "I must look like the wreck of the Herperus." She dragged in a weary breath.

"Ah, no. Her eyes were as green the fairy-flax, and her bosom white as—"

"She had blue eyes, and don't worry about my bosom."

He shrugged, his expression still amused. "Poetic license. Mr. Longfellow wouldn't mind the color change. Come along. I'm hungry, too." He led her past the stairway and along the short yellow painted passage. Indicating the first door, he stood back, showing her his bedroom.

Indifferently clean red velvet curtains hung at the window. A tiled wash-stand holding a leaf-patterned jug and basin and an ivory-handled chest of drawers with a shaving-mirror on top occupied the space not used by a heavily carved, four-poster tester bed with the curtains missing.

She gave him a look that caused him to raise placating palms and back into the passage while she removed her hat. Lacking a comb, she took the net from her hair and shook her head. The frizz escaped. Years of practice helped to finger-comb the lot at the back and twist a strand around to hold the mass in place. She reapplied the net tightly and added her little hat with her single pin. The water was cold, of course, and she washed her face and hands.

Not in her wildest dreams had she expected that a gentleman who spoke in a cultured voice and seemed instinctively courteous would lodge anywhere so ordinary. She'd pictured him in a gracious house filled with bustling servants.

Before leaving, she stared out the window at the tiny yard below, at the weedy garden, the clothesline sagging between two posts, and the little wooden building with a crescent moon cut into the door—a privy, apparently. This had been built against the back lane for the convenience of the night cart. For a single man, perhaps this tiny space was adequate.

When she re-entered his main room, he was wearing his tan gloves, and he tapped his wide- brimmed hat against his thigh, clearly impatient to leave. He led her back down the stairs, where she noticed a small kitchen lurking behind one of the downstairs doors. "Your lodgings are very compact," she said, more in surprise than criticism.

He shrugged. "I don't need anything bigger, really only my sleeping quarters upstairs. I rarely use the kitchen other than to heat water for my bath. I keep the bath in a room off the kitchen."

She glanced at his face. "What about the office front on Rundle Street?"

"That's a surveyor's office."

"Not yours?"

He shrugged. "I don't have much use for an office."

"Where do you work? You *do* work?"

"Occasionally. And I buy and sell land."

"Is it profitable?"

"What? The land trading? No. Not yet."

She couldn't imagine what sort of money might be made out of *occasionally* trading land, but whatever he did to support himself at least paid for his lodgings. Surprised by his lack of ambition, she followed him out the door, past his untended garden, and back onto Rundle Street.

Food, clothes, shoes, leather goods, saddles, horses—anything really— could be bought on this busy thoroughfare. Some buildings looked rickety and insubstantial, and some had been built to last centuries. However, she didn't have time to take her bearings, for he hurried her along the street, nodding at everyone he passed. She kept her gaze lowered, hoping not to see anyone who knew her.

They sat down to lunch in the front room of a pastry shop she'd never before patronized. With all her meals provided by her employers, she saved where she could. A few small tables had been set out. Pretty girls in striped brown aprons served the respectable-looking customers: ladies who spoke in low tones and dressed in extravagant tea gowns. Most wore small hats loaded with flowers, or birds, or ribbons, all in the latest styles. Most wore simply-braided hairstyles. Some bunched their hair up and hoped for the best.

In her plain blue gown and her low-crowned straw hat, Wenna squirmed with embarrassment. Normally, she didn't eat with her betters. Nevertheless, she consumed a meat pie covered with pastry flaky enough to melt in her mouth. The tea in the pot was the perfumed variety Mrs. Brook drank, not the thick brown brew offered to her servants. All in all, Mr. Courtney had treated her well, but she still didn't have a place for the night or a job.

"After all that fuss before, I can barely force myself to return to the labor exchange." she said, massaging her forehead to relieve a dull ache.

"I don't think the exchange is the place for you to find a job." He settled his forearms on the table and linked the fingers of two shapely, well-kept hands together. For reasons unknown, this made the blackguard look earnest.

She heaved a breath. "I need to regroup and examine my options. I must know someone who can help me find employment. Heaven knows I've always been hard working and respectable."

"My best contact, the previous governor, left the colony last year, unfortunately, or I could have taken you to his wife. She would have found a placement for you, because she knew all the ladies in town."

She inclined her head, letting her face express her disbelief. "Isn't that always the way? You promise to help a woman find a job and suddenly you can't."

"You're a harsh taskmistress. I promised to help, and I will. But I've had another idea." He rested his chin on the points of two meeting forefingers. "You want to go to Cornwall. I have to go back to Cornwall this year. I could take you with me."

"How kind. Would you put me in your trunk?"

"I would put you in my cabin." He frowned.

"Of course you would. You've done nothing but proposition me since you first saw me. What do all the other women in this colony have against you?"

"You might think you are the only one, but I do have other choices." He sounded annoyed. "It's just that, well, I *could* marry you." Leaning back, he frowned as if he didn't quite credit the words he had said. "In fact, I'm beginning to think you would be the perfect choice."

"That's very flattering." She suppressed the urge to push him off his chair. "But I would rather be a lady's maid than a gentleman's cabin comfort."

His eyebrows lowered farther. "If you marry me, you'll have a fine house in which to live, with enough money to support your grandparents."

She sighed and smiled politely. "Then, that's a very good idea. Shall we marry right away?"

"I wouldn't think we could get a license right away. It might take a few days."

"During which time I would stay with you?"

"Yes."

"Oh, dear. I must look like a droplet just come down in the rain." She glanced out the window at the blaring sun. "You can't be that desperate. Some women would call you handsome, and until I saw your grubby little rooms I would have thought you were well off."

"Grubby little rooms? You are, of course, used to living in gracious mansions." His eyebrows tilted disdainfully.

"The *most* gracious."

"In the servants' quarters." He nodded, assuming he had put her back in her place, which he had. "With a good scrub, my rooms wouldn't look too bad. I'm a bachelor. I'd hardly need a big house full of servants."

She lifted her chin. "I suspect you're an adventurer, a good-looking single man who knows on which side his bread is buttered. You spend your life as a guest in other people's houses, eating their food, being waited upon hand and foot. You would never want to marry unless you could find someone rich enough to support your indulgent lifestyle."

"That's quite a speech." His mouth formed a grim line. "You might remember that had I tried, I might have added Patricia Brook to my string of prospective brides rich enough to support me."

"You're not that stupid. Miss Patricia would have wanted you at her beck and call. She would have held the purse strings. You would want someone meek and mild."

He gave her a strange glance. "As a matter of fact, Miss Know-It-All, I think you would suit me very well. I wouldn't have proposed, had I not. And no one in the world would call *you* meek and mild. I'm astonished that you lasted so long as a lady's maid. I wouldn't have thought you could hold your tongue long enough to flatter a mistress."

"I was sorely tried, on occasion. But when I thought of the money I was earning, I kept my opinions to myself."

"Money. That's practically all I've heard from you."

Suddenly her throat hurt. "I hate you, you irresponsible lecher," she said in a clogged voice. She wiped at a tickle under her chin and her hand came away wet. Her nose had blocked, and she realized she was dripping with furious tears. "You've messed up my life, and you've left me in a fix, and all you can do is sit there looking harmless."

"I know what I did," he said, his expression stark. "And I know I can't put it right, not today, not straight away."

"You're such a rag of a man."

His lips relaxed. "Should I assume that's a 'no' to my proposal?" He handed her his clean-enough white handkerchief again.

She blotted her face. "You didn't mean it."

"So, will you marry me?"

She gave a long deep sniff, not about to blow her nose in front of him. "All you want is someone to clean up that place of yours."

"That would certainly be a bonus." He watched her face.

"There's no point in me trying to find a job as a lady's maid for weeks. Everyone is away for summer, or *everyone* who is anyone."

"How does one qualify to be *anyone*?"

"Money, that word you despise. That's the only measure in this country unless you happen to be a prince."

"The same as in the old country. So, you won't be looking for a job immediately?"

"Which means I'll need somewhere cheap to stay for a few weeks." She tried to read his expression but couldn't, and she wouldn't give a second's consideration to his proposal, which he'd clearly made in the spur of the moment, perhaps hoping to impress her with his gentlemanly ways. The darned man couldn't. She certainly *did* have his measure. "What's behind the door of your other upstairs room?"

"This and that."

"Which and what?"

"Boxes, mainly."

"You owe me lodging since you lost me mine." She folded her arms across her chest.

"You want to lodge in my spare room?" His eyebrows almost hit his hairline. "Surely you would rather send *me* there?"

"No. That would mean more work for me. The spare room will do. Since all my prospective employers are out of town, none will know I'm staying with you. And, I won't be wasting any of my own good money."

He eyed her. "This trip to Cornwall—it's really so important to you?"

"I don't break promises. I told my mother I would always care for her parents, and I will." She found her gloves on her lap.

"Well, if I'm about to have a lodger, I'll need to busy myself with some extra furniture. We'll go back and you can look around the room and tell me what I need to buy." Adopting a look of purpose, he rose to his feet.

Doubtless, given time, he assumed he would get under her skirts, but he wouldn't. She didn't like the way men pushed into women. Although about six years ago, she thought the pain might have been worth the effort, had she not discovered that the carpenter she had set her mind on was also dallying with a lowly tavern maid.

Two ladies arrived in the entrance of the shop and looked around. The older one glanced at Mr. Courtney, scrutinized Wenna, and put a gloved hand over her mouth to whisper something to the younger, who laughed. No doubt they'd speculated about seeing a poorly clad spinster with a fashionable gentleman. Wenna's cheeks warmed as Mr. Courtney held out his hand to help her arise.

Noting her focus, he glanced behind him, spotted the ladies, smiled, and said, "Good afternoon," as he moved toward the doorway with Wenna.

The ladies fluttered. "Good afternoon, Mr. Courtney," replied the older one, while the younger coyly batted her eyelashes. She seemed about to engage him in conversation, but he nodded politely and escorted Wenna outside.

The man had protected her.

With her chin atilt and her expression tight, she walked beside him—until she had a dreadful thought. Those ladies might not have been discussing the discrepancy between a scruffy redhead and a golden god, but whispering gossip about the beauteous Mr. Courtney leaving Stirling with his *doxy*. No. Surely not. The story could not have travelled to town so swiftly.

She needed to stop seeing herself as everyone's focus. Ladies wouldn't discuss her, other than to make certain that anyone who could afford to employ a lady's maid knew the name of the rare temptation for husbands and male guests. Although such humiliation was hard to bear, she marched back to Mr. Courtney's rooms as if she belonged with him.

Until she found her next job, she would hide away, and hope the incident would be forgotten.

Chapter 4

Leaning against the doorway, Dev watched Wenna assess his dingy second bedroom. He imagined, being a lady's maid, she was used to better. "How old are you?"

"Twenty-six," she answered, toeing a box near the window. "What's in this?"

"I don't know." Merely his age. Interesting. He had always preferred older women. "My father sent them on to me after he'd cleared out my mother's possessions." The early afternoon light from the window painted a pink halo around her hair and outlined her shapely silhouette.

She gave an exasperated sigh. "See if he sent anything useful. If not, stack two boxes in that corner for me to use as a bedside table, and move the rest behind the door."

"No sooner said than done." He opened the nearest box and picked through the paper wrapping. "Plates in this one."

"Take them to the kitchen." She sounded as though she meant to put order into his life. "This one seems to be framed paintings. You can hang those up." She straightened, glancing at him with her fine red eyebrows raised. "Shall I go through the rest while you buy a bed? We don't have many more hours of daylight left."

He tugged out his fob chain to check the time, and remembered. "My watch first," he said, palm out. "And my ring, too, if you please."

Her mouth considered. She blinked. "Oh, yes, your watch. Now that I have a place to stay and all my things, you should have your sureties back." From somewhere in the folds of her skirt, she casually pulled out his valuables.

He donned both, annoyed that she accepted his trust as her ransom. "You're a mightily suspicious woman. So, I'll be off now to buy you a feather mattress."

"Feather?" She gave him a smile he could only describe as long-suffering. "That would be too much to ask."

Expecting an expensive mattress that with luck would not be used more than a few days *would* be unreasonable, but challenged, he left without answering. He would buy her a damned feather mattress, if only to confound her.

A few lanes farther along the street, he bought a bed, which the maker sent two boys to deliver. Dev hoped Wenna would let them in, or he would need to carry the thing upstairs alone, not that the lightly-made frame would weigh more than a few pounds. Finding a feather mattress was another matter. The colony had a surfeit of hair mattresses. Finally he was forced to buy one, knowing she would continue to think him entirely useless.

On his way back to the first shop he had tried, the closest to his lodging, he heard his name. "Ah, the Honorable Devon Courtney, if I'm not mistaken." Strictly speaking, Dev was Lord Dellacourt, but not until last year, when the second of his brothers had died. As the only son now, Dev would hold the title of the heir to the Earl of Marchester, but certainly not in this country. He glanced at the speaker, a tall, outrageously handsome chap wearing a tailored suit and a faultlessly placed hat.

"Dev to you," he said chidingly to Nick Alden, assuming Nick was ragging him, as was the colonial habit when confronted with aristocratic lineage.

Nick's mouth tilted at one corner. "I'm sure you are still perfectly honorable."

"I prefer not to seem like a twat, if you don't mind." Dev examined Nick's face and shook his head. "You didn't get a shiner from that ball yesterday, I see. I can only spot a slight bump and a bruise on your face."

"You're on the wrong side of the bruise. From my side, it's a headache for which I fortunately have the cure." Nick gave a jaded smile, indicating the tavern. "I don't seem to have the self-protective instinct these days to play cricket."

Six years ago at Cambridge, where the two had met, Nick had been carefree and charming, although as irresponsible as the rest of the South Australian lads. Before Dev had arrived in the colony, Nick had returned from England with the others, but he'd found greener pastures in New

South Wales, from which he'd only recently returned. At the cricket match yesterday, Dev had briefly seen a changed man who no longer cared for anything he couldn't find in a bottle. Word was that alcohol could be addictive. Dev wasn't sure. He could take a drink or ignore a drink, depending on his mood. "Did you come back to town this morning?"

"Yesterday. My father banished me from the hills the moment he saw the lump on my head. Thought I should see a doctor. The doctor mumbled something about drunks and fools. Since I'm a combination of the two, I'm immune to hard knocks, or so he led me to believe. Whither thou goest, my fine young man?"

"Off to get a mattress."

"Then I'll go with you." Nick stumbled slightly onto the path and righted himself. Years of practice, no doubt.

"Good. I was wondering how I would carry it home."

"It?" Nick gave him a strange glance. "We didn't have a chance to talk yesterday before I was removed from the field. I hear you've been in Adelaide for a couple of years." He began strolling alongside Dev. An unwary woman approached, glanced at Nick and, open-mouthed, walked into a lamp-post. He had that effect on females, though he didn't seem to notice, or he'd had years of practice in not noticing. "Your father's idea?"

Dev nodded. "He thought a couple of years in France would do me well. Then, no sooner than I began to take an interest in the growing of wheat on the home farm, he decided I should come out here with the governor's retinue. As you can see, I didn't return."

"How long will you get away with that?"

"Not much longer. I'm booked to return on the Hougoumont, which will be here in June." Dev stopped, swooping an arm in the direction of a narrow doorway. "In here. This is the place where I plan to buy a mattress."

Nick glanced around, frowning. "A mattress? I thought you said a mistress. I was interested to see where you would get one you had to carry home. I keep mine in her own house. So much more convenient." He stepped back. "I'll leave you with your *mattress*."

Dev put his fists on his hips. "If you've nothing better to do, you can help me carry it back to my lodgings."

"Through the streets?"

"Are you about to perform your dainty act?"

Nick gave a twisted smile, Dev paid, and Nick reluctantly assisted him in moving the mattress to the foyer of Dev's lodgings.

"We'll keep your business as your business," Nick said. "I've forgotten about your lofty relations, if that would suit you better."

"It would." Dev watched his formerly carefree friend leave, somewhat reassured that Nick couldn't mention the title, since he appeared to know nothing about Dev's brother's demise. Dev dragged the mattress upstairs, with its proposed occupant in mind.

Wenna stood in the doorway of the spare bedroom. Twists of curls escaped the confines of her net, and wanton tendrils clung to the sweaty skin of her face and neck. From the moment he had met her, he had wanted to bed her. Seeing her with her hair loose and flying around her head had brought back memories of love and sunshine, laughter and happiness. He wanted those carefree days back.

However, those days would never return. Jenny was lost to him and Wenna was single-minded, opinionated, and a handful. She challenged him, but a diversion in his duty-filled life wouldn't go astray. "Did the bed arrive?"

"Just in time for the mattress," she said with the first real smile he'd seen from her. Her momentary happiness transformed her face. With her hair loosened, she looked younger, softer, and infinitely desirable She stood aside so that he could wrestle the mattress onto the frame.

The room had changed in the time he'd been away. The grimy lace curtain had disappeared, and the hot afternoon sun twinkled on the motes streaming in with the light. She'd covered a couple of boxes with a fancy tablecloth beside the bed. Black skirts and bodices lay across the other couple behind the door.

"The mattress is horsehair. I couldn't find anything else on the spur of the moment, but I have a couple of feather comforters in my room, under the bed, I think. You can use one."

"Do you also have spare sheets and pillows?"

"I do." He turned on his heel and grabbed a pillow off his bed and clean sheets from his bottom drawer.

"Your father sent you quite a trousseau," she said when he returned. "You could have been living comfortably if you'd deigned to look."

"That's my girl. Back to your usual critical self. Now, what's your next job for me?"

"Take those two boxes downstairs and then you can please yourself."

Judging by the distracted look on her face, he doubted she would let him *please himself*, and in lieu of bouncing her onto his bed, he resignedly hefted the two large heavy boxes to the kitchen.

* * * *

Having worked as a maid most of her life, Wenna quickly made up her bed using the finest linen she had ever seen, monogrammed with the letter M twisted with flowers. Mr. Courtney disappeared into his uncomfortable little sitting room when he returned from downstairs. The story that his aunt had been the governor's wife might be true, judging by the quality of the goods his father had sent. The boxes had also contained silver candlesticks, crystal bowls, and flatware. Wenna had him move the tableware down to the kitchen, leaving her a nice room once she'd draped another lace tablecloth over the rod above the window. The dirty lace curtains could be washed tomorrow.

She hummed while she worked. This was the first time since her father died that she'd had a space she could imagine was hers. If Mr. Courtney wasn't interested in the kitchen either, and he wouldn't be, she could make that hers, too, even if only for a few weeks. In the meantime, she wondered about her meals. Surely he would pay, since he had lost her three months' wages. Perhaps not, given that she'd already cost him a new bed and a mattress.

"Meals," she said, hovering in the doorway of the sitting room. "Do you have food in the kitchen?"

He sat at the desk minus his jacket and, with the sleeves of his white shirt rolled up to expose his sinewy golden tanned forearms, he looked more approachable and entirely male. Without a doubt, he was the most attractive man she had ever met, physically. Mentally, he left a lot to be desired, being irresponsible and entirely too casual about money and possessions. If he had spent part of his life with nothing, like she had, he might have been more careful.

He lifted his gaze from the stack of papers in front of him. "Normally, I eat out."

She sighed. "As I thought. I'm sure you'll never run out of gullible women."

"Unfortunately, I don't have a gullible woman awaiting me tonight," he said with overdone politeness. "I thought I would eat at The Pig and Whistle across the street, instead."

Hearing no invitation in his tone, she dropped her gaze. She must remember not to be so critical. At least she'd had a pie today. She wouldn't starve, and tomorrow she could buy food to keep in her room. Eventually she would have to break into the ten shillings she'd picked up with her clothes at the Brooks' house, but she would hold off as long as possible. "Do you mind if I use this sitting room when you're not here?"

He looked surprised. "Of course not. Use any room you like. Sit with me for a moment, because we need to talk about our situation."

She moved into the room, not knowing what to assume about him. "If we're going to be living together for a couple more weeks, we should try to get along. I'll keep the place tidy, because I can see you don't, and I'll cook meals if you pay for the food. I think that should work." She sat in an over-padded armchair, after moving a pile of papers onto the floor.

"Isn't that rather one-sided?" He had turned his chair to face her.

"You'll have me cooking and cleaning for you," she said, offended. "That should more than pay my way."

"It does pay your way. But *should* you pay your way when you're in this position because of me? Seems to me ... I should keep my mouth shut. I have a very good deal. A paragon like you—why is it that you are not married?"

"I don't need a man," she said, her jaw tight. Her father had wanted a houseful of boys. He had only been given a girl, who had from the start done her best to match up to his expectations. Then he died, and all his dreams for her and her dreams for herself had been put on hold while she worked with her mother to survive. "I'm perfectly self-sufficient."

"Though, as you said, you might not be able to get the job you want." He kept his eyes focused on hers. "When the story of last night is retold, and if I know Patricia it will be, you won't be described by name. You'll simply be 'the redheaded maid.' On the other hand, my name will be told, but my part in the whole thing will be glossed over. The chaps will wink and nudge me, and the ladies will pretend to be deaf." He meshed his fingers across his flat belly, his gaze a challenge.

She pressed her lips into a straight line. "And I'll be seen as the immoral one, not you, if Miss Patricia tells. I don't suppose a redheaded lady's maid will be employed for months." She kept her tone waspish.

"You could dye your hair black."

"Very amusing."

"Or you *could* marry me. I did offer to take you to Cornwall with a promise of more money and comfort than you've ever known."

She let her head fall forward, wearied by his ridiculous proposition. "Yes, you did say that."

"*Now* will you listen?"

She laughed wryly. "You might think me being unemployable is a joke—"

"I don't. I'm offering reparation. Would you grant me the honor of your hand in marriage?"

"It would serve you right if I said yes." She crossed her arms.

"It might serve us *both* right if you said yes. The fact of the matter is that I want a wife and child."

"The one usually follows the other, but if you want a wife, I'm sure you won't have any difficulty finding one amongst your own class."

"I need a very special wife. One who wants to live in Cornwall. The red hair ..." His expression looked annoyingly charming. "Well, that's a bonus. I should tell you from the start that I wouldn't be marrying a woman who didn't have the first attribute. That's an essential. And the child. My family needs an heir."

"You are *serious*?" She stared at him, knowing he could find a hundred women who would snap up the chance.

"I'm proposing a marriage of convenience, you might say, but as convenient for you as for me. We'll both have what we want."

"I wouldn't be the only woman in South Australia who wouldn't mind living in Cornwall. It seems to me, you're snatching at someone who would be a poor match for you."

"It seems to me that you shouldn't look a gift horse in the mouth."

She tried to read his face, but saw nothing but a man waiting for an answer. "When something seems too good to be true, it usually is."

His gaze remained unwavering. "You only need to ask yourself if you could...ah ... do the conceiving with me."

He sounded slightly hesitant; an act, no doubt. Any woman who wanted a baby would happily do the conceiving with him. Since her first sight of him, she'd been undeniably attracted, but not even close to losing her head. He was nothing but a credible rogue with an open-hearted smile that could charm the birds right out of the trees—the sort of man to keep at a distance.

"I think it's the conceiving act that interests you most." She must have looked suspicious, because he gave her a harmless smile. If he was speaking the truth...but of course he wasn't. Golden gods like him didn't marry scrawny spinsters like her. She rubbed the side of her neck and still couldn't think of a credible objection.

"What do you have to lose? Oh. Are you a virgin?"

She pressed her lips together. "I'm twenty-six."

"And truthful."

She gave him a quelling glance.

His shoulders rose and his mouth hitched up on one corner. "I want to bed you, Wenna."

"But you really don't want a wife."

"I really want a child. Legitimate."

She stared at him, puzzled. "An heir. To what?"

"My family estates in Cornwall." He tapped his fingers on the arms of his chair.

"So, you want to marry me, poke me, give me a baby, and take me off to Cornwall to live as happy as a pig among the daffodils?"

"Daffodils?"

She waved a hand casually. "Everywhere. Up the hills and down the dales. Green pastures full of daffodils and violets."

He laughed, filling the entire room with a joyous sound that somewhat fuddled her brain. "In private gardens, perhaps."

She didn't know what to make of him. He'd been kind since the carriage trip to town. He might not be rich, and he might not be moral, but he had certain qualities, one of which was optimism. She wouldn't mind if he spread some into her life. For years she'd thought she would be able to elevate herself and, despite only being a daughter, replace the successful son her father had hoped for, but this latest setback put that dream out of her foreseeable future.

"When are you planning this wedding?" she said, realizing a marriage of convenience would suit her, too. Love matches were only for the fanciful.

"I'll have to see about a special license first. Don't think me unenthusiastic, but it's been quite a day so far. I'd rather rest for a while and see what I can do tomorrow."

"Then, should I make a cup of tea?"

"The perfect way to pass time. The stove will be cold, though." He angled a query at her.

With another sigh, she rose to her feet. Having a task to perform gave her some direction. Now with a more immediate aim in her mind, she could mull his sincerity about marriage. She took the stairs down to the kitchen and entered a small room with another two doors in the far wall. A woodstove had been set against the wall between a working bench built with an indoor tap and a set of shelves containing a small pile of tumbled wood and a basket of kindling. Against the wall in common with the building next door sat a small wooden table with two chairs.

She stacked the kindling beneath the hob and lit a small fire. As soon as she'd added four thick twigs to the flare, she filled and placed the blackened kettle onto the hob. In a slatted food cupboard above the working bench, she found five chipped mugs, a brown teapot, a tin of tea, and a bag of sugar. Mr. Courtney had said he bathed, unlike the poorer people who didn't have the opportunity to do anything other than wash. Pleased, she opened the first of the two extra doors, built adjacent to the laneway at the back of the building. Here she found a hipbath, a large bucket, and a floor drain. Another tap would have been nice, but she'd spent her younger days in the country and knew how to cope with the bare necessities.

Behind the second door was nothing but a shelved storage area holding only the two boxes Mr. Courtney had moved from her bedroom and a few pots and pans. She removed a big black pot, which she put on the hob beside the kettle and filled with water. She hadn't had a bath in a week, but the water would take some time to heat. The kettle boiled, she made the tea, filled the two mugs and, with the basin of sugar balanced on top, took one mug upstairs.

"I put water on to heat so that I could take a bath. You don't mind, do you?"

He raised his gaze from his papers. "If you're heating water, I wouldn't mind a bath. This morning I had nothing but a cold wash." He accepted the tea and raised a palm at the sugar.

"I'll put on a second pan for you." She hoped he understood that she wouldn't use his bathwater.

He nodded. "The towels are with the sheets in the bottom drawer in my bedroom." His gaze went back to his papers, so she assumed she had permission to go into his bedroom for a towel.

When she opened his bottom drawer, she found his shoes resting on the towels and the sheets. Having agreed to work for her board, she opened each of his drawers to find a more suitable place. Shirts had been scrambled with trousers, and his trousers had been folded incorrectly. With an impatient click of her tongue, she occupied her time taking out his clothes, refolding, shifting his shirts, socks, and underwear to the higher drawers and his trousers and jackets to the lower. She found more clean sheets and towels scattered among his clothes. After piling the linen onto the bed, she decided his six pairs of handmade leather shoes should be in the lowest drawer, and the towels in the bathroom. She carried the linen into her small room for storage.

Assuming that by now her water would be boiling, she grabbed her clean underwear and towels, and hiked off down the stairs again. She spotted her cold mug of tea and drank the lot in a few gulps. The big pot of water was enough for her bath with the addition of another pot of cold water. Puffing after the exertion, she put a second pot on the hob. Making sure the door was tightly shut, she undressed, took his bar of soap from the window sill, and settled into the bath. Glorious. Somehow she wriggled right down and soaped up her hair.

And then she completely lost track of time. She opened her eyes to the sound of footsteps on the stairs, and had barely hauled herself out of the water before hearing a rapping on the door. She snatched up her towel, covered herself, and opened the room to Mr. Courtney. "I would have called you when I had finished."

"I've never known anyone to take a bath for a full hour. I thought you might have drowned, either that or run off with my silver." He looked amused.

She flicked her dripping hair back from her face. "Call me a fool," she said, with the glimmer of a smile, "but given the choice of a bath or struggling under a box of silver, I would rather have a bath."

"I can't fault you for that." His face softened. "With your hair like that, dripping wet, you look like a mermaid."

She smiled cynically. He tried—she had to give him credit for that, at least, but she didn't look any better wet than she looked dry. "Give me time to dress. Then I'll prepare your bath for you."

"Wrap yourself tightly in that towel, take your clothes, and go upstairs to dress. I'll empty your cold water and prepare my own bath."

Since he'd already seen almost all of her, dressing modestly to leave the room would be a waste of her time, and so immodestly dressed, she did as he said.

After donning her blue gown again, and toweling dry her hair, she sat on her new bed, thinking. Now she'd left service, she didn't need to keep wearing her neat braid, or netting her hair. She'd invented a dozen different styles for three different ladies, but she'd never done anything interesting with her own hair. She tried a complicated knot on the back of her neck, but didn't know how she looked. She hadn't heard him return, so she went to his room to use the mirror.

She tried Miss Patricia's bigger hairdo, but her hair stuck out at the back and sides like a dry mop. Giving in, she combed her hair, plaited a braid, and gave herself a figure- eight knot at the nape of her neck— slightly different but not exciting.

She didn't hear him pad up the stairs. She almost leaped out of her skin when he suddenly appeared in his doorway dressed in nothing but a towel. In clothes, he was a golden god. In a towel, he was a Greek god. She glanced away. "I needed to use your mirror."

He dropped his clothes on the bed. "Don't let me scare you away. I know you won't look at me while I'm naked, and so I'm feeling quite safe."

"I don't feel at all safe while you're naked. I'll come back when you're dressed."

"Don't be a prude. When we're married, we'll be sharing a bed." He loomed close.

Flustered, she tried to move past him.

He blocked her exit by opening the top drawer and glancing in. "What happened here?"

"I tidied."

"Where did you put my shirts?"

"In the next drawer down."

He smiled and scratched his shoulder. The muscles in his back rippled as he opened the second drawer. She breathed out. His grace of movement fascinated her. His manliness fascinated her. He had smooth, tanned skin and shoulders possibly twice the breadth of hers. A grid of muscle sat across his abdomen. His hips were taut and lean, and his legs long.

"Let me pass."

"I thought you'd say that," he replied with amusement glittering in his eyes. He pulled out a clean shirt and kept barring her progress by pushing his arms into his shirtsleeves. Clearly he didn't plan to don an undershirt. "Wear something prettier," he said, eyeing her. "We're going out to eat."

"This is my best gown. I don't have anything else other than my uniforms."

He frowned. "You can't wear that or black to our wedding. You'll have to buy something else."

"I don't want to waste my money on clothes."

He stared at her. "You can waste mine. As long as you don't waste too much. Money's short at the moment."

"No wonder, if you eat out all the time."

He gave a reprimanding click of his tongue. "I don't need anyone telling me how to spend my money." Then he faced her, his eyebrows raised. "I'm not the one willing to take any offer. You are."

After a long assessing glance at the full length of her body, he let her pass. She marched off, sure she hadn't accepted *any offer.* She certainly hadn't accepted that he would marry her, and she had offered to work for her keep.

If anyone had accepted an offer, he had.

Chapter 5

After eating dinner with the offended redhead last night, Dev slept well. He'd been friendly, he hadn't made a single attempt to inveigle her into his bed, and still she'd criticized him. She would be the perfect daughter-in-law for his father, both seeing all Dev's faults and both unable to please. This, of course, gave him plenty of scope to keep trying; not to be good enough because he attempted to be successful in all his endeavors, but to find a way of having his efforts recognized.

In the morning he went for his usual run, washed and changed, and found Wenna waiting for him in the kitchen with a dish of porridge. Although he rarely bothered with breakfast, he appreciated her thought. Since she seemed to want to rush him off, he thanked her, ate, and headed into his sitting room, attempting not to look like a man with a mission.

In his enforcedly aimless life, he had only once wanted to make a home for himself. A few months back, he had been unable to resist buying a block of land in the foothills, facing the sea. The Mediterranean weather in the colony mimicked that in the south of France, where he had spent two years living and working with artisans and dabbling in various food-growing industries, which had been meant to keep him away from Jenny until he came to his senses. Instead, when he had arrived in this faraway country, he had noted the many opportunities waiting to be grabbed up by a man with his agricultural background.

As a younger son with an inheritance from his dead mother, he had money to invest in new ventures. The price of land in the colony had been kept cheap to attract more settlers. Although he was very much attracted, he would have no chance to settle here. Now that the last of his brothers had died, he was urgently wanted back home. The most he could do would be to leave a completed project behind. One day his descendants might be grateful for his foresight.

Although he would have liked to spend his day as usual on his foothill's property, he couldn't leave Wenna to settle into her new environment alone. Expecting her to disturb him at will, he settled into his study to read his correspondence, checking letters from overseas suppliers of fruiting stock, bills from tradesmen, and quotes for new work. Again he went over his finances. Every three months, money from England was deposited into his bank account. As usual, he had overspent. The bank would give him leeway, but he needed to be somewhat more parsimonious if Wenna decided to marry him. Women wanted various knickknacks that men needed to supply. He hoped she wouldn't want too many. The less she had to leave behind, the better.

Fortunately, the blunt little redhead appeared to be occupied in the kitchen, rearranging the items in the cupboards. Sometime after noon, she brought him a plate of cheese and pickles. "Your cupboard is now bare. Would you like me to buy more food?"

He blinked, reminded that she needed to eat, and felt for money in his pocket. "Is this enough?" He gave her ten shillings.

"Am I cooking a meal tonight?"

"We'll eat out. Buy whatever food you want when you want it. I'm not normally here during the day." Leaning back, he ate the hard cheese, reminded that he couldn't continue simply pleasing himself. He had asked this woman to marry him, not because he loved her, not even because he desired her, but because he didn't care whom he married. The fact that she was a redheaded maid would set up his father's back, highlighting his needless edict all those years ago. This gave Dev a curious sense of completion.

To keep his word to Wenna, he now needed to seek out a wedding license. He'd already discovered that she wouldn't leap into his bed without a ceremony. As Nick Alden was the only person he knew who wasn't still holidaying in the hills, Dev rose to his feet and donned his jacket. The Old Queen's Arms in Wright Street boasted blackjack tables and a roulette wheel, and therefore, possibly Nick, who spent most of his time either in a tavern or gambling

After a comfortable stroll in the April sunshine, he reached the corner where the painting of Queen Victoria and the cast iron balustrade identified the hotel. Wandering into the taproom, he glanced around. The bouncer at the door rose to his feet, scanned Dev, and sat back onto his stool. One bored barmaid wiped glasses on a grimy towel, while another strolled to a booth in the corner carrying two glasses of ale. Dev's gaze followed.

One of the few patrons, Nick sat sprawled with a painted female beside him. The woman appeared chastened, and Nick indifferent.

"Are you sober?" Dev called as he strode toward the couple.

Nick looked up and spotted him. "I don't know," he said in his world-weary voice. He offered a smile that could charm the angels out of the clouds.

The woman cast her gaze downwards. Obviously she'd had no luck with Nick, but her stiff posture said she didn't want to stop trying.

"Off you go, sweetheart," Nick said, pressing a coin into her hand.

She glanced at the money, heaved a sigh, scooped up one of the newly delivered ales, and moved to the bar where she propped her elbows, awaiting her next potential customer. Dev slid onto the wooden bench seat in her place while Nick quaffed his fresh drink.

"It must be my lucky day." Dev flattened his palms on the sticky-ringed wooden tabletop. The ceiling in the room was also wood, which kept the area cool and dark. "This is the first place I looked for you. I thought I might have to leave a note at your father's house."

"So you haven't come to join me for a drink?"

Dev shook his head. "I can't waste the time. I want to get back to work as soon as I can."

"You'll never change."

Dev smiled. "I need a favor from you, Nick. I want to marry, and quickly. Do you know how to procure a special license?"

"Probably."

"Would you do that for me?"

Nick's eyes focused on his face. "What's the rush?"

"She won't share my bed without a license."

Nick's mouth twisted cynically, and he nodded. "No wonder you want me sober." He pressed his hands over his jacket pockets. "Do you have notepaper and a pencil? No?" He called, "Pencil and paper," through the echoing space to the barmaid. Like every other woman in the world, she scurried to do Nick's bidding, and within minutes he had a grubby, curled piece of paper in front of him and a chewed pencil. "I need particulars. Your full name, your address, and your date of birth."

Dev told him.

Nick raised his gaze. "The lady's name?"

"Wenna Chenoweth."

"Her date of birth and address?"

"She lives with me, she's twenty-six, and I don't know her date of birth."

"No matter. I'll give her one. I'll see about finding you a special license within the next couple of days." Nick drained his glass.

"Is that all it takes?"

"I don't think it's too complicated, Dev." Nick was already searching in his pocket for the price of his next drink.

"And you don't want to ask me anything about this?"

"I understand the problem. You want to bed the lady and she wants to see a piece of paper first. Seems to me that you have enough experience to get her on her back without this paper, but who am I to judge?" He stared into his empty glass.

"I've tried asking nicely. The woman is unreasonable."

Nick shaded his amusement. "They prefer being persuaded. A license should do the trick for a feckless lump like you."

"Well..." Dev hesitated, but Nick seemed happy enough to see the back of him. He stood. "Thank you."

Nick didn't glance up. Dev buttoned his jacket and left for the brickworks to supervise the loading of a new batch of red bricks.

* * * *

Plates clattered, glasses clinked, and the yeasty smell of hops filled the barroom. Dev idly circled the base of his beer mug on the alehouse's hewn redwood table. He'd finished his supper: roast beef, roasted vegetables, and a potato mash. Wenna had picked at hers.

He moved his gaze from the waitress with the nicely rounded rump to Wenna. "Would you like a cup of coffee before we leave?"

"Coffee? Here?"

"If not, I'll order one for me." He raised a hand. The waitress, Maisie, hurried over. He glanced at Wenna, who nodded, and he ordered two.

The brew that arrived was thick enough to hold a spoon upright, and Wenna sipped quietly with both palms around the mug. She'd had little to say, but the way she rubbed her forehead from time to time gave the impression that something troubled her—being with him in a tavern, no doubt, but the place was filled with respectable tradesmen, most of whom he knew.

"Tell me about Cornwall," she said, tucking a wayward ringlet behind her ear. "Your family, Mr. Courtney. Do you have brothers or sisters?"

"Mr. Courtney? Since we're about to marry, I think you should call me Devon." He leaned back and positioned his palms on his knees. "I have no siblings now. I had two older half-brothers, but they both died without issue."

"Without issue? Is this why you need an heir for your father's lands?"

"My father never thought his youngest son would inherit," he said, shrugging. "He trained my older brother, William, to take over after him. But Will was thrown from his horse a couple of years ago and died instantly. He and his wife had no children. The next heir, my brother John, was with the army in India at that time, but before he could come home to take Will's place, he was killed in a skirmish. My father is panicking. He seems to fear that none of his sons will live long enough to take over from him."

"It must be dreadful to lose one's children." Wenna's large green eyes met his, her face stark. "It's hard enough to lose one's parents."

He nodded, having lost both, one parent to death and one to suspicion. "My mother died young. I barely remember her."

"Both my parents died young," she said in a husky voice. She dropped her gaze. "First my Da, and the next year my mother died, too. They say she died of a broken heart." Dropping her gaze, she swallowed, staring at her lap. Then, her face hardened imperceptibly, and she shifted her empty coffee mug to the outer rim of the table. "Do they ever clean the tables here, or just leave customers with the mess?"

The place didn't look particularly messy to him, or maybe he wasn't as fussy as Wenna. "The barmaids clean up as they wander around."

"I'm not used to eating in hotels. In private houses, the service is more formal."

"Yes, but now you are not governed by those rigid rules."

Her mouth considered, her bottom lip disappearing for a moment. "I suppose not. At least I'm not doing the work. Devon. It's a nice name, unusual."

"Devon is the county next to Cornwall. I was named after land. My brothers were named after ancestors. I suppose there's a message in that." He laughed cynically.

She looked puzzled for a moment. "Perhaps your parents saw you as less likely to follow tradition."

"My father certainly saw me as different." He shrugged. "I was the only child of his second wife. He didn't treat me the way he treated my half-brothers. Each graduated from Cambridge. He sent me to run the home farm at eighteen, and when I turned twenty, he gave me two years at Cambridge. No sooner had I settled in there than he packed me off to France. For the past eight years, I've barely spent a week at home."

"Count yourself lucky. I started work while you were still playing with your tin soldiers."

He heard her tone and blinked. Not too many colonials reprimanded the son of an earl. She'd had no good opinion of his rooms and had been critical about the way he lived his life. She certainly didn't seem impressed by The Pig and Whistle. He had no need to impress her, but he didn't like being seen as privileged and complaining by a woman he wanted to strip naked and drape all over himself. He drew a deep breath, trying to see her as his father would, though he doubted the earl would see past her working-class background and her red hair.

Allowing himself to smile at the thought, he leaned back and hooked his thumbs in his waistcoat pockets. "If you've finished, we should leave." Finding the price of the meals in his pocket, he rose to his feet, placing the money on the table.

A local tradesman with a fistful of beer mugs stopped behind Wenna. "Always was a lucky dog, wasn't yer, Courtney?" he said with a wink. "Got a real looker, this time."

Dev knew "looker" meant "good-looking" and smiled at Wenna. "I surely have," he said, appreciating the compliment to her.

However, her chin lifted and she stalked in front of him out onto the dark street, clearly offended. "This time? What did you have last time? A donkey?"

"That was just his little joke."

"I suppose everyone around here counts off your women as they trudge in and out of your lodgings?"

"My, but you're easy to offend. A man calls you a looker and you want to start a fight?"

"Yesterday I lost a high-paying job. I had my teeth jolted loose during a trip down from the hills. I spent some time staring at ceiling of the labor exchange, and I didn't find a job. Today I cleaned your kitchen from top to bottom. Tonight, the locals think I'm just another woman who is about to share your bed."

"Grin and bear it. You'll be my wife soon enough, with a new list of new complaints," he answered, disgruntled.

Share his bed? That might make up for her harsh tongue and her constant criticisms of him. Lord, but he wanted her. Every time he glanced at her, his body clenched with desire. He saw himself between her legs. Siring a child would empower him to make his own choices for the rest of his possibly misbegotten life. He imagined her head thrown back; heard her gasps of pleasure. If he could, he would marry her on the spot so that he could make love to her again and again, and stop thinking he'd missed some vital point along the way.

The gas street lighting, newly supplied, showed the way to his gate. From there, he moved to the door, inside which he kept a lamp. He lit this for Wenna's benefit, as he knew each step of the way. Once inside and up the narrow stairs, he guided her to the sitting- room door. "I'll light the lamp in your bedroom for you."

"No need. I can undress in the dark."

"Do you intend to retire now?"

"I do. This place is untidy, and I can't sit in a mess. I'll have plenty of work to occupy me tomorrow in making this place suitable for human habitation."

"Not this room." He frowned. "This is my office."

She glanced around, tilted her finicky nose, and took herself off.

In the light of the lamp, he turned the pages of a landscaping journal he found under a pile of old newspapers. Normally, he kept his papers filed on the floor, but since she didn't like untidiness, perhaps he should review his habits. He frowned. True, he desired her, and they would please each other in bed, but he didn't plan to start behaving like her lap dog.

He tossed the magazine back onto the floor and sat leaning forward with his forearms loosely over his knees. His fingers meshed as thoughts of her undressing passed through his mind. He could imagine her concise movements as she unbuttoned her gown and let the skirts drop to the floor. No. A fastidious woman like her would catch the garment and carefully drape the folds over the boxes. Next she would step out of her petticoats, or maybe her shoes, and they too would be neatly dealt with. He leaned back, imagining her in a corset and stockings. His cock hardened.

He could see those efficient fingers of hers unhook her corset, leaving the chemise beneath clinging to her warm skin. Her nipples would unfold in the fresh air while she pulled her chemise over her head, slowly, letting her beautiful, imagined, white breasts free. Would she cup them as he longed to do? Would she watch her nipples harden and smile with pleasure?

He stood, shaking out the muscles in his thighs. He didn't know what she would do, but he knew what he would see. Her hair would be tightly braided and she would be wearing a pristine white cotton nightgown that hid the shape he'd noticed beneath the towel. He'd seen the mouth-watering movement of her unconfined breasts and he'd made assumptions based on his needs. No longer could he do that. He could make assumptions based only on their plan. They would breed together. But by hell, no rule stated that neither could find enjoyment at the same time. She would, if he made certain of it— and he thought he could—but clearly she wouldn't let him tonight. Not until he had married her.

He snuffed out the lamp and let the moonlight guide him to his bedroom. In a state of full arousal, he undressed, for once ignoring his need. As he took off his clothes, he hung each garment on a hook behind the door. For some reason, tonight he couldn't leave his clothes where they dropped, nor could he put them away as neatly as she had. Fifty push-ups took care of his problem, and he eased into bed with a sheen of sweat on his body and slightly aching shoulders.

With one arm under his head, he stared at his ceiling. During the past six years, he had learned to live with his grief over losing the woman he loved. Now he had the means to force his father to accept a redheaded servant as the mother of the legitimate heir, something he'd been powerless to do all those years ago.

If the thought of natural justice didn't give him a peaceful sleep, nothing would.

* * * *

Wenna woke at dawn as usual, blinking and stretching while she acclimatized to her new surroundings. Planning her day, she shut her eyes again, just for a wee moment. The next time she saw the daylight, she threw herself out of bed and into her black gown, not knowing how much time she had lost by dozing off. After she tightly braided her hair, she tidied the room, and walked out into the passage.

As she passed Devon's room, she glanced in, but his bed lay empty. A pinkish gray light filtered through his red velvet curtains. She imagined him in repose, looking younger and gentler with his thick lashes resting on his cheeks, lying with his covers to his waist, showing the broad shoulders and hard chest that had so impressed her yesterday. With a rueful clamp of her mouth, she went down the stairs to visit the privy and wash. When she'd finished, she made herself a cup of tea.

"Hello," said a light husky voice behind her. "I thought I heard someone. Mr. Courtney didn't say that he had a woman here. Not that he does, usually. Sorry. I shouldn't oughter have said that." The young man, sixteen or seventeen years old she guessed by his downy upper lip, blushed and glanced at his shoes.

She wanted to blush and glance at her shoes, too, but if she did, she would look guilty. "Where did you come from?" she asked, keeping her tone polite.

"Let me introduce Ernie, the surveyor's assistant, Wenna." Devon appeared, wearing light trousers and old shoes, the magnificence of his upper body highlighted by a cotton shirt made transparent by sweat. He blotted his forehead with his shirttails. "He works in the office at the front. Wenna is my wife."

The young man glanced at him and back at Wenna, his face filled with embarrassment. "Nice to meetcha, Mrs. Courtney," he said awkwardly. "Guess I'll get back to work." He practically scuttled out of the room and through the doorway to the front of the building.

One side of Devon's mouth lifted. "He and the surveyor use this kitchen for occasional cups of tea. Now that you're here, I suppose they'll have to make other arrangements."

"I don't see why," she said, strangely pleased about being introduced as his wife. He hadn't left her hung out to dry as his *doxy*, which either showed natural courtesy or a good upbringing. "It's not as if I expect to live in the kitchen."

"Well, for now, if you're making tea, make enough for four."

"Should I make porridge for four as well?" She concentrated on the teapot, not trusting herself to look at him again. Although she had seen sweaty men before, with his thin unbuttoned shirt stuck to the perspiration on his skin, he looked too blatantly male.

"Porridge? Every day?" He sounded surprised.

"That's what I eat every day."

"I take a run every day. I'm just back. When I'm out in the morning, I can buy whatever you want."

She shot another quick glance at him. Near the waistband of his trousers, his shirt had parted, showing his hard abdominal flesh. She cleared her throat, trying to ignore her quick and impure interest. "That would be a waste of time and money when you have oats here."

"Porridge for *two*, then," he said, sounding as if he'd made a concession. "After we've eaten, *I* can go out and buy whatever *you* want."

He pushed one hand into his pocket and came out with a creased five-pound note. After frowning at the money, he passed the bill to her. "Here. You might as well buy a wedding gown too. I imagine it's enough. Is it enough?"

"For a wedding gown?" Her heart thumped. She shared the money with both her hands, staring with bemusement at his largesse. "With five pounds I could buy a trousseau. And a pair of carriage horses."

He relaxed his mouth. "Were that possible, my treasure, I would marry you twice over. I know it's not much, but later on you'll have all the money you want."

"I plan to keep two pounds of this," she said, facing him. Not even for more money than she had ever seen in her own two hands would she melt under his generosity like a pat of butter in the sun. "Which is the money I lost in wages when you had me dismissed." She nodded her head for emphasis.

He laughed. "I wouldn't hire *you* as my accountant. You've got five, woman, and what's mine is yours, literally, for the rest of your life, if we go through with this marriage. You haven't changed your mind?"

"I don't recall agreeing to your proposal in the first place," she said, using a precise tone, determined not to succumb to his charm. No matter what she said or how she acted, the man remained courteously patient, a virtue she completely lacked. She would not let him make her feel like an ungracious wretch.

"No 'no' is a 'yes.' Don't you know that a double negative is the same as a positive?" He gave her a wide grin, spun on his heel, and left.

She thought of three things she could have said, like "I'm not going to marry you because I would far rather work as a scullery maid," or "I know you only want to get me naked," but the first was untrue and the second didn't seem at all dreadful. Clearly she had lost her mind.

Nevertheless, despite his fine words, she remained skeptical, unable to believe that even a poor gentleman would concede to marrying a maid. He would fool around with her for a while, trying to get her into his bed, and when she wouldn't concede, or after she had, she would be tossed out on her ear. Prepared for whatever might eventuate, she cooked porridge for two and ate alone while the kettle boiled again. When he returned, he ate his porridge and she filled the teapot, which he took through the green door to the surveyor's office along with three empty mugs. Apparently he didn't need companionable breakfasts with her.

The lure of spending five pounds beckoned. For the first time in her life, she had an opportunity to buy a stylish gown. Her steps light, she went back upstairs, tied on her straw hat, and walked out into the sunshine. Many a time she'd collected hats and gowns for Mrs. Brook from the street's exclusive shops. For Devon to give her such a large sum meant that he wanted her to look very much like a lady for her supposed wedding.

Adelaide's most coveted dressmaker sold her designs in a shop two blocks away. The sun had just reached the top of the buildings and the early autumn weather was perfect, not too hot, but not shawl-weather either. Ducking and weaving past footpath conversations and hawkers with loud voices, Wenna set her mind on a cotton gown, perhaps in a blue or yellow pattern.

She arrived at the front of the shop and hesitated. The money in her pocket would let her choose whatever she wanted, but Mrs. Miller took measurements and rarely finished a gown in under a week. Wenna might need her gown tomorrow, or the day after, that was, if Devon truly meant to marry her. She stood, indecisive, staring in the window, noting the draped fabrics, the feather and bead accessories, and the elegant full-length evening gloves.

Farther inside the interior, she could see three customers, all acquaintances of Mrs. Brook. Wenna's chest deflated. If she bought a modish gown in full view of these society matrons, they would speculate about where a maid would find the money for an exclusive design. If Mr. Courtney didn't marry her, then stories about her leaving the Brooks' country house with him would spread and be added to, and she would be painted indelibly scarlet. Her chances of respectability would be dashed.

Swallowing her disappointment, she turned on her heel and hurried back in the direction from which she came, her heart pounding loud enough to make her eardrums echo. When she reached Seymour's Emporium, a more fitting place for a lady's maid, she strode in, her assumed confidence recovered.

On the ground floor, she bought herself a pair of brown fabric shoes with elevated heels. Upstairs, she bought a layered crinoline hoop and a full, gathered petticoat, arranging to have all her purchases delivered. Next, she skimmed through the racks.

Finally she chose one skirt in a deep russet brown and another in cream, and one cream and one floral Basque bodice. Next, she travelled to the fabric department and bought various lengths of cotton fabric and a length of black braid. She also bought a pair of scissors and a packet of pins, threads, and needles. Back in the haberdashery downstairs, she looked at hat shapes and turned up her nose. She could do better than stock shapes disguised by cheap artificial flowers, but not today. First, she needed a plan. Having spent just over two pounds, she pocketed the two Devon owed her and took the smaller parcels back to his lodgings.

After drinking a large glass of water, she took the basket from the kitchen and strolled down to the East End market, where she took her time choosing suitable foodstuffs. Back home—was it home?—she thought about making a meal for Devon, who had disappeared. In lieu, she ate an apple and a hunk of cheese. Her parcels arrived, and she sat in an armchair in his upstairs study to alter the first of the bodices she had purchased, a cream cotton patterned with flowers of pink, blue, and russet.

As neither of the bodices had been small enough in the waist, she had eight seams to unpick and redo. Left alone, she finished the first quickly. She tried this on with the russet skirt. Although she couldn't see her full reflection in Devon's shaving mirror, she could feel the fit. The skirt swished with a pleasing fullness now that she owned a satisfactory crinoline. Wishing she had bought netting snoods, she pondered over her hair. The new combinations called for a far more sophisticated hairstyle than the braid she had worn that morning and the night before.

She tried four different styles before she settled for the first. Her arms ached as she made a loose chignon on the nape of her neck. After narrowing her eyes at her appearance for two or three minutes, she changed back into her black gown and made her way to the kitchen. With an old towel tied around her waist, she put a roast on to cook. With the leftovers, she could make pies tomorrow.

She could barely breathe in the heat of the kitchen. In most of the houses she'd worked, the stoves ran all day, but she'd worked for wealthy people who had large homes with many other rooms. The heat of the one room didn't impact on anyone's comfort, other than the kitchen staff.

The shadows lengthened while she prepared vegetables and set the tiny table. She might have used the plates from the box Devon had brought downstairs, but she'd noticed a raised gold patterned edging and didn't dare. The thick white plates in the kitchen looked good enough with a daintily embroidered tablecloth from one of his boxes in her room.

As she pondered, trying to find something alive in the garden to put in a mug as a table decoration, she heard the lobby door open. She lifted her head and watched Devon walk toward her, trying not to care that he was the handsomest man she'd ever seen.

"My, something smells appetizing. And what do we have here?"

She stood back, thinking he wanted to look at the table setting, but he was looking at her hair.

"Turn around," he said, a strange look on his face.

She did, nervously smoothing her black skirts.

He let air through his teeth. "That's more like it. At last your beautiful hair is visible."

She swallowed. He approved. She wished she didn't care. "I bought four different outfits with the money you gave me. And a pair of shoes."

"With five pounds? Ah, no doubt your cooking will be a credit to my budget, too. While the stove is going, I'll put on the bath water. Are you interested?"

"In taking another bath? Yes, of course. I'd never thought to have one daily. Is that what you do?"

"When the stove is hot, that's what I do. Now, what have you been cooking?" He lifted the lid off the carrots, beans, and peas. "Will I carve the meat for you?"

She nodded, removed the roast from the oven, and sat down to a normal family meal, the first she'd had since her mother had died. His legs didn't fit under the small table as well as hers, and when he sat, the flatware bumped.

She rearranged her skewed fork. "What should I do with the laundry? You don't appear to have a washhouse outside."

"I leave the items I want washed in the foyer, and the woman who does my washing collects it from there, weekly." He moved a little to the side, and his foot cracked against the table leg. "Add yours."

She put her feet beneath her chair, knowing she ought to do the washing to save him money and occupy her time, but the thought of someone else performing the mindless task was too good to withstand.

"And meals," she said, noting that he'd stretched one leg out from under the table. "Morning and midday. Should I make those for you?"

He finished his mouthful and moved his chair back a little. "I would be satisfied to start each day with breakfast, but I'm not often around during the day. I'll leave money for you to buy whatever you want. And, you really don't need to cook the evening meal."

She nodded, catching her bottom lip with her teeth. Despite his polite enjoyment of her cooking, she couldn't expect a man his size to sit at a table that trembled with fear whenever he moved. "And I've been thinking about the men in the office. I could make them a cup of tea while the stove is hot in the morning, around ten. And another in the afternoon when I might want one myself."

"That's a very good plan. They'll be delighted to have two cups of tea a day, and it will keep them out of here." He smiled.

Unable to prevent herself, she smiled back, wondering. In Seymour's Emporium, the hat shapes had given her a yen to work further on her sketches. If Devon didn't marry her, she would either have to find work as a maid or support herself another way. While she was idle, she could work on her idea. If she didn't try, she didn't deserve to succeed.

Chapter 6

After a sparse, hurried breakfast with Devon, Wenna made pastry, which she filled with the leftovers from last night's roast. While the pies baked in the oven, she meandered upstairs, knowing Devon kept pencils and paper in his desk. She sat on his scuffed leather chair and pulled open a side drawer, finding not only lead pencils but also a ruler. In the next drawer down, she found notepaper and a finer page likely meant for letters. Beneath both, she saw foolscap, which was her preferred size. Since he owned a full package, she decided not to worry about the cost. Apparently, *he* didn't.

Hesitantly, she began to draw the back and side view of a hairstyle she had designed in her mind last night. Gaining confidence, she filled the next page with another, both with and without the hat she decided would be the perfect foil for the shape.

The little filigreed carriage clock on Devon's desk said she had taken half an hour. Barely in time to save her pastries, she scooted down the stairs and put the kettle on to boil. The staff in the shop-front office would expect a cup of tea now, if Devon had informed them of her plan. After making two mugs of tea, she pasted a polite smile on her face and opened the green connecting door to the room, a space that dwarfed the study above due to the position of the stairwell.

Ernie sat at a desk strewn with paper, tapping a pencil on his lips. His head turned toward her and he gave a sound of surprise. His scrubbed young face creased with a smile. "Morning, Mrs. Courtney."

"Good morning," she said, glancing around the area. The view of Rundle Street was partially blocked by a pair of green brocade curtains, fringed and tied back to let in the early morning light. An older man in a dark suit, seated at a large map-covered desk on the other side of the room, stood when he saw her. Shelves stacked with folders and papers ranged behind him.

"Where are your manners, lad?" he asked Ernie.

Ernie's chair scraped back and he said, "This here is Mrs. Courtney."

"So I surmised. How do you do, ma'am? I'm Tom Finn, surveyor." Mr. Finn inclined his balding head courteously. To compensate for the lack on his pate, he grew a magnificent set of side-whiskers down his cheeks.

"Wenna Courtney," she said without a quaver, stepping over to him to shake his hand. "So, you do the surveying?"

He nodded. "A never-ending job in a new colony."

"Are you the only two working here?"

"How much more staff did you expect?" His eyes narrowed with amusement.

"I had no expectations, Mr. Finn," she said, smiling back. "Enjoy your tea. I'll bring another at about three in the afternoon."

Ernie gallantly opened the door for her as she left. She took a deep breath. Without being married, she was now Devon's wife. With the rest of the day to herself, she sat down again to alter her cream bodice and add the black braid, military-style, around the collar and cuffs. Pleased with her efforts, she ate a pie for her midday meal and plotted her next hat and hairdo designs.

She had barely finished her first drawing when the lobby door swung open, and Devon appeared.

"Nick's done it." His smooth-skinned face lit with one of his devastating smiles, and he waved a sheet of stiff paper at her. "We can be married this afternoon. I knew he would come through."

"Who is Nick?"

"A friend from long ago," he said, evading her gaze.

She didn't note his answer. "Married." Her thoughts sped too fast to catch, and she stared in horror at her black gown. "What time this afternoon?"

"Five o'clock. Not only did Nick organize a special license, but he organized the venue, too." He grabbed Wenna into his arms and whirled her about.

When her head began to spin, she spiked both elbows into his chest to force him to put her back on her own two feet. He let her slide down his hard body, but he didn't let her go. He stood with his hands lightly on her hips, his blue eyes triumphant.

"Finally married," he said in a satisfied voice. His mouth curved into a smile she saw as deliberately lascivious. "Now we'll be able to share a bed."

Knowing what he meant, she tightened her face. She hadn't even kissed the man. She certainly didn't want him grunting over her. Perhaps he didn't know that a woman needed courting before she wanted to open her legs for him. A small amount of courting. Or, perhaps more companionability than a quick breakfast together and a glance or two over a rustle of newspapers in his study at night.

She'd been able to put the thought of him poking her to the back of her mind while she'd had everything her way. His way wouldn't be so comfortable. Now she had to be what he wanted: a convenient wife who knew her role as a breeder. Naturally, a woman with her background and looks expected no better; in fact, not half as much, if truth be told. She'd had no expectation of marrying a tall, handsome tradesman, and even less of marrying a gentleman.

Somehow, she'd landed on her feet in more ways than one. Devon, a gentleman with impeccable social contacts, would be a great catch for a woman with funds of her own. For a woman who had no foreseeable way to earn an income, an irresponsible, entirely-too-careless wastrel was an impediment. However, he was also even-tempered, good-natured, and— she breathed out—unbearably attractive. Whenever he touched her, her skin tingled. Possibly, she could make something of him.

In fact, he might even be the perfect man for her, one who could be molded and pushed by the right wife, and end up successful with her prodding.

If she added a little more money to her savings, she could contribute to his coffers. Although he would return to Cornwall as a son hoping for a handout, if his wife looked confident and prosperous, his father would be more inclined to be generous. In Cornwall, she could bring up healthy, happy children, though she didn't intend to breed until Devon could show himself well able to support a family. She couldn't place much importance in his story about her having as much money as she wanted when she lived abroad. He'd seen that as a lure, but the lure was going home to the place she was meant to be.

Married! Something inside her opened up and warmed. He honestly meant to marry her. No female could not be impressed by his manly body or his chiseled face, or the way his eyes gleamed bright blue when he smiled.

She kept her expression nonchalant. "I will share your bed if you wed me," she said, using her gracious tone.

"If?" He glanced away. "I've been planning to wed you for days. I've been hoping to bed you for even longer, as you know." He nuzzled his nose into her hair, and his breath blew a whisper on her skin. "You're so fresh and clean, and thoughts of you naked drive me wild with lust."

She swallowed. "Now you're being fanciful." Her face and neck suffused with heat, and she pushed him away, her heart tumbling around in her chest. While trying to breathe, she had thoughts of him naked, too, and wondered about the size of his *oldjohn*. He was a large man. Her hands shook.

"We men do have these thoughts, faced with sharing a bed." His expression turned indulgent as he tugged a curl of her hair that had somehow escaped.

She shifted away, trying to put sharing a bed out of her mind. Sharing a table had been awkward enough. Likely the bedding would be as quick as the meal last night, and assuage his needs. "We women have more practical thoughts, like shopping, cooking, and cleaning."

"Forget your practical thoughts. We'll be celebrating tonight and eating out." He sounded miffed.

She adopted a languid "Miss Patricia" tone. "In that case, I'll lie on my bed reading your newspapers before I prettify myself for the most momentous day of my life. Do you mind if I use the mirror in your room this afternoon?"

"Do what you will," he said, already turning to leave. "I'll be back after four to dress."

"Have a pie before you leave. They're still warm."

He snatched up two and disappeared.

In the early afternoon, she unpicked the waist seam of her older black gown and took apart the bodice, giving herself the beginnings of a new skirt and a bodice pattern. The town hall clock struck three before she'd barely tidied the scraps of material and the broken threads. She had an hour and a half to ready herself.

Before she changed into the combination she'd decided on for her wedding, she took a laundered white shirt with a starched collar out of Devon's tallboy, brushed his dark suit, and cleaned his black shoes. Knowing he owned the correct attire for an afternoon wedding, she found the black silk cravat she'd placed with his other neckwear in the top drawer. The clock struck the half hour.

Now for herself. Being the prettiest of her outfits, she'd planned her cream skirt and the cream-based floral bodice for the wedding that might never have eventuated. For the first time, she pulled on the crinoline hoop and dropped the extravagant petticoat over her head. The skirt took almost no time to fasten, and the swish and sway of the material fascinated her for a few moments, but her clammy fingers slipped with her stays. Her bodice had been altered to emphasize her small waist and the back hooking took quite a bit of contortion. Finally, she walked as gracefully as any lady back into Devon's room to use his mirror for her hair.

For the second time, she formed the loose chignon that Devon had noted, but this time she added a pattern of thick strands to lightly decorate the spread. Using a hairclip, she separated a few curls to soften the edges around her face and neck. She stared at herself for a few moments, certain she looked as smart as any of her mistresses. When she heard him take the stairs at his usual rate, two at a time, she hurried back to her bedroom. Although he couldn't avoid seeing her before the ceremony, she somehow needed to prolong the moment.

Her palms sticky, she sat on her bed. She didn't have gloves. Her plain black pair would look appalling with her light outfit. And she didn't have a reticule to hold her handkerchief. No matter. She wouldn't cry. A bride didn't cry on her wedding day.

Too soon, Devon stood in the doorway, dressed for the wedding, his hands shoved deep into his trouser pockets, silently staring at her. He said not a word. His face looked tight, tense. He tapped his black hat on this thigh and glanced at the gloves he held in the same hand. "Thank you for readying my clothes," he finally said.

She heard a crow outside calling, "How? How? How?" and her lips stretched into the shape of a smile. How foolish to expect a compliment. Better to be thanked for a good deed done than admired for the way she spent his money on decorating herself. He was only marrying her because... Why, why, why? A man with his looks and connections could choose from a long line of rich, beautiful young brides. Surely. Unless he was the wastrel she suspected he was, paid to stay away from England and hoping to be invited back if he sired a plump child to be fed sugarplums by his doting grandpa.

She glanced at Devon again. In black and white, the man looked like a lord: formal, remote, invulnerable, and the handsomest man in creation. Unable to suppress her shallow thoughts, she pushed past him through the doorway.

She held her posture during her entire wedding ceremony, keeping her eyes wide, refusing to blink, afraid that sentimental tears might gather. She wished her parents could see her today, standing tall beside a man who would provide strong, healthy children. Although she couldn't be any more to Devon than the breeder he wanted, she had the idea that he could too easily be more to her, but she would guard against that. A love not returned would be wasted.

His friend had organized the ceremony in a stark building beside the almost fully constructed town hall. Two witnesses, strangers whom Devon quite blatantly paid, stood staring while the man dressed in street clothes who had introduced himself as the registrar asked Wenna to take Devon for her husband.

Neither she nor Devon had given thought to a ring, and she accepted his green signet in lieu. She murmured "I will," and after the same phrases, Devon also said "I will." The whole procedure, including the signing, took no longer than ten minutes. She stepped out of the tall building and onto King William Street a married woman. "Mrs. Courtney," the registrar had pronounced her.

"I'm afraid of losing your ring." She glanced at the town hall clock, whose minute hand had just passed the quarter hour. "It's far too big. You'd best take it back."

"I'll get you another," Devon said indifferently, taking her by the elbow. "But a ring isn't an essential. We made our vows in front of witnesses, and no more than that is required. A church ceremony takes far longer to set up, and it would have meant nothing to me. I'm not a believer."

"I can't argue about religion. I've always gone to church on Sundays, and I've never seen the need to question."

"You've never hesitated to question me, or my motives."

"You're hardly a higher being."

"What? You don't admire me?"

"You have your good points."

"Would you care to elaborate?"

She stood stock-still and looked him over from head to toe. "You look well in a formal suit," she said drily.

He laughed. "I thought I was a rag of a man. Well, at least I own a block of land."

"Let's hope you'll be able to sell it before you leave."

He made a doubting mouth. "It's an investment."

His hat fashionably angled and, without speaking, he walked her back to The Pig and Whistle. Inside the noisy place, he took the same seat as before and told the same waitress he wanted a bottle of the best wine. The wine, which Wenna thought was extravagant, bearing in mind the state of his shaky finances, came with two thick-stemmed glasses. Since a celebration seemed to be in order, she sipped a little, too.

Devon's gentlemanly dress appeared to impress the waitress, who listened to his order with her eyelashes lowered and then rushed to do his bidding. Wenna didn't know what the waitress or the other patrons presumed about her. Not wearing a ring, she didn't look like Devon's wife, but since she knew she'd married him, she assumed an outward confidence.

Halfway through the meal, a little man with a curly fringe of white hair and an enormous nose came over to the table. "Everything in order, Mr. Courtney?"

"Sit and have wine with us, Snow. Milady has hardly taken a sip, and I don't want to quaff a full bottle by myself."

"Don't mind if I do." The little man dipped his head and appropriated a beer mug from one of the few empty tables. "Is tonight a special occasion?"

"I'd say so." Devon poured the wine into the mug. "This is my, ah, wife," he said, indicating Wenna. "Snow is the host here. I think he owns the place, too, although he won't admit it."

"Garn with you." Mr. Snow grinned at Devon. "You don't think a rough old miner like me 'ud get a job here if I didn't own the place, do you? Good t'meetcha, Mrs. Courtney. Thought it would only be a matter of time 'til this young buck settled down. A lotta ladies gonna be disappointed, though." He quaffed his wine as fast as most men drank ale.

Devon laughed. "You still don't have a taste for the good stuff."

"I'm a simple man. You two enjoy yourselves, and I'll get back to work. Jest wanted to inspect the lady. Everyone's interested, like." Mr. Snow took his empty mug and left.

"I'm surprised you eat in this place." Wenna watched the little man speak to the waitress, whose face fell as she glanced back at Devon. "The other patrons are working people and none would touch wine."

"Maybe they should."

"Wine is too expensive if we're wanting to get back to Cornwall."

"Are you enjoying the meal?" he asked politely.

She looked at the fine grain of her beef and the fluffy, buttery vegetable mash on the thick white plate. "It's beautifully cooked."

"So, please leave me to decide how I spend my money."

She glanced at his face. Yet again she'd annoyed him when she was only trying to help. She'd never had a way with men, likely because she was too plain-speaking. Perhaps she needed to learn when to keep quiet. Finally, the half-empty bottle was re-corked. With Devon carrying the remains, she walked in the failing daylight across to the lodging with him, steeling herself for the night ahead.

She lit a lamp and waited in the study while he put the water on to boil for the baths. Though by rights, as his wife, she should do this, he said he had done the task for months and would continue. When she heard the rattle of the pan being dragged off the hob, she undressed down to her chemise, collected the fresh towels to hide her legs, and descended to the kitchen.

The stars outside the window began to emerge in the gray sky. After her bath, she lit up her bedroom, took out the sponge she had bought some years before, sprinkled on the vinegar she had poured into a jar from the kitchen, and inserted her womb guard. Then, she dropped her clean nightgown over her head and sat on her bed. She didn't cry. Brides did not.

* * * *

Dev couldn't imagine being more tense. He'd planned to impregnate Wenna, breed a son or two and live his own life, but the look of her in her wedding gown had tempted him to call the whole thing off. She'd looked calm, beautiful, and full of hope. He'd expected her to look satisfied to be going ahead with their plan, like a business partner ready to sign the contract. Instead, she'd looked like a sweet young bride.

And now he planned to put his baby inside her. Fortunately, his body was a step ahead of his brain and didn't mind that they were almost strangers. His towel around his waist and already half-aroused, he walked into the light of his bedroom.

"What the devil?" he muttered.

She'd turned down the covers of the bed, but had made herself scarce. She couldn't be nervous. She'd been loved before, which any man would have expected given her age. Some women of the same age would have eight children by now. He reversed and followed the lamplight to her room.

"Changed your mind?" he asked the redhead who sat neatly on her single bed.

"I thought it would look a little gauche to be waiting for you in your bed."

"Gauche?" he said. "For a maid, you have quite an extensive vocabulary."

She gave him a smile full of cynicism. "I wasn't born a maid. I was trained to be a maid, and maids learn from their masters and mistresses. For example, my first mistress said to me, 'You look like a gauche country girl.' Then she had me hide my hair."

"I expect she couldn't stand the competition. Now, would your ladyship join me in my bed?" He stood aside so she could walk before him, which she did.

He followed her night-braided hair, her squared shoulders, and her white cotton-tented body, his bare feet padding on the floorboards while he struggled to breathe evenly. This composed woman aroused him like no other. He watched while she neatly folded his suit into a lower drawer and paired his shoes into the bottom. Apparently, she would rather act the maid than share his bed.

He didn't bloody well care.

He would have her unless she left him right here and now. He would take her without emotional involvement. She needed no emotion, either. She wanted to leave this country, he wanted to stay, and neither needed to complicate matters. His hands clenched while she began to fold his shirt. "You're delaying, my dear."

"I'm tidying up after you."

He dropped his towel. His erection hit mid mast, jutting at right angles. Her eyes focused on his rod, and she backed a little.

"Then, I'll tidy up after you." He stepped forward, only slightly impeded by his now full erection banging on his belly, scooped up the hem of her nightgown, and lifted the pristine white cotton over her head, trying to roll the damned thing while the sight of her nakedness left him dry-mouthed.

She stood, lifting her chin, daring him to stare at a slender white body unmarred by a single mole or freckle. The palest of pink nipples, barely a skin tone darker than the rest of her, tipped her surprisingly lush breasts. Telling a beautiful woman how beautiful she looked was as pointless as complimenting a genius for his brain. He could see that she wanted to cover herself with her hands, and he appreciated her determination not to be coy.

"You should stay naked for the rest of your life," he said in a forced voice.

"I don't have a choice at the moment. You have appropriated my nightgown."

With that, she snatched, and trickled the garment onto the floor. Her breath tingled on his shoulder while her palm brushed the underside of his rod, which jerked in anticipation.

"Mm," she said.

"Mm?'

"You should leave *this* on display, too. Your social calendar would then be full."

He could barely breathe, which ended up not being a problem because she fastened her mouth across his. Just as he prepared to take her lovely bottom into his two palms and lift her onto his upright rod, she ended her kiss and moved back, eyeing the bed.

Accepting her clear invitation, he lifted her by the waist, threw her onto the bed, and dropped beside her. One roll, and he took her onto his chest. Her heart thundered against him and he arranged his cock between her thighs. "This is a wildly inappropriate moment," he said, wishing his brain hadn't started functioning while his tool wanted to guide him. "But are you clean?"

"I had a bath just before you."

"I mean, disease-free."

She pushed up from him and stared right into his eyes. "I'm not a whore, and I suspect you've diddled quite few. Are *you* clean?"

He cleared his throat. "I haven't been with a whore. I, ah, would normally use a contraceptive sheath. With you, I'm not using anything because we want a baby. Now, lie on me while I fix your hair." His fingers slid to the back of her neck, and she let her soft breasts compress against his chest while he removed her clips, which he tossed onto the floor. When he found the end of the braid, he pulled off the tie and combed his fingers through the heavy mass, freeing her locks. "That's better."

She shook her hair, letting the curls trickle across his chest. Her hand lifted to the top of his shoulder, and she tinkered over his skin for a moment, her mouth sulky. "Get on with it."

He lifted her hair out of the way, stroking the silky softness as he rolled on top of her. His thighs parted hers, and he angled his hips, desperate to begin the act that would end with the hot rush of his semen into her.

Her unconfined hair spread across the pillow, and in place of Jenny's soft loving smile, Wenna's face wore an expression of wariness. He gently dropped his mouth across hers and she responded by lifting her knees. Other than that, she kept still.

This wouldn't work, and he didn't know how to proceed. He'd never had a woman who didn't want him, didn't grab his buttocks and urge him on. Ridiculously, he'd thought she shared his desire. Why? She'd never been anything other than cool.

"I'll turn off the lamp," he said gruffly. He reached over and drowned the wick.

When he rolled onto his side again, he drew her into his arms, running the flat of his palm down her smooth back and delightful bottom. Eventually she did the same to him. With his mouth just under her ear, he put her hand onto his heavy erection. Breathing audibly, she explored. Her breath heated on his cheek and her palm found a frustrating rhythm, too slow, too gentle. He kissed her, took her hand in his, and settled it on his chest. She'd relaxed. For tonight, that would suffice.

* * * *

A drawer squeaked. Surreptitiously, Wenna cricked open her eyes and watched Devon drag his old trousers over his linen under-drawers and his even-older shirt over his head. He collected his soft-soled shoes and, without washing or shaving, left the room. She heard the downstairs door slam.

She yawned and stretched. Without a doubt, Devon slept on a better mattress than hers. His sheets were the finest cotton money could buy, but better than comfort and luxury was the fact that he hadn't pushed his huge *oldjohn* inside her. Last night, after he'd fallen asleep, she'd taken out her sponge, and then she'd worried that he might try to poke her some time during the night. She needed to learn his habits.

The town hall clock struck six. Lately, she'd been sleeping an extra hour, but since he appeared to be an earlier riser than she suspected, she clumped out of bed, washed quickly, and dressed in her black gown, assuming he'd gone for his daily run. As a wife, she should take an interest. As a wife, she bundled down the stairs with his shaving mug and lit the stove.

While the wood crackled and smoked, she shot back to the bedroom and tidied. For a moment, she paused to examine her face in his shaving mirror. She didn't look any different for having spent a night in a man's bed—in her *husband's* bed. He'd had his hands all over her body and he'd kissed her. She wouldn't mind at all if he did both again.

And she'd caressed his silky-hard *oldjohn*. *My.* She hoped he didn't remember but she suspected he would. The man was a reprobate and had encouraged the touching. Her cheeks warmed. She was hardly a virgin, but no man's hands had smoothed her the way his did, and no man's eyes had seen her naked body. None had handled her hair so reverently.

She gathered together the sheets from her single bed and took them downstairs for the laundress. After she filled the kettle, she put the oats on to cook. While setting the small table, she examined the plates that sat boxed in the storage cupboard. Each plate she drew out was gold-edged with bouquets of flowers painted in the center—large plates, small plates, bread-and-butter plates, dessert plates, cake plates, lidded vegetable dishes, and serving platters. No two plates were exactly the same. Nonetheless, the set matched. His mother's plates, he'd said. His mother had died. Why did his father not use them?

Her mouth quirked into a rueful smile. He didn't use them because they were too beautiful, each a work of art. Wenna couldn't use them either—not in a set of rooms behind a shop front with no dining table, and no point in having one, not for two people like her and Devon, who had nothing in common, who wouldn't sit over candlelit dinners discussing their dreams. She shut the door of the cupboard and took out the thick plates and mugs she used for breakfast every day.

The door squeaked, light momentarily appeared in the foyer, and then the doorway darkened.

"Good morning," her husband said with the sort of smile that made her insides hum. Perspiration beaded his brow, and his shirt clung to his chest. "I thought you would sleep longer."

"If you're up and about early, I should be, too."

"I went for a run around the city perimeter. This morning I stopped off at the market and bought fruit for breakfast." He walked into the kitchen with a newspaper-wrapped bundle, which he passed to her.

"I cooked porridge."

"We can have both."

"Just a moment, and I'll pour the hot water into your shaving jug."

He blinked at her. "I usually use the cold water. Wenna..." He took a deep breath. "Thank you."

He left with the jug. Her heart resumed a steady beat. That's what impressionable brides hoped would happen when they'd married a golden god. She sighed. Now a wife and with virtually nothing to do, no washing, no cooking, she was in a position to be a particularly supportive wife—if she found the courage to follow her plan.

Chapter 7

When she'd been nothing but a lodger, Wenna had assumed she couldn't change anything in Devon's bedroom. Now a wife who shared his bed, she thought she could freshen up the area.

First she took down the velvet curtains and whacked them on the clothesline outside until the nap stood up again. The multi-paned window looked almost gracious when she replaced the revitalized fabric. Pleased with herself, she shifted the washstand to catch the morning light beneath the window. This left more space at the end of the bed, and more space for her to get to work polishing the enormous bed, starting at the foot.

As her rag moved over the ornate wooden embossing, she found carved figures among the leaves and flowers, persons who appeared to be...she peered closer and stared. Her mouth went dry as she gaped at the appalling sight of bodies writhing into unlikely positions with unlikely beings. Her husband slept in a bed lewd enough to take the place of pride in a brothel. Short of breath, she examined each exaggerated phallus and every sexual depravity known to man, woman, or beast.

By the time she'd been reluctantly enlightened, the carvings gleamed a golden red and the silver travelling clock in Devon's study chimed the hour of ten. A trifle late, she delivered the morning mugs of tea to the office, afraid her cheeks still held the warmth of titillation.

Now free until three o'clock, she patted her neat chignon, brushed down her black gown, straightened her collar and cuffs, and jammed on her elderly hat. Now or never.

Assuming confidence with a ramrod spine, an elevated chin, and a determined smile, she put her drawings into her cloth bag and left for the hat shop. As luck would have it, the only customer left as she arrived on the doorstep. The bell jangled as she walked in, alerting Mrs. Busby, the middle-aged proprietor of Madame Fleur's hat shop, to her presence.

"Good morning, Miss Chenoweth." The woman's professional smile spread across her well-worn, comfortably plump face. Like Wenna, she wore black on her substantial frame, but for another reason entirely. When fitting hats on ladies sitting in front of a mirror, she needed to be the background for the hat and not let her gown distract from the color or design she hoped to sell. "Another order for Mrs. Brook?"

"Not today, Mrs. Busby. I have an idea I'd like to discuss with you, if I may?"

"Of course you may. Your ideas in the past have been good for my business, which is why Mrs. Brook has always had a special price from me."

Wenna rested her bag on the nearest seat, a red padded velvet with a carved wooden back. "Mrs. Brook brought you extra customers because her hats looked so stylish with her hairstyles. As you know, I designed her hairstyles using the latest pictures from France. These days, the ladies like large, complicated hairdos. This means the hats need to be small to set them off."

"And your idea is?" Mrs. Busby raised her thin black eyebrows.

"I've left Mrs. Brook and branched out on my own now, Mrs. Busby, and I have a few drawings I would like to show you." Wenna set her four pages across the countertop where Mrs. Busby usually made out her accounts. "I have depicted various hat shapes and the hairstyles that look best with them. When ladies try on hats, often they buy the first one that fits their hairstyle. This might not be the best in a fashion sense, or to suit the occasion, or even to suit your pocket. If the ladies had a hair stylist, perhaps in the back of your establishment, hair could be designed to suit any hat. I think this might be good for both of us." With a certain amount of trepidation, she watched the milliner's face.

Mrs. Busby's tongue rolled over her teeth while she thought. "You would be the hairstylist?"

"I can work from half past ten until half past two every day. Today, without charge, I'll style the hair of any lady who would like to see the effect." Wenna held her breath.

"Would you like a small glass of sherry, Miss Chenoweth, while we discuss this?"

Wenna left at half past two wearing a cream fabric pillbox decorated with black leaves—bought for a discounted price. She'd styled five heads, sold ten hats, and managed to remain "Miss Chenoweth" the whole time. Tomorrow, she would earn six pence per head. Smiling, she

paused on the street to admire the cut flowers in buckets for sale outside
the toolmaker's establishment. A posy of pink roses absorbed her for a
moment. Even from some feet away, the heady fragrance perfumed the
surrounding air. Knowing she shouldn't buy frivolities with her meager
funds, she turned away.

"Lovely, ain't they?"

She smiled at Mr. Snow, the tavern owner. "I love roses. I love the
delicate perfume."

"A newly wed, pretty young woman should have some. Let me
buy you a bunch."

She blushed. "Thank you. No."

"I'm an old and ugly man. Your husband won't say a thing." Mr. Snow
had an expression of little-boy mischief on his face and a definite twinkle
in his round brown eyes.

She laughed. "What a shame. I'd love him to be wildly jealous."

"Done, then." He pushed his hand into his trouser pocket,
searching for tuppence.

"You're very generous, Mr. Snow, but I don't have a vase. I couldn't
take something so lovely and watch it die."

"Reckon I could find a spare pickle jar or two from The Pig and
Whistle, if you think they would be good enough to hold your flowers."

"I think they would be perfect. Thank you, Mr. Snow, for your practical
suggestion." She watched him choose the prettiest bunch. As he presented
her with the posy, she said, "I see they're digging up the road in front
of your hotel."

"Gas pipes," he said in a morose tone. "Street lightin' is all very well,
but not when we keep havin' problems with the pipes. Twice they've
changed my nearest, and twice they've dug up the road. Needs to be
finished before winter, or we'll have bogs in the street the way we did last
year. I'll walk back with you."

She walked beside him through the crowded street. Wagons trundled
by, and various men greeted Mr. Snow, staring at her. Previously, she'd
been glanced at and dismissed. Selling her idea had added a lift to her
confidence. She would need this tomorrow, when she charged money for
her services. "I've heard that we'll all have gas lighting in our houses
within a few years."

"I wouldn't be surprised. Progress keeps creepin' up on us. No more'n
twenty years ago, this street was mostly tents, and look at it now."

"So much has been done in such a short time." She gazed around, focusing on the new buildings, nothing more than thirty years old, and realized for the first time that she saw history in the making.

"Mr. Snow!" Maisie, the shapely barmaid from The Pig and Whistle, pulled to a breathless halt on the footpath in front of them, glancing at Wenna's hat before turning to Mr. Snow. "I'm supposed to tell you the cook's drunk and he's throwing his knives all over the kitchen."

With a quaint bow from the waist, Mr. Snow said, "Excuse me, Mrs. Courtney, but I must deal with the emergency. Maisie'll come over later with them pickle jars."

The couple hurried off to deal with the problem while Wenna strolled home. She sat the blooms in a basin until ten minutes later, when Maisie came to the door with two big jars. "I was noticing your hair before, Mrs. Courtney, and I was wondering where you had it done."

"I do my hair myself, Maisie."

"Fancy that." Maisie's blue eyes shaded with disappointment.

"I can do yours, too, if you like, when you have the time, and teach you how to do it yourself," Wenna said, assessing the barmaid's straight brown hair.

"Fancy that!" Maisie's face lit up. "Soon as I finish serving the lunches, I'll have time."

"Well, I'll see you in half an hour?"

An hour later, after her hair had been meticulously styled with braiding that started at the top of her head and ended at her nape where the plaits crossed and twisted into a bun, Maisie agreed to tell the hotel's customers that she had her hair done by a Miss Chenoweth who had set up in Busby's hat shop. Visible to at least twenty women per day, she would be a great advertisement for Wenna.

Wenna made the afternoon tea, sighing with unutterable boredom, and then settled into the study to sew the new bodice for her russet skirt.

* * * *

Dev pulled up the creaking hired wagon containing his second load of bricks. He'd delivered his first early this morning. This would be his last. As the least skilled of the builders, Dev had been the natural candidate for the job.

The mason, Jim, a short, sturdy, gray-haired man about fifty years old, came over and stood near the tray. "Just in time. The lads have finished the foundations." He indicated his four grinning muscle-bound sons, dressed like him in dusty shirts and trousers, with brightly colored handkerchiefs tied around their necks to catch the sweat.

Four months ago, Dev had begun building in the foothills. He had a grand plan, but had started with a compact house in which he, or the next owner, could live while the later building took shape. He had named this "The Gatehouse" in his mind. During the first month, he'd had an underground tank excavated to make sure of the water supply. His laborers had dug the room-sized hole, lined the area with stone and mortar, and brick-vaulted the top. Gutters, yet to be bricked into the soil, would guide the run-off from the rains toward his tank.

Dev had planned this first design like most settlers' cottages, a central passage with two rooms either side, and a kitchen, a laundry, and a bathroom built at the back. The days of having a separate building for these last rooms had passed, fire not being as prevalent in the stone-built houses as in the old wattle and daub.

He knew Wenna was curious about what he did all day, but since she thought land was bought to be sold, she would see him as a fool to be building a house. Perhaps he was a fool when he would be leaving within the year, but he had been assured the main construction could be completed by then—the walls, the floors, and the roof. Since he worked as his own laborer, too, the job should be done sooner, and he would see something of himself left behind.

"I'll unload, and you'll have your bricks in a trice." He leaped down from the flatbed and began hefting his load into piles, helped by two of the so-called lads. His land had been cleared of the native scrub, but he'd kept a few tall she-oaks for the shading of his houses. As he worked up a sweat, he thought about living in this beautiful stark country and being his own man. A dream—no more. As the heir to his father's title and estates, he was expected back in Cornwall to do his duty, some of which he had pre-empted by marrying. Producing an heir, well, that would happen soon enough.

During the heat of the day, the walls had arisen as he watched, and had heightened as he learned how to mix the lime mortar. He'd never been another man's laborer, but he enjoyed being his own, seeing his sweat pour into a substantial building.

Satisfyingly worn out after helping build another outside wall, he drove the flatbed wagon back to Adelaide, a little more than two miles away. The horses plodded, swishing away the flies and the dust, while he resigned himself to another night of frustration.

Wenna—lovely, maddening, obstinate Wenna—wasn't ready to welcome him between her legs yet. Perhaps she looked like Jenny, but the beautiful, willing dairymaid hadn't needed to be readied. The first time she'd passed him a cup of fresh sweet milk and offered her wholesome smile, he'd wanted her. The second time, he'd realized he could have her, but he resisted temptation.

Although she was older than he, in her twenties, she was a maid, and gentlemen didn't dally with maids. Instead, dry-mouthed, he noted how brightly the sun shone on her red hair and how patiently she listened to his gauche ramblings. Somehow, talking to her while she squirted the milk into the buckets absorbed his emptiness, left him feeling at peace, less frustrated with his disciplined life.

He'd shamefacedly told Jenny's back that his brothers said he looked exactly like a past tutor of theirs, blonde and lanky, and she understood the implication. She scraped out her milking stool, arose, and walked into his arms, her fingers pushing his hair out of his eyes.

"You're beautiful," she said. "You look like a picture in a storybook, like a prince. Your brothers—they're jealous." She raised her soft mouth to his.

"I love you," he whispered.

In silence, she stroked his hair, passing her fingers through, sifting. Unmanly tears filled his eyes. His mother had used the same soothing touch when he'd gone to her with a problem.

"Shh," Jenny said as she rocked him. "I feel love for you, too, and I can see that you do need it."

She unlaced her bodice. When she put his hand on her soft breast, he forgot about his gentle, golden-haired mother who had died ten years before. The fresh scent of Jenny's skin, the freckled white of her breast and the aching hardness between his legs took over from memories of the distant past. With heat spreading throughout his body, he kissed her.

Her fingers tangled in his hair. "I am yours for the asking."

"I can't marry until I'm twenty-one. We'll have to wait."

Jenny ran a thumb across his cheek. "We can never marry, but I do so want you." She drew him farther into the milking shed and, frantic with lust and longing, he took her the first time in the hayloft. Later, he held her in his arms, worrying that he might have given her a baby.

"Hush," she said. "We will make sure you don't." And she taught him how to protect her.

Over the following months, he knew he wanted to love and protect her for the rest of his life. He needed only two years to turn twenty-one, and then he could marry without his father's sanction.

However, his father heard about Jenny and, without consulting his powerless youngest son, found a husband for her, a local farmer. He dealt with Dev by enrolling him at Cambridge. Two years wasted studying law and he was pushed off to France to learn self-sufficiency, or so his father said. The banished cuckoo in the nest, Dev learned as much about viticulture as he could. When stories of the new land Terra Australis began to filter through to him, he snatched up the position of the secretary to the next governor of South Australia, likely offered because of his mother's connection to the governor's wife. A title would never be his, and a new start would suit him. He held this position until the governor finished his term.

In the meantime, his unhappily married older brother, William, Viscount Dellacourt, died. John, the second in line for the title, was recalled from his base in India, but as a colonel in the British army, he had responsibilities. Word arrived that he'd been killed in a skirmish, and Dev succeeded to the unwanted third-hand title of Viscount Dellacourt, heir to the twelfth Earl of Marchester and all his properties. His laugh when he read the notification sounded bitter even to him.

The wagon turned onto King William Street, and Dev dropped off his rig at the Saddler's Arms, where he'd hired the horses. He walked back to his lodging, hot, sweaty, and dirty, but elated. As he opened the door into the foyer, the office door squeaked open.

"I picked up your mail with Mr. Finn's when I went to the post office," young Ernie said, grinning and waving a bundle of papers.

"Good lad." Dev accepted his mail and glanced through. The Earl of Marchester, his father, dutifully enclosed a report of estate matters three monthly. Not, however, this month.

* * * *

Wenna heard feet pounding on the treads.

Devon called out, "Good evening," as he passed the sitting room. "The bedroom looks different," he said, returning to the doorway after he had washed and changed.

"A small amount of cleaning and a slight rearrangement of furniture does wonders for the look of a room. You live your life in a shambles."

She glanced up at him. He wore a dark suit, and he'd brushed his hair into gleaming corn-silk softness.

"I'm a rag of a man who lives his life in a shambles, am I?" A slight smile softened his face. "You must have seen something in me, or you wouldn't have married me." His expression one of challenge, he took her sewing from her lap, placed the fabric on the side table, and drew her to her feet. Staring straight into her eyes, he slid his hands onto her hips and set his body right up against hers.

Her wretched heart gave an excited leap. "I married you because I want to go to Cornwall," she said, her tone regrettably uncertain.

"And in return, what did you promise? If you can't remember, I'll give you a small hint." His hands spanned her waist, and he gave her a brief kiss. His gaze met hers, and his eyebrows lifted to a query.

She put one hand behind his neck and, unable to suppress a smile, drew his mouth down to hers. Darned man. His soft lips fastened on hers with just the hint of his tongue teasing across. She wouldn't open to him because she disliked that disgusting probing, but at the light touch of his tongue on hers, she stood on tiptoes, digging her fingers hard into his shoulders. His arms tightened around her. The kiss deepened, and her whole body heated.

Last night she had been unable to stop caressing his hard, silky-smooth part, and she'd wallowed in the wickedness of his encouragement. The lewd bed, no doubt, influenced his ideas. When this man, her husband, touched her, she wanted to be whatever he wanted her to be: his wife, his lover, respectable, wanton, smart, or silly. When he smiled, she was his to be molded. When he gave her space, she turned back into the disciplined person she'd always been, one who never forgot her goal.

He walked her backward to his desk, lifting her skirts as he sat her atop. Her crinoline hoop subsided after first aiming for her nose. One tilt of his hips pushed the hoop out of the way, and he stood between her thighs. Like a wanton, she undulated against his ready hard part, making a soft noise of surrender. His hands cupped her buttocks, drawing her even closer, and his mouth swallowed her sounds of eagerness. Her fingers dug into his back. She could think of nothing but the sensation between her legs. His unwilling wife had turned into a molten heap after the barest touch. The creak of the floorboards beneath his feet brought back her sanity.

She pushed at his shoulders. "You'll have to stop," she said in a soft, indecisive tone she could scarcely recognize. "We're both neat and tidy and ready to go over the road for a meal."

He laughed. "And you think everyone will know what we've been doing?"

"*I'll* know."

"Indeed. But this is what happens to women who tell their husbands they are useless. The husband tends to think he should prove he's a man, at least."

"I suspect most people you meet know you're a man." She covered his seeking mouth with her hand.

"And tonight you look all woman." He angled his head so that her hand covered his cheek almost like a caress. "There's nothing more tempting than a tidy woman waiting to be mussed."

She wriggled back a little, sliding her center of pleasure away from all temptation. "You're quite impossible."

"True," he said pleasantly. "Let that be a lesson to you." With an inscrutable smile, he rearranged the shape in his trousers.

She slid from the table to the floor, using one hand to check her hair, not certain of the lesson she should have learned, but knowing the one she *had* learned. Lust for him could control her too easily.

However, she had discovered he liked her gown and her hair. With two choices of bodice and gown— four combinations as well as her best blue gown—her outfits wouldn't look new forever. Her plan to incorporate her black gowns into her wardrobe culminated today when she'd put a waistband on the black skirt of the newest, wearing that with the cream bodice she had trimmed with black braid. The new cream-and-black hat completed her outfit.

If she could do nothing more, she could merge her body with his and bear his child. When she did, she would own a part of him forever. Her attraction to him melted her bones. Perhaps she didn't understand him. Perhaps she could never empathize with those not born to work. Perhaps she could never match him or be good enough, but she could appreciate the perfection she had married.

Huffing out a sigh, she followed him down the stairs and into the street. The churned dust had settled and the place had quieted, though the shops wouldn't close until dark, a little more than an hour away. He held open the door to The Pig and Whistle for her, and she led the way to his usual spot when Maisie appeared.

"We have a window table free," the waitress said, a firm smile on her face.

Devon looked surprised but pleased as he sat at a table with a view of the outside street. "What do you suppose prompted an offer of a window table?"

Wenna watched a rather-satisfied Maisie walk away. "We're a couple. They need the tables closer to the bar for the men. I've been thinking. A bath in the morning would suit me better than a bath in the evening. Do you mind changing?"

"Not at all," he said in his cultured voice. "I don't have a bathing preference. I heated the stove in the evenings because I don't spend the day at home." His thick lashes shaded the expression in his eyes.

Tonight would be the night; she knew that. She knew Devon wouldn't wait forever for the tupping he'd wanted to do from the start. If she hadn't decided to clean his bed, she wouldn't be so nervous. When she had finished polishing, she'd understood that he wouldn't be content to have her lying beneath him staring impatiently at the ceiling.

She gave Maisie a seedy smile as her meal was deposited on the table.

Maisie waited, staring down at Devon. "Notice anything different about me?"

He leaned back and gave her the once-over. "You look very smart, Maisie. Far too smart to be working in this establishment."

"I got me hair done." After a significant glance at Wenna, she swished off, the elaborate styling of her hair making much of her back view.

"That's a compliment to *you*," Devon said as he cut his beefsteak. "She's copying your hairstyles. You might change the fashions around here."

"I might," Wenna said, paying attention to the peas on her plate rather than the man who would service her, one way or another, tonight. Her confidence had vanished after seeing the couples, and even triples, carved on his bed. Should Devon be interested in that sort of thing, she didn't know how she would react. Protectively, she pulled the high-buttoned neck of her bodice tighter.

"Are you chilly?"

"I'm not very hungry."

He shrugged. "I hope you will excuse my appetite, in that case."

She reared her head, staring at him, hoping he didn't mean his appetites in bed. Last night he'd been so nice, and last night she'd thought she would let him do anything to her as long as the whole act could be over and done with quickly. Instead, he'd shown her men liked to be touched and he'd shown her where. She now knew how immediately he reacted when she touched him there, and last night that reaction possibly thrilled her more than him. Tonight he would want more.

He finished his meal and ordered coffee. She examined his face, and saw beyond his beauty. He had an aura of strength and quiet power. She would never have this man groveling at her feet, despite his desire for her. Her only influence on him would be what he chose.

"What do you do when you're out all day?"

He stared straight into her eyes. "Today I was looking at a house in the foothills, built on a rich clay loam. The view from there is extensive, all the way from the port to the city." And he rose to his feet.

Clearly, tonight would be the night.

Chapter 8

Although her bargain with Mrs. Busby had energized her, Wenna's cleaning frenzy during the day had somewhat eroded her confidence in further experimentation with Devon tonight. Given the choice, she would certainly vote for a good sleep. However, she could see by the unholy expression on Devon's face that abstinence didn't feature in his thoughts. With a decided lack of enthusiasm, she trod up the stairs.

Trying to concentrate, she sat with her everlasting sewing in an armchair while Devon flicked the pages of magazines and checked various articles with his handwritten notes.

After about an hour, he turned to her with his eyebrows raised. "Bed? Or do you intend to sew all night?"

She folded the bodice, and, without a word, she left for the small bedroom to disrobe. After firmly closing the door, she stepped out of her skirt, unhooked her bodice, and put her underwear into the wash bag. Almost nervously, she donned her cotton nightgown. That done, she inserted her vinegar-soaked sponge and began to prepare herself to be a wife again, first taking her pins out of her hair. With her brush in her hands, she left for Devon's mirror. Though he still occupied his study, a lamp burned in his bedroom.

The yells of roisterers echoed through the street outside, and a golden halo from the nearest street lamp glinted on the wavy imperfections of the window glass. She closed the curtains and began brushing her hair. As she reached the halfway mark of her long bedtime plait, Devon arrived, dressed. Immediately, the small room shrank. He sat on the end of the bed, leaning back on his elbows while he watched her.

"I can do this elsewhere if you want to change into your night attire."
Her fingers worked faster than her tongue.

He gave a lazy smile. "I don't want to change into my night attire,
and I don't want you elsewhere." His white teeth flashed as he removed
his jacket and his waistcoat, hanging both on a hook on the door. His
shirt followed speedily, tossed into the corner. And she kept watching him
while he flicked off his shoes and unpeeled his socks. One long bare foot
lifted to the tallboy where he rested his toes, effectively barring her way.

Her shoulders stiffened with apprehension. The silence lingered while
her gaze flittered over his golden tanned chest, idly wondering why he
would have removed his shirt in the sun. He sprang up suddenly and landed
on his feet beside her, looming so near that she needed to step backward.

"Don't wear a nightgown," he said, his voice a whisper on her cheek.
"Let me see you."

She heaved a breath. "Turn down the lamp."

He laughed and dropped his trousers and under-drawers in one swift
motion. She didn't want to look at his *oldjohn,* but the moment she did,
she realized that the word she'd heard with a snicker to describe the male
part sounded ludicrous when applied to him. His penis was brand new,
rearing to his waist and hoping to be handled.

"Let's get you naked, too," he said in a husky voice. He scrunched the
bottom of her nightgown in his hands and lifted. The fabric momentarily
caught on her hair, but she'd never been so naked so quickly in her life.

She covered her chest with one arm and the junction between her legs
with her hand, staring at her toes in embarrassment.

When he didn't say a word, she tilted her head up to look at him.

His eyebrows lifted. "Do you want me to throw you onto that mattress?"

She raised her chin, spun around, and climbed onto the window side
of the bed. He made a dive onto the sheets and grabbed her almost as
soon as he landed.

"Stop being so defensive," he said in an indulgent voice, propped
on his elbow and facing her. "I'm your husband, and I wanted to see
your beautiful body. I don't hear that as a shocking request." He
caught her to him.

"I'm not used to undressing on order." Almost resentful, she used two
palms on the firm flesh of his chest to distance him from her.

He stroked his thumb over her upper arm. Despite being a ne'er do-
well from the old country, likely sent here because he'd misbehaved at
home, and for all she knew a ne'er do-well here, too, she couldn't imagine
being with anyone but him. Physically, he was perfectly put together and

so touchable that she had to curl her fingers into a ball to keep herself from latching onto him. Although she had never liked the sex act, her body began to react to his nearness by relaxing into a slow melt.

She wasn't meant for a beautiful man she wanted. She was meant for a man she could push and prod into making something of their life together. But pity help her, she wanted Devon. Not for all the tea in India would she let him know, or before she could turn around, he would be trying to take advantage of her, as charmers of his ilk did.

"Get it over with," she said in a forced voice.

"Not a chance." His mouth pressed to the skin of her throat. He moved her hand to his groin, sliding her palm with gentle ease over his hard penis, his breath noticeably short.

Her own breathing almost halted. She wished she didn't love touching his silky smoothness. Before she could fully explore his reaction, his mouth angled across hers, his lips hot and greedy. His tongue flickered into her mouth and out, and he nipped at her lips until her hand grasped him hard.

"Move me to where you want me," he murmured thickly.

"As if I could push a man your size out of bed," she muttered with derision, trying to sound cool and calm and fighting not to wriggle herself onto him.

He laughed. That laugh of his made a well inside her chest that clenched onto the sound, wanting to keep the joy forevermore. However, he took her hand off him and sat up. Apparently, he'd had enough of her sharp tongue, as others had before him. Without a word, he left the bed and the bedroom. Her throat clogged. She'd driven him away as she drove everyone else away, but she wouldn't care. He wanted a baby, and he would persist. She turned down the lamp, her eyes hot and prickling.

She didn't fall asleep in her few minutes alone, and she heard the creak of the floorboards. The bed lurched as he landed beside her, and her back stuck against the sweaty wall of his chest. In the dark heat of the muggy night, he rested his stubbly chin on her shoulder. Comforted by his return, she slept.

Some time later, she awoke to the delicious hot sliding of a hard length of penis between her legs. She edged her bottom closer, angling slightly, desperate to have him inside her, but he teased and teased until she thought she would die of wanting him to fulfill her. No matter how she twisted, she couldn't angle his rigid penis into the desired spot. Finally, she edged away and rolled over to look at him.

In the early dawn light, his lids covered his eyes and his soft lashes rested on his cheeks. He seemed not to care that he could have her now.

Her throat thickened. She leaned over him, brushing his cheek with her fingers. His mouth twitched. She circled his ear with a tickling touch. He took her hand in his and tucked her fingers beneath his chin. She moved closer and lifted her knee over his hip and when he did nothing, she pressed her lips to his neck. His hand moved lazily to her behind, which he cupped. She shifted herself right up against him.

He breathed out and his eyes opened. "You need to be careful when you wake a man in the early morning," he said in a rumbling voice. "You might get more than you bargained for." His thumb angled her chin for his mouth and, as he kissed her, he rolled atop her. His buttocks clenched and tightened, and in this position he seemed to have no problem finding the way inside her. She wasn't sure she was ready, but the slide and withdraw forced a gasp of pleasure through her throat.

He buried himself to the hilt. His thighs forced her legs wider, and he went deeper. She clutched at his buttocks, her fingers frantic while she urged against him. She thought she might reach paradise when he stilled, breathing hard. With a harsh groan, he rested his forehead on her shoulder.

"You agree to have my child?" He lifted, bearing the weight of his upper body on his arms and the weight of his lower body on hers.

"Yes. Yes. Don't stop."

"Witch," he muttered. Still inside her, he sat on his haunches, his knees shifting under her buttocks until the back of her thighs rested over the top of his. Then he lifted her hips higher. With only her shoulders on the sheet, he had her at his mercy, but he seemed in no hurry. He touched the bones of her face, carefully exploring her jaw line and her chin with his thumbs.

She turned her head and kissed his palm, pressing her heels into his buttocks to urge him on while he remained hard and unmoving inside her. He leaned forward, sliding his lips to her ear and teasing back to her mouth. Rocking against him, she found an aching excitement even in this reprehensible position, her lower body far more exposed to his vision than she thought seemly. His expression unbearably tender, he leaned forward and took one of her nipples into his mouth while he teased the other with his fingertips. She dragged his head up, and he took her lips hard again while she undulated beneath him, her body weeping for release.

Finally she realized he was as slicked with sweat as she, and that if he wished, he could end this torture. Tired, but not yet sated, she stilled her movements, noting the tension in his arms. When she moved her hands to his shoulders, his gaze met hers. He gave an unreadable smile and she saw how much he wanted her and how unwilling he was to be in the thrall of passion. The man wasn't the heartless charmer she'd thought.

Longing to understand him, she put her hand on the back of his neck and exerted a gentle force. With a near groan, he lowered himself down on her again and took her mouth carefully. He swelled inside her, beginning to slide rhythmically in and out, hard, hard, hard, frantically, pleasuring her almost more than she could bear. She whipped her head from side to side, desperate for she knew not what, until his fingers parted her and his thumb urged at her pleasure spot.

She exploded in wave after wave of bliss, while he slammed into her. Within moments, he stilled. His breath came in ragged gasps. His palms soothed up her arms and down again, repeatedly, as if learning the shape. Eventually, his breathing evened out, but he stayed, tightly holding her to him. In the aftermath euphoria, her fingers played on his skin, not urgent now, merely wanting to feel the texture. Too long she had needed someone to soothe her, to hold her, to want to be with her.

In the pre-dawn light, she stayed close to her husband, basking in the security of his big body. Somewhere outside, a chorus of birds began to question each other and answer. A kookaburra cleared his throat for his morning laugh, and then he began. She silently laughed with him. Perhaps for the first time in the past few days, reality hit her.

She'd craved a place to belong all her life. After Da had earned enough money managing the mine, he'd planned to take her and Mumma back to their homeland, where the sun didn't burn the landscape, where the rain fell and kept the foliage green, where the past and present met in tradition. They'd wanted her to have the family connections they had lost.

Now she could fulfill their dreams for her. Now she'd taken the last, irrevocable step. In consummating her marriage, she'd committed herself to leaving the land of her birth with her new husband and going to live in Cornwall.

* * * *

Dev awoke early. He swung out of bed, washed quickly, and dressed for his run. After he returned, he changed quietly, careful not to disturb Wenna. She slept soundly with an opened palm beneath her cheek. He paused for a moment, fascinated by her lovely coloring, so familiar, so like Jenny's. Wenna, however, was Jenny's polar opposite in every single way. Wenna was greedy in bed rather than loving. When he couldn't have the second, he would settle for the first. However, he enjoyed her boldness, and the way she would take the pleasure she wanted.

His balls already tightening with his thoughts, he let out a long breath, turned, and pattered downstairs to eat the bread and cheese he'd bought from a market stall. Yesterday's ignored mail sat by the office door in the foyer, five letters in all, among them the dry accounting from his father's man of business, who oversaw the management of Dev's funds. He checked and found the usual quarterly bank draft enclosed.

He now had the wherewithal to finish his gatehouse and set out his vineyard if he wished. The idea was sound, even if he wouldn't be here to see the fruits of his labors. He took his correspondence upstairs to his study, disgusted that while he was idling around with the gentry of Cornwall, his legacy would be enjoyed by another forward-thinking businessman.

He would like nothing more than to live on this continent, which called to him somehow. He loved the way the sun sat on the horizon before lifting over with a burst of frantic color. He loved the brilliantly marked birds, the exotic wild life, and the warmth that seeped right into his bones. He loved the endless summer, the mild winter, and the even length of the days. With Wenna by his side, helping to furnish their own house, working toward a common goal.... He moistened his lips. Wenna.

He hardly knew the woman, but he had to admit that legal coupling was far more enjoyable than his usual furtive connections. A man almost didn't have the right to gain as much pleasure as he had out of sex with his wife. For a while last night he'd even forgotten that his purpose was merely to impregnate her, but she didn't want to stay here. She thought of nothing other than going to Cornwall. He would be a fool to dream.

Sighing, he sat as his desk and opened three invitations for weekend entertainments, which reminded him that he needed to cancel his plans for this next weekend. He couldn't leave Wenna alone as a newlywed, but expecting her to settle comfortably into his social group when only a week ago she had worked as Mrs. Brook's maid would be nothing short of unreasonable. He lifted his head when he heard a rap on the door connecting his lodgings to the office and, determined to leave Wenna to her sleep, he silently pattered down the stairs.

Finn stepped into the lobby, glancing around. "Sorry to disturb you. The City of Adelaide docked this morning, two weeks early. Will you be collecting your vines, or do you want me to send Ernie?"

Ernie appeared behind Finn, looking far from enthusiastic. "The missus is making scones today," he said in protest to the surveyor.

Dev frowned at the lad. "She's not awake yet. You can't sit around waiting."

"She's right behind you."

Surprised, Dev turned, and saw an elegant redhead wearing a black skirt and a floral patterned bodice standing in the doorway.

She offered him a polite smile. "Good morning." Although she looked dewy soft and kissable, he saw no sign of self-consciousness about the night before on her face.

"What's this about scones?"

"They won't be ready until ten o'clock." She glanced at Dev as if she couldn't quite remember who he was.

His grin came and left. He could give her a reminder the moment he could get her alone. "I'm in half a mind to stay home to sample a few myself," he said, wondering how much of the conversation she'd overheard. He didn't want to explain the vines to her at this stage, or tell her he worked as a laborer on his own property.

She shook her head. "I'll save a few for you. I'm sure you don't want to be under my feet all day in this tiny cramped space." Her eyes indicated the kitchen.

"You're right. A kitchen is no place for a man."

"Men should be out earning a living," she said, nodding in agreement.

"Careful. You'll give Finn and Ernie the impression that you can't wait to be rid of me."

Finn cleared his throat. "You have a good wife, Courtney, no doubt about it."

"She's certainly not a mealy-mouthed miss."

"I do have a tendency to speak my mind," she said in a careful voice. "But I have much to do, and I work best alone."

"She's made the upstairs look very comfortable," he said to the others who couldn't keep their gazes off her. She was, without a doubt, an elegant woman.

"I didn't think you'd noticed."

"I had other things on my mind yesterday, but yes, I noticed." He couldn't meet her stare. If he did, he knew he would smile in a far-too-intimate way. He wanted to press a kiss on her soft lips, and he wanted to grab her and carry her upstairs again. In working hours, he shouldn't. But hell! "I appreciate everything you do, Wenna," he said, his voice going husky when he thought of the pleasures of the flesh he could enjoy until she conceived. "Well, I'm off. I've plenty of nothing to do today, too. See you tonight."

Wenna smiled. "Tonight," she said, with no special inflection in her tone. She walked backward and disappeared up the stairs.

He had his vines to collect and his house to build. His mind already plotting the planting of his vines, he left by the door of the lodgings, an almost satisfied man.

Chapter 9

Wenna rubbed the butter into the flour as the kindling under the stove crackled into a flame. From the look of him, young Ernie didn't take the time for breakfast, and scones were the cheapest and easiest filler she could make to feed the lad. Fortunately, she'd bought jam, but she should have bought cheese, too.

By ten o'clock, Ernie and Finn had had their morning tea and the kitchen had been left clean and tidy. As she had done yesterday, she collected her combs, her tongs, her clips, and her capes, and hurried off to Mrs. Busby's hat shop.

Yesterday she had arranged to do Maisie's hair first, a simple touch-up before the midday rush at The Pig and Whistle. A few other waitresses had also shown interest, and all agreed that using "Miss Chenoweth" rather than "Mrs. Courtney" as her working name would spare her husband quite an amount of embarrassment. "I'll explain to Mr. Snow," Maisie had said, fingering the top button of her bodice. "Mr. Courtney is a great favorite of his, not that he believed Mr. Courtney married you. No disrespect meant. Mr. Snow has a common-law wife himself."

For a moment, Wenna had been unable to answer, but her lack of a wedding ring supported the suspicion the locals had about her wedding. She might have suspected the same had she not seen the marriage lines. However, with the barmaids more than willing to protect a facade they didn't credit, she had the perfect cover for her activities. Not for a moment did she assume Devon would approve of her working. Only a slacker would accept a woman adding to his coffers, and she had no intention of overtly humiliating him. She wanted pin money to help him out, not a great fortune.

Today, since Maisie had shown such a keen interest in hairstyles, Wenna planned to teach her how to create a simple coronet braid. If all went as planned, Wenna could take on the waitress as her assistant. Using her as a model had certainly paid off, and the opportunity to have more of the hotel staff showing off "Miss Chenoweth's" hairstyles seemed too good to miss.

Wenna had dreamed up this idea in a larger way a few years back. Had she not married, she would have eventually opened a little shop, where she would have made a living out of the complicated hairdos currently in fashion. Few people could manage the styles, but as a lady's maid, she'd had picture books to copy, and she knew all the latest designs. The big chignon she wore was currently very popular in England. Since they were planning to leave for Cornwall in a few months, her business idea would be largely useless, but nevertheless a money-earner in the meantime. Also, she could do some good by training others.

Without even asking Devon, she knew he would not approve. He seemed to think she could occupy herself as a lady, but a lady without a house and servants was simply an idle woman, and she had never been one. She needed occupation, let alone money, which Devon didn't appear to understand. While she used Mrs. Busby's back room and shared her customers, he would never be humiliated by anyone finding out that his wife was a working woman.

"Remember to spread the word about where you have your hair done," she told Jane, as she reflected the back of the barmaid's hair into the big mirror. "Mrs. Busby's hat shop. No one needs buy a hat if they don't want a hat, but the more people who come in, the more who might like to buy one."

"I'd say so," Jane said, turning her head and preening. "Real fashionable, I look. I might even want to buy a hat meself."

Wenna stood, squinting as she critically examined her efforts. The young woman had thin blonde hair, which Wenna had combed through with a weak sugar solution to hold the shape. The coronet braid ran from her nape to the crown of her head, making her narrow face rounder. Jane certainly looked smarter. "Wait there, and I'll show you which hat would look best with the style I gave you." Two steps into the other room, and she found a basic shape with a small brim she turned up at the sides. "Wear this forward on your head with a ribbon tie behind. Mrs. Busby could advise you on decorations."

"I could." Mrs. Busby had followed the hat into Wenna's area. "I can decorate these small hats quite economically, too, with ribbons, or even leaves and flowers."

Jane left with the smartest of hairstyles and a discounted hat.

Mrs. Busby made an astonished face at Wenna. "You made her look very nice. If you style all those barmaids, Miss Chenoweth, they'll soon look too smart to be barmaids."

Maisie glanced at Wenna. "Just what Mr. Snow said when he first saw my hair. Gave him an idea, it did. You might notice a change in the hotel tonight."

"What sort of change?"

Maisie tapped the side of her nose. "A good change. Wait and see." She stayed to help with the hairdos until midday, and then she scooted off to work.

In the afternoon, Mrs. Busby sent in four paying customers to see Wenna. At sixpence a head, she did well. She thought she could manage eight a day, which would make her more than a pound a week, not bad for a woman working in her spare time. The average wage for a man was a pound a week. Maisie could earn twelve shillings, more than half that if she could help Wenna each morning, and then Wenna could manage to make even more money.

She arrived at the lodgings in time to occupy herself with finishing a black-and- white striped bodice before Devon came home looking weary. He smiled at her, removed his cotton jacket, rolled up his sleeves, and began to have a cold-water wash in the sink basin. "Were the scones successful?"

"Ernie seemed to think so. Mr. Finn ate a few."

"None left, I suppose?"

"If I'd thought you were serious, I would have saved you a couple. I just didn't imagine you would eat something as ordinary as a scone."

"I can lower myself occasionally," he said with a glint in his eye.

She was beginning to know that look. He wanted to tup her again.

She backed. "I must change for dinner," she said hurriedly. Although her body had responded with an excited thud, without her contraceptive device, she couldn't let him touch her. "The daylight is starting to fade."

He gave an offhand shrug, and he changed into a dark suit. Together they strolled over the road to eat. When they reached the entrance of the hotel, he opened the door for her.

She moved inside ahead of him and then stopped. "Well, now. What has happened here?" She glanced in astonishment around the room.

"Snow appears to made the dining area separate from the bar area." Devon indicated a waist-high wooden partition, which now divided the big room. The section of the bar parallel to the window was now a space where drinkers could stand or prop on stools. The remaining half of the room had been set up with the tables and chairs.

Maisie sashayed over, wearing a plain gray gown with a white apron. "Let me show you to your table," the newly re-made waitress said, her gracious arm-swing into the room a trifle overdone.

Jane, standing behind the bar in the dining section and wearing the same uniform, winked. With their new hairdos and gowns, both women looked very smart. Wenna hitched her shoulders with delight, knowing they'd be asked numerous times about their hair. After she'd been seated, she watched more and more couples enter, stare around the room, and look pleased to be seated away from the noisy bar.

"Seems to me, Snow's clientele will change. Men will bring their wives in here more often."

Devon inclined his head and pasted a lordly smile onto his face. "You can't complain about me. I take you out every night."

"I can't say I've appreciated that until tonight." Beaming back, Wenna sat mentally counting her pennies. She could see Maisie's and Jane's new look being closely examined by the wives, mothers, and sisters in the room. Before long, Wenna might have a solid clientele.

Devon fingered his clean-cut jaw. "Did you know about this?"

"I was told to expect a surprise."

"The barmaids are copying your hairdos, which is very astute, because you do have style. Did you know that? Did I also tell you how charming you look tonight? In the lamp light, your hair looks a delightful shade of auburn."

"Charming," she repeated with a smile, not sure how to take the compliment. "You look charming, too, but because you *are*, not because of the color of your hair."

He grinned. "I can take a compliment. Thank you. So, I'm charming and you are beautiful. You are, of course, but it never seems quite fair to compliment a woman for her looks. Your coloring is stunning—that bright wonderful hair and your clear white skin, but you would have inherited that." He made a throwaway gesture with his hand. "You make so much more of your coloring by the gowns you wear. It's your style that's to be complimented, because your style is all your own."

Tonight she wore her russet skirt and her black-and-white striped top. She cleared her throat, amazed to hear him say she was beautiful. No one had ever thought that; in fact, quite the opposite. "Thank you. I *am* complimented. Did you have a satisfactory day?"

He nodded and rose to his feet to be introduced to the wife of a man he knew. This happened twice more during the course of the meal, and he scrupulously introduced her, too. Her new husband had a natural courtesy, but of course anyone could see he was a gentleman. Certainly the tradesmen and their wives treated him as such.

"Tell me about your garden, Devon," she said when she finally had his attention again. "Describe it to me."

"We don't have a garden. You've seen it. It's just a clothesline and some rubbish bins."

"I mean at home. In Cornwall."

"Oh, *that* garden." He narrowed his eyes in concentration. "You'll understand that the cricket pitch was all I needed. That's at the side of the house near a small garden planted with herbs. At the front, we have a long carriageway lined with pines on either side to the front gates. Behind the house, we grow a few acres of flowers to be picked and sold."

"It sounds wonderful. Your father is a flower grower?"

"I suppose you could say that."

"I'm glad he has nothing to do with the mines."

"He owns mainly farming lands." He took a deep breath and leaned back, his brow crinkled with thought. "My mother had a pretty little garden outside her bedroom window. She grew lavender and roses. She might have grown violets, too. I'm not certain. Along the path to the big main garden were two statues of naked women." His mouth curved into a devilish smile.

"I suppose you examined them thoroughly."

"I have to admit I was rather fascinated. These days I prefer the real thing."

"I'm glad." She blushed. For too many shallow reasons, she enjoyed her evening meal tonight.

Mr. Snow came over as Devon put the price of the meal on the table. "What do you think of my girls?" he asked Devon, glancing in the direction of the bar.

Devon shook his head slowly, his smile complicit. "You'll make a fortune, you sly dog. This is exactly what the colony needs, somewhere for respectable people with limited incomes to eat."

"That's what you told me months ago. Then the barmaids had the idea about the uniform–thought they might look better as waitresses." Mr.

Snow pushed his hands into his pockets and leaned back on his heels. "We'll try this for a while and see if it makes a difference."

Devon gave a noncommittal nod and pulled out Wenna's chair as she stood. She could easily get used to his fancy manners. As they walked together over to the lodgings, she held his arm.

"So, the idea of the dining room was yours?"

"Not really. One day I had a discussion with Snow about the great hotels in London and the aristocratic people who patronized them." He opened the front door for her. "I also mentioned the prices of the meals."

"Let's hope he doesn't put his prices up, too."

"Ever-practical Wenna. You should be happy to be eating in a place where you don't have to compete with extended cleavages and bottoms begging to be pinched."

"You're quite mistaken if you think women want their bottoms pinched."

He put his arm around her waist and turned her into him, planting a soft kiss on her mouth. "I've found they'd rather be kissed." His breath warmed her cheek.

She pushed his firm chest. Although he could melt her with his smile, her determination not to have a baby until she knew she would have money enough to look after her grandparents in Cornwall could not be overridden. Smoothing her thumb over his cheek, she smiled and wriggled out of his grip. Devon's father might want an heir, but he certainly wouldn't want a few extra strangers to support, no matter how well-fixed he was.

Clearly, his father didn't support Devon in a life of luxury, although he owned beautifully cut suits and shoes made from the best leather money could buy. Likely, he had needed these accoutrements while he had worked for the governor, but his savings wouldn't last if he took her out to dinner every night. If he looked around for a proper job, he would find one, being as personable as he was. Then they could find a more congenial place to live.

She took the first stair tread, realizing that that idea was impractical. If they were leaving the colony in a few months, she should make the best of these lodgings, because moving would be a waste of money, even if she managed to earn enough for a move. Better to stay here and spend her earnings on essentials.

Despite her husband's idle lifestyle, or perhaps because of it, he excelled in bed sports. That night he explored her and her reactions with meticulous attention to detail. She rode him while he laughed up at her. The man was irresponsible, a slacker, a charmer, and the best lover a woman like her was ever likely to have. No one had ever made her smile as often as he had.

Life with him could be very comfortable if this burgeoning relationship grew, but she doubted he would remain faithful. His sort didn't, but if he kept his promise to take her to Cornwall, she would be a good wife to him… the best, as long as she remembered to remain emotionally aloof.

To fall for him or his charm would be an irretrievable mistake.

* * * *

Waking before Wenna in the morning, Dev realized he hadn't married her because his thoughtless flirting had lost her a job. He had not a single noble bone in his entire body. However, the idea of presenting a redheaded maid to his father as the mother of the next heir had appealed to him. Why not? One woman was the same as the next, and to set his father back on his heels had seemed like a good idea at the time.

Now Dev realized he had made the best of bargains for an entirely puerile reason. His thinking had been unworthy of him. The earl had been well within his rights to resent having a cuckoo in his nest. Perhaps he didn't treat his youngest son the same as his brothers, but in all, as a youngest son, Dev had been given a good grounding to make his own way in life.

The sooner Dev returned to England and faced his unwanted responsibilities, the better. He owed this at least to the earl, who was man enough to appreciate Wenna for herself. She would give his father a run for his money, though. Wenna said exactly what she thought, and she wouldn't be intimidated. Her sense of style had been a revelation, too, given the miserly funds he had supplied. Clearly she could manage wonders on a budget. Well and good. Since she wouldn't be cobbling a place for herself in Adelaide's society, she had no need for an extensive wardrobe—not yet, not until they reached England.

A splurge in Paris with his sister-in-law would most likely suit both women, and Wenna might impart some of her sense of style to his brother's dowdy widow. Devon looked forward to Wenna showing the English aristocracy the freshness of a colonial upbringing. This in itself had been a welcome surprise. Her lithe healthy body and her sensuous enjoyment of his had been a revelation. Judging by her initial tight-lipped assessment of him, he'd expected her to be a woman who would slap his hands away when he touched her and keep her knees closed until he begged.

He rolled over onto his back and saw she watched him. Her sleepy gaze wandered to his penis, which sat large and sluggish on his belly. She reached out her hand and stroked him from the base to the tip, where her fingers lingered. Idly, she pulled his foreskin to the glistening head and watched his cock swell further. Short of breath, he watched, too.

This inexperienced maid had quickly learned how a man liked dallying. She'd gone from a woman who would merely lie on her back, to one who wanted to experience anything and everything. She stretched him a few times while his languorous lust expanded and then she said, "What do you plan to do today?"

"The same as I do on weekdays," he said, his tone husky with need.

Her hand stopped moving. "That would be to idle around with your worthless friends?"

"Not many of my friends are worthless or idle."

She straightened her fingers, her palm just a whisper above his skin. "Which isn't an answer to my question."

He put his hand over hers to keep her touching him, but he no longer had her full attention. "I work as a laborer," he said unwillingly.

"Well! I couldn't see how looking at land would make you so dirty every day." Her eyes met his, and her delighted smile was a joy to see. "You do get paid, don't you?"

"It's certainly worth my while."

She shook off his hand and began exploring his penis again, this time tracing a torturous vein until his member jumped. "Do that again." She laughed.

He liked her in this teasing, relaxed mood. "It's involuntary. You need to work out how to make me do that again."

"Oh, my, you're a devious man." She rolled over and sprang out of bed, her nightgown a tent over her delicious body.

Suspecting he was the pot talking to the kettle, he, too, swung out of bed. "I'll start up the stove and put the water on." He dressed in his running clothes while she went to the privy, leaving before she came back.

By the time he returned home after his run, she'd bathed and dressed, and she had her oats prepared for breakfast. He'd discovered a plateful fortified him for a good day's work, and he no longer glanced at the unappealing gloop with disdain. He sat with her in the kitchen to eat, though the area was scarcely a dining room. However, this didn't bother him, for she kept the whole place neat, she kept him fed, and she did more than her wifely duty in bed.

He grinned at her. "What do you plan to do today?"

"I think I'll get to know the neighbors. I need a little female company." She kept her gaze on her plate.

"I do, too, but if I mentioned female company, I doubt I would please you."

"You please me well enough if you mean my company, but I would rather you earned a pot of money." She lifted her head. "If you mean other female company, I imagine you could get that without a pot of money." Her mouth moved into a wry tilt.

"I meant yours. I would be a fool to say otherwise." He stood up, considering a quick kiss on her cheek, but decided to leave her wondering exactly what he had meant.

At this stage, she was his perfect foil, still unsure of herself and him, which kept her being his delight. If they remained here rather than scurrying off to Cornwall, she would be a far more suitable wife for him than one of the spoiled darlings he constantly had presented. In Cornwall, Wenna might receive a chilly reception at first, but his father would soon see his son was teaching him that societal designations depended on class rather than birth. Wenna was nothing if not classy, being able to change at will.

"But you're right. I need to leave for work. I won't be working tomorrow. Are you a churchgoer?"

"I've always attended a Sunday service." She clasped her smooth hands in her lap. "Except last week because, as you know, I was being dismissed from my job."

"I'll take you to church if you like, but I'll be playing cricket for the rest of the day." He paused, tilting his eyebrows in query. "Would you like to come and watch?"

Her eyes wide, she spread her splayed hand protectively across her upper chest. "Who will be there?"

"The men you saw playing cricket at the Brooks' last week, and the wives and mothers and daughters you also saw there. We usually play on Sunday. That Saturday game was only scrambled together because most of the team was in the hills."

"The mothers and daughters." Her mouth twisted. "I'm not quite ready to confront Mrs. Brook and Miss Patricia."

Dev eyed her, appreciating her fine, narrow nose and the elegant curve of her cheekbone. "When the time comes, I'll do the confronting. You needn't worry I'll let them patronize you. I won't."

"Nevertheless, I need more than a week to learn my new place. I spent more than twelve years as a servant."

He paused, curious. "How old were you when you started working?"

"I worked to support myself from the age of thirteen, but I needed to help Mumma after Da died. That was the year before." She rose to her feet, collecting the dirty plates.

He followed her into the kitchen. "What did your mother do?"

"Laundry. Endlessly. I used to do her damping and starching, thinking I was a great help. Looking back, I spent far too much time rattling about with my friends." She smiled wryly.

"I'm sure she understood."

She nodded. "Too well. She tried to encourage me to better myself." Turning, she poured a little of the hot water into the sink dish. "Perhaps, if she hadn't died, all would have gone as she had hoped. But in the end, I achieved the same household position she did."

"In which part of Cornwall were you born?"

"I was born here in South Australia."

"I thought you said you wanted to go back home."

"Cornwall was Mumma's home." She scrubbed the plates. "This land is flat, brown, and ugly. I want to see the beautiful sea mists and the granite cliffs of Cornwall."

"How can you say that? Just step outside and you'll see two contradictions to your words. And as for ugly, we have blue skies, green hills, and—"

"Brown water."

"You're too hard to please. The weather is perfect—"

"It never rains. The dust never settles."

"Because it doesn't rain all the time. Our clothes don't go moldy and nothing smells of decay. The people here are new, too, with fresh ideas and an enthusiasm that you rarely see elsewhere. Here, it doesn't matter who your parents were—"

"Unless your mother was the local washer woman," she said, her tone bitter.

"That doesn't matter here." He took the hot water off the stove. In winter he would want an evening bath, but they would be gone before the worst of the weather. "Where in Cornwall was your mother born?"

"Near Falmouth, on the Marchester estate. She always worked for the Marchester family. Before she married Da, she was personal maid to Lady Ann, the earl's second wife."

Dev's breath caught on a lump in his throat. Her mother had been his mother's maid.

He took the big pan of water to the bathroom, filling the hipbath halfway. "What about your father?" he called. "What did he do?"

She came to the door, a dishtowel in her hand. "In Cornwall he ran a small mine. The tin petered out. He heard about the copper here, and he was instantly snatched up as a mine manager. The job was well paid. He and Mumma had great hopes, but he was killed during cave-in."

Dev stripped off his shirt, frowning. "Managers work in offices, not mines."

"He ran in to help. He saved two lives before he was trapped by another cave-in, a bigger one. Because of his bravery, Mumma and I lost the kindest and nicest man in the world. Our house, too. That was part of his wages."

"Weren't you paid compensation?"

"We might have, had he been meant to be in the mine, but he only went in because he heard the miners' cries. Mumma and I ended up with nothing. She couldn't take a job as a lady's maid because she had me. Lady's maids don't have children. So, she worked as a washerwoman." She shrugged.

Dev examined her expression, which had hardened. "I'm sorry," he said simply. "Your Da was a hero. His widow should have been treated better than that."

"In Cornwall, she would have been given a pension."

"I doubt it. Compensation would be at the owner's discretion. Did he do nothing at all for you?"

"We had free housing. Mumma had too much pride to accept anything less than earning her way. If I had been a boy, I could have taken a job in the mine and earned a good wage. But girls have to lower their expectations." She stood, wiping the cloth over the plate, her gaze idly wandering over his body.

"Somehow, I don't think you have ever lowered your expectations." He stepped out of his pants and into the bath. "I think my father will be very pleased with you, especially when you give me a child."

"What if the child is a daughter?"

"I would prefer a son for my father, but for myself, I'd just as soon have a daughter. Let's have both, and be off with you, woman. I've lingered long enough and now I have to ready myself for a hard day's work." He grabbed the soap and didn't take long to wash and dress.

For a month now he'd been carrying bricks, mixing mortar, and generally laboring. A day a week playing cricket relaxed him. She didn't seem to mind being left alone. He had the idea that he'd married extremely well.

The next week she made an announcement about her monthly days, giving him to understand that he couldn't touch her during this time.

Nevertheless, he held her in his arms at night, appreciating the scent of her skin, appreciating the shape of her, the way she thought and the way she spoke. She was his perfect fit.

Yet, his father was the earl of Marchester. Her mother was his mother's maid. He couldn't tell her. Not yet. First he needed to prepare her. He had to stop hiding her, as if he might be ashamed to present her to his friends. She needed to realize she was more than an equal—she was a delight, and she made him proud.

Chapter 10

For the week that Wenna insisted she was indisposed, Dev mulled over siring a girl. From a family of boys himself, he hadn't considered the matter before. He had expected his firstborn to be a son and heir. Naturally, the entail depended on a living male child. Females didn't inherit earldoms. Despite the fact that he had married and was diligently trying to make a baby, he may well have been wasting his time. Well. Not wasting his time because he enjoyed his wife's body.

Then again, no matter the sex of the child, male or female, Dev would be the earl until he died. He would never be able to come back to this country, and he may as well become accustomed to the fact rather than seeking the ins and outs of his situation.

He pulled out Wenna's chair, and she seated herself at the usual table in The Pig and Whistle.

Snow came over, rubbing his hands. "We've got a mutton stew tonight with fresh green peas."

Wenna smiled at him. "That sounds very nice, Mr. Snow."

"We'll also have a bottle of wine, Snow."

Snow grinned at Dev and moved over to the bar to order.

"You should stick to ale," Wenna said with a frown. "Wine is expensive."

"The Barossa claret, my little miser, is not as costly as the imports." He leaned back in his seat, eyeing her. "And I'll spend my money however I wish."

Wenna raised her fine red eyebrows. "If you can afford wine, I can afford a new hat."

"You appear to have a roomful of new hats."

"I have three constantly refurbished hats. None would have cost as much as one of your handkerchiefs."

"You can have a new hat any time you like," he said, annoyed. She looked as smartly dressed tonight as she always did. Instead of the greens redheads usually wore, she stuck to warm colors or black and white. He admired her taste, but her focus on money irritated him.

"How long do you think the handout you gave me to buy a wedding gown will last when I need to buy food every day?" She straightened her knife and fork.

"Since you never asked me for money, I assumed you had as much as you needed."

"Oh, I'll never have as much money as I need."

He suppressed the urge to empty his pockets and thump all his spare cash onto the table. This cool, precise redhead was not the patient Jenny of his dreams. Wenna was a constant exciting challenge. She could slay him with a look and cut him down with a word, and the more she nipped at him, the more he had to quell the desire to conquer her.

The wine arrived. He filled his glass and hers and noticed she matched him sip for sip, which seemed to be a pattern with her. She would never be the sweet submissive guardian of either his excesses or his morals. She challenged him. Nobody knew better than he how much he needed a challenge in his life, and he wanted her in his life forever-more. He would never get enough of her—of her feisty tongue, nor of her passionate lovemaking. Although he'd casually chosen her as his wife, he couldn't have made a better choice had he considered for years.

"It's becoming a chore to keep you hidden away, you know." He leaned back, watching her reaction while his stew was put in front of him.

Her head angled to the side, and her lips pursed. "I thought you were quite happy to go to your cricket matches without me."

"I am, and I understand why you don't want to be there, but you're not the sort of secret I like keeping from my friends."

"Which has me wondering about the sort of secret you usually keep from friends." Her expression neutral, she began eating.

She had given him the perfect opportunity to explain who he was. His friends from Cambridge knew him as the third son of an earl. As such, he had no title and didn't stand out from the crowd. He hadn't apprised anyone of his new situation. As matters were, if Dev told Wenna, he might embarrass her with the knowledge that her mother had been his mother's maid. She already nipped at him for being *a gentleman*. Or she might spread the story and embarrass them both.

He wanted to stay the man he had always been in this country: *"one of us."* His gaze lifted as he watched his wife eat. Her table manners were impeccable. Being a lady's maid had shown her how to act like a lady, except in bed, where she'd had no example to follow. His mouth curled with silent appreciation, although he didn't want to think about her body in public, knowing how *his* body would react. The novelty of having a desirable woman in his bed each night had certainly not worn off yet.

He cleared his throat, putting aside her comment. "If you meet my friends before attending a match, you'll have their undivided attention while I'm on the field." He tilted his glass. Tonight, he planned to take her until she begged for more. Somehow, he could never get enough of her.

She glanced away from him and gulped down her drink. "I don't like this heavy red wine," she said in a considering voice. "I think I prefer sherry."

"You can sip sherry as much as you like. I won't force you to drink wine. I won't force you to do a single thing you don't want to do. Fortunately, you like doing what I like doing most of all." His gaze caught hers, and he smiled.

"I have never said I like doing it," she said, making a hopeless attempt to look scandalized. Instead, she looked amusingly unfocused.

"Yet you know to what I am referring."

"Your mind never leaves the subject, though I don't understand why you're in such a rush for a baby. I think we ought to wait until we get to Cornwall."

"Speaking of Cornwall." He tapped his fingers on the starched white tablecloth. "Your mother worked for the countess of Marchester. Did she ever discuss Lady Ann?" He idly twirled his wine by the stem of the thick glass, wondering what she knew about his mother. Servants gossiped about their employers, and if his mother had been having an affair with his brothers' tutor, her maid would surely know.

Wenna blinked and frowned, her soft lips pursed. "When Mumma married, she had to leave Lady Ann. She thought it was a shame that married women couldn't work. I don't remember her saying anything else. Why do you ask?" Her last few words sounded tangled.

"Everyone in Cornwall likes to know all they can about everyone else."

"I know she was quite sad about leaving Lady Ann." Her brow wrinkled with concentration. "Lady Ann was the earl's second wife. He doted on her, according to Mumma, but not enough to keep Mumma on. He thought her first duty was to her husband."

"Duty. Earls know all about duty." He put his empty glass on the table. His mother would have understood the word. The earl's sons certainly did. Will knew his duty was to learn all about the estate. John knew his duty was to find a respectable profession for himself in the army. Dev, the spare son, had no duties other than to keep himself scarce.

Naturally, a proud man like his father wouldn't ever admit he knew Dev wasn't his son. The earl would pretend forever, but everything Dev did from the time he could remember had been carefully supervised. First his long education at home. Next his stint on John's inheritance, the home farm, until a scant two years at Cambridge and the two years in France. The earl certainly had suspicions. However, Dev's far-from-pampered life had toughened him up and led him to find his own place in the world.

Maisie took the empty plates, and he rose to his feet. He automatically crossed to take Wenna's chair as she stood. She stumbled slightly and clutched at his arm for balance.

All the way across the road she clung to him. The wine must have gone straight to her head. Normally, she didn't reach out for him. As he unlocked the door to the lodgings, she gave him a nose-wrinkled smile, circling her arms around his waist. "I've got a falling-down feeling," she said, pressing her cheek against the back of his jacket.

"Good. When we're upstairs, I'll fall down on top of you."

"Why wait until then?"

He tried to read her expression. "You want me to take you on the stairs?" Turning into her, he lifted one of his hands to each side of her face. "Tempting. But impractical."

"Don't you want me?"

"Yes." He angled a slow kiss on her mouth. "Upstairs."

She moved with him into the foyer, but before he could take another step, she nipped at his bottom lip with her teeth.

He gave her quick kiss and moved her in the direction of the staircase. "Here, Devon."

"We'll be more comfortable in bed."

She shoved herself out of his grip and leaned against the wall, her face a picture of obstinacy. "Here or nowhere."

"The bed's only a flight of stairs away. I'm not in the habit of rutting on the floor."

"Tonight, it's your only choice."

He tried to take her arm, but she swung out of his grip. Although he had no moral objection to tupping his wife on the stairs, he had a real objection to sex on order. "Walk or I'll carry you."

"Interesting." With a challenging tilt of her chin, she crossed her arms and stood her ground.

He sighed, lifted her right arm, bent, and swung her across his shoulder. Without too much difficulty and with a lot of regret, he carried her up the stairs. Tonight, instead of making her beg for more of him, he would be treated to a cold back.

"I'm upside down and the world is spinning," she said in a sing-song voice. "I think I'm going to be sick."

"I wouldn't advise it." He dumped her onto the middle of the bed and went back down to the kitchen to pour her a glass of water.

In the short time he'd been gone, she'd fallen asleep. He sat her up and she blinked fuzzily at him. "Drink this." Pressing the glass against her lips, he tilted. With no other choice, she swallowed.

"I used to think you were kind." She coughed as the last mouthful trickled from the corners of her lips.

Without answering, he undressed her and slipped her between the sheets. He didn't know what had possessed him to let her drink half a bottle of wine. Even he, used to the stuff, obtained a faint pleasant glow from that amount. He lay awake for a while, arms behind his head, finally acknowledging that he needed to take better care of her.

Her wellbeing had grown rather more important to him than he had expected.

* * * *

Gentle hands smeared across Wenna's wet face, drying her tears. She'd been dreaming and now half awake, she tried to remember. What? Green fields. Flowers. Two people beckoning her. She should go.

She snuggled into a warm chest. Lips pressed on her eyelids and a bristled chin rubbed against her cheek. Loved and comforted, she slept again.

In the morning, she awoke with a slash of pain behind her eyes and a dry mouth. She didn't want to get out of bed, but Devon would be out running now, and afterward he would go off to his laboring job. As soon as he left, she would prepare her tools for the day, and trudge down the street for her appointments in the back room of a hat shop—if the dull thud inside her head would let her stand.

For the past month, she'd earned a wage not only for herself, but also for Maisie, who would soon leave her job as a waitress and take on styling full time. Mr. Snow approved. He liked the new respectability of ushering smart women through his establishment.

With little enthusiasm, she wandered downstairs to prepare breakfast. Her head pounded. Despite her distaste for wine, she'd foolishly matched Devon drink for drink. No inducement in the world would encourage her to drink wine again. Why on earth she couldn't behave as her husband expected a lady to behave she didn't know. Or perhaps she did. For reasons she suspected, but tried to keep out of her mind, she wanted him to see the real her, not the impressionable maid he thought he had married. In the time they'd been together, she'd learned to respect him. He didn't have the same respect for her, though he could certainly be kind. Sometime soon she would have to tell him about the money she earned, but she knew without being told that he would put a stop to her activities.

Nothing could be surer than he wouldn't want to introduce his wife to his rich friends as a working woman, but if he wanted to get ahead, he needed her money. At this stage, although he worked as a laborer, having a gentleman farmer as a father put him a step or two above her on the social scale. A step or two was not as lofty as she'd supposed. Before her father had died, he and her mother had mingled with the newly rich and the mine owners. Wenna's childhood friends had been the sons and daughters of the wealthy. Da's death had brought her mother down a peg or three on the social scale, but Wenna had reason to assume that her background didn't make her entirely unacceptable to the gentry.

* * * *

Dev arrived back from his run hot and sweaty. He emptied Wenna's bathwater onto the scruffy garden outside, while she stood over the stove stirring the oats. "What do you plan to do today?" He grabbed his pot of bath water from the stove.

Despite denying himself an opportunity to pleasure himself with his tipsy wife the night before, he was glad he'd stood his ground. Glad, but horny as all hell. Wenna had practically kicked him to death during the night, moaning and thrashing around until he'd held her. She'd calmed, showing that she appreciated his presence.

She looked pale and tired, but nonetheless still appealing. "Perhaps I'll start making a new gown. I'll need something else for Cornwall."

He poured the hot water into the bath and topped up the level with a pot of cold, realizing that his wife had no life. Perhaps that's why she'd drunk to excess, to ease her boredom. He'd married her and settled her into his bachelor lodgings, then he disappeared each day except Sunday to work on his new house. On Sunday, he dropped her off at church and went to play cricket with his friends. Every night he ate with her and took her home to bed. She'd rarely refused his attentions. He could say with complete truth that to date she had been the perfect wife, and he had been a rat.

Clean and dressed in his dusty work clothes, he sat down to breakfast with his clean and impeccably dressed wife. He eyed her as he ate. "What would you want to do if I took a day off work?"

She jerked up straighter in her chair. "If you took a day off work, you'd miss a day's wages."

"Would you like to go to an art show?"

"I want us to have enough money to get to Cornwall."

"I have enough. You could buy yourself a new hat and take a stroll with me along the river."

"Why would I want to stroll along the river?"

He shrugged. "Fresh air. Sunshine. Why not?"

"I shop for food every day. That's enough for me. And you take me out every night."

He drew a deep breath. "I've put off my regular engagements for the past few weeks, but I can't ignore my friends' invitations any longer. Tonight I plan to have dinner with them at The Castle, and later a few hours upstairs. I might be late but I won't disturb…." He stopped when her face froze. "I can't take you. No other women will be there."

"Do as you wish. And I'll do as I wish. A cold collation here would suit me nicely. The small bedroom would also suit me nicely."

"Are you telling me I will lose my husbandly rights if I go out with my friends?"

She crossed her arms. Her eyes narrowed. "I won't be sharing a bed with a man who ruts with prostitutes."

He drew his eyebrows together. "How on earth did me going out with friends change into me rutting with prostitutes?"

"I know you'll take another woman as soon as blink."

He examined her expression of disdain. "And would that matter to you?"

"Certainly not." Her chin lifted.

"Why, then, are we discussing the subject?"

She moistened her lips. "You are married to me."

"I have no intention of being unfaithful."

She lowered her gaze, taking a long breath. "I'd believe that if I knew you weren't going to the upstairs rooms in The Castle," she said to her plate.

"I don't imagine I'll spend more than five pounds."

She stood so quickly that she bumped the table. The dishes clattered and his teacup tilted dangerously. The furious expression on her face warned him, but since he didn't know what she would do, he didn't think to move his foot away before she stamped down hard on his toes. "Don't even think of it!"

He grabbed her upper arms and jerked her onto his knee. Her hand clenched, but before she could punch him, he covered her fist with his palm.

"I can't believe you'd spend so much on a whore." Her bottom lip trembled.

Discussions of money had a powerful effect on her. He pondered for a moment. "Gambling." Wincing, he wriggled his toes. "I don't buy favors."

"Upstairs at The Castle," she said in a precise voice, "is where men buy favors."

"The rooms are for hire, but we hire ours for card-playing and smoking."

"I wish I could believe that."

He leaned back. "You seem to think I'm inexhaustible. A man who is satisfied at home has no need to go elsewhere."

Her lips pursed, and she tried to rise from his knee, but now he had her so close, he didn't want to let her go. He gazed into her eyes, and she lifted her hand to the side of his neck, giving him a light and rather insincere smile. Her body tensed as if to leave. Before she could, he tightened his arms around her waist and lifted his mouth to hers. From there, he took the tasty delight of her tongue as he would take her nipple, drawing it into his mouth and rolling it around. Her breath eased out and she arched, rubbing her breasts on his chest. What with that and her buttocks on his thighs, he was more than ready to unbutton his trousers, daylight be damned.

He brushed the backs of his hands against the side of her breast as he played in her mouth, drawing away and returning. Her fingers left the nape of his neck, moving his hand to the underside of her breast. She lifted her head. "Will you be very late?"

"What?"

Her lips wandered along his jaw line, her breath a soft whisper on his neck. "Tonight. Will you be back at a reasonable hour?"

"No later than midnight," he said huskily, gently positioning her face so that he could again kiss her soft and willing lips. His hand shifted to the hooks at the neckline of her bodice.

Her breath eased out as he began the unhooking, and her fingers sifted through the hair around his ear, sifting, sifting, caressing his ear and his jaw. "Midnight seems a long time to wait to have you in bed with me."

"We won't wait." Breathing hurt. "I can take you now, here."

Leaning back, her eyes half-hooded, she let him undo her bodice to the waist, her face a picture of sensuality with her lips pouty and moist. Then she slowly opened his shirt, concentrating far too long on each button. The anticipation left him dry-mouthed until she finally bared his chest. While waiting, he had done nothing except frame the sides of her breasts, and when she began to run her hands over his skin, his own nipples hardened. She bent her head and licked one. His heart pounded against her face.

"You can't imagine how you tempt me," she said onto his skin, and the whole of him vibrated with her words.

Then, she sighed and pushed herself upright, closing his shirt and shrugging his hands off her.

He snatched back her hands and held them in his, against the wall of his chest. "Wenna, you can't stop now. You want me, and I want you," he said, the desperation in his voice surprising him.

"I do. But I don't want a quick tupping on the table. I want to spend hours in bed making love to you." She heaved a long sigh.

"Then, I could take the day off."

She shook her head slowly. "I need the daylight hours for my sewing. And you must make a living." Her expression regretful, she stood, staring down at him. "And tonight...I might be asleep when you get home."

He nodded slowly, finally understanding. "And you won't be in the mood if I wake you?"

"As to that...." Her shoulders lifted in a shrug.

His mouth tilted on one side. Lord help him. She would use sex to manipulate him and, starved fool that he was, he would let her. "As I see my choice, I can stay home tonight or I can take you to The Castle with me?"

Her head tilted slightly to the side as she stared at him, considering. "Yes."

Despite an arousal harder than the willow on his cricket bat, he laughed, raising his palms in surrender. "So, I'll take you to The Castle. Whatever we do, we need to eat." He stood, buttoning his shirt. "I'll be home at the usual time, and I'll see you then. Dress is formal."

Chapter 11

With six ladies booked for styling that morning, Wenna walked to the hat shop soon after she'd made tea for Ernie and Mr. Finn. Despite having to deprive herself, she had put a halt to a surprisingly exciting interlude, all to change her husband's mind. She couldn't think of a single incidence in her previous life when she had lowered herself to manipulation.

Half-ashamed, but *only* half, she would now meet his upper-crust friends on her own terms. She tugged open the hat-shop door. The unashamed half of her knew that meeting the males first would put her in a better position when she had to be confronted with their various sisters and wives, and that time would surely come. Devon would do himself no good by hiding away his hastily married wife.

She and Maisie managed the complicated styles requested before Maisie sat Wenna down in front of the mirror. "So, where might you be going tonight with that handsome husband of yours?"

"The Castle. I know it's known for the food and not for the other entertainments, but it's the other entertainments I'll be trying. Before you look too scandalized, I'm going to attend a card evening."

Maisie put on a mock prissy face. "I wasn't about to be scandalized. Your husband is a gent. He wouldn't be hiring fancy women. Do you play cards often?"

"No." Wenna didn't expand. She had played Slapjack with the other servants until she'd been elevated to the position of lady's maid five years ago, but she'd never gambled. "Do you remember that big looped plait I showed you? That's how I want my hair styled for tonight."

Maisie's lips pulled to the side while she thought. "The one where I loop strands over and over? I don't know if I can remember the whole thing."

"Try." Wenna explained the braiding with a mirror at her back, but the looping needed to be practiced and Maisie hadn't had the hours. Eventually Wenna settled for a figure-eight braid along the back of her head. She pulled out a few curls to soften her face, knowing she couldn't have managed even this uncomplicated braid on herself. "You've done a very good job, Maisie. We'll practice all the other styles I've shown you when you have the time, but it's almost midday now."

Taking a break of her own, Wenna strode to King William Street with the money she had earned at the hat shop wrapped tightly in her handkerchief. Every three months she sent off a bank draft to her grandparents. After a short wait, her bank deposited the cash and made out the notification, which she marched off to the General Post Office.

As she watched the clerk slide her envelope down the chute, she said, "Do you have any mail for Miss Wenna Chenoweth, formerly of Dutton Terrace, Medindie?"

The clerk sighed, searched for the Walkerville box, and found a dog-eared letter from England, most likely a message dictated by her grandparents who, born in the eighteenth century, couldn't write. "Returned a month ago. You should always leave a forwarding address."

"I'll write one for you now." Naturally, because she had a hair appointment pending, she had to fill in a long and complicated form under the eye of the clerk. "I've had a change of name, too. Courtney."

The clerk glanced up at her. "Courtney of Rundle Street? Wait, then. I have mail for Mr. Courtney, too." He rummaged around in a cabinet behind him while she tapped her foot. "Ah, yes. The Honorable Mr. Courtney."

Amused by Devon being called "honorable," which he usually was, or at least in his dealings with her, she put his letters with hers and hurried off, with so much to do and so little time that she plotted tasks as she walked. First she had the four heads of hair to style, and then she would modify a skirt and bodice to wear tonight, lacking an evening gown.

After finally arriving home, pushed for time, she still had the envelopes in her hand when she opened the door to the store cupboard. In one of Devon's mother's boxes, she had seen a tablecloth trimmed with elaborate lace, which she thought she could use on her gown tonight. Knowing she would be back to tidy up, she left the letters with the fabrics she had scooped out in her search.

She had barely an hour to work before Devon's homecoming. Sitting on the carpet in the study, she cut into the lace tablecloth. With a modicum of guilt and a silent apology, she carefully removed the long corner, which she repurposed as a shawl collar for her cream bodice, after removing the black braid. The lace softened the rigid neckline and draped to a point near the waist in front. The exquisite pattern would disguise her outfit's plebeian origins.

She undressed quickly and even more quickly stepped into her cream skirt, adding her newest refurbishment. A careful examination of her appearance in the cheval mirror quite satisfied her. The elaborate lace against the plainness of the cream ensemble looked restrained and tasteful. She would pass as a lady.

Experimenting with a carefully pronounced "How do you do?" she hurried her lace scraps down the stairs and replaced various tablecloths, pillowcases, table napkins, and embroidered doilies back into the box, grabbing up the letters she'd left. Her own sat on the top. Her mouth curved into an expectant smile as she lifted the seal.

It is my sad duty to inform you that your grandmother died on the 20th of October and your grandfather followed her to the grave a week later. United in life, and united in death.

Formal words. Her smile died, and her eyes misted. Neither shocked nor grieved, for she had never met either, she experienced a huge well of disappointment. She would never meet her only surviving relatives.

Sighing as she gathered up Devon's mail, she trailed back upstairs. She now had no one of her own but her husband, the man who had married her because she wanted to go to her grandparents in Cornwall. Despondent, she left his mail on his desk before putting out his evening suit. She had no need to leave the colony now.

Trying to shake off her new loss of direction, she took out Devon's shirt. Her honorable husband looked wonderful no matter what he wore, but he looked especially handsome in formal clothes. Any woman would be proud to be with him. She'd barely cleaned his shoes when she heard his quick footsteps on the stairs. Soon she would be faced with a pack of young irresponsible gentlemen who would surely look down their noses at her.

Instead of working up a case to despise the over-privileged, she stood, racked with nerves, facing her husband in the doorway.

He stopped and his gaze swept over her gown. "Very elegant."

"Thank you. Let's hope I pass muster with your snooty friends." She couldn't make herself tell him that her grandparents had died. If she no longer had a reason to go to Cornwall, he had married her for naught. She had married him because she had yen for this particular irresponsible young gentleman.

"Since they're all male and unmarried, I don't imagine you will have any problem passing muster." He began to remove his shirt. "One of my friends married recently, though, but he dropped out of the card-playing group. I expect he would rather be with his new wife than with a pack of bachelors."

Trying to ignore the fact that he saw himself as a bachelor, she squared her shoulders. "He must be very much in love."

He shrugged. "You shall be able to judge for yourself when they return to town." Turning, he soaped his washcloth and began to wash his face and chest.

She stayed, fascinated by the play of the muscles in his back. Were she confident of him or of herself, she would run her hands over his bare skin and lift her mouth for a kiss. Despite knowing where that would lead, her urge to have him inside her quickened her pulse. However, she couldn't be impulsive when she needed to protect herself from pregnancy. Her womanly places tingling with need, she turned her back and left for the sitting room.

For the next quarter hour, she occupied herself by worrying about the ramifications of her grandparents' deaths. A good wife would go to Cornwall with her husband, and she would bear his baby. Devon's situation hadn't changed, only hers had. She now had a moneymaking business, which would be hard to leave when she could see how easily she could expand. Her not-so-successful husband had nothing here except a seasonal job. In England, their positions would reverse.

She picked at her fingernails until he appeared in the doorway. In the severity of his evening suit, he looked remote and untouchable. Tall and good-looking, chiseled from ivory, topped with gold-flecked amber, even the way he inclined his head spoke of innate class. If he had said he was a prince rather than the son of a farmer, she would have had no difficulty believing him. She rose, ready to leave, hoping not to put a foot out of place.

His mouth relaxed into a smile. "You look lovely. I'll be a proud man tonight."

Her heart almost stopped. Lord, she wanted to make him proud. She had wanted to make her father proud, too, but he had told her that as a female, her best option was to be a good wife. That appeared to depend on a husband's requirements, and her husband had expressed no need of her except in the bedroom.

She wanted more, much more, always had. Her business was small, and would remain so or her husband would look foolish to his friends. She couldn't do that to a man who had thus far done the right thing by her.

* * * *

Half an hour later, Dev strode with his new wife past a suit of polished armor to the reception desk at The Castle. The maître d'hôtel approached, looking mildly ridiculous in a medieval tunic and hose. "Mr. Courtney. Good evening. Your room is ready."

The man turned and led the way past the dining room, where the well-heeled patrons sat at long tables in high-backed medieval-style chairs. In a way, the place reminded him of home, drafty and stark, but this aspect was much admired by the homesick colonials. The studied antiquity clearly implied class. Glasses clinked and the smell of roasting meat wafted from the kitchens.

Dev indicated precedence to Wenna, who followed the man past the old tapestries to a reserved back room. Inside was more of the same: a long table, uncomfortable chairs, and paneled walls. "My wife and I will drink barley water. Will that suit you, my love?" He raised his eyebrows at Wenna.

"Oh dear. You're martyring yourself for me. You may have barley water if you insist. I'll have watered wine." She smiled firmly at the maître d'hôtel, who blinked at Dev.

"In that case, I'll share your wine," Dev said, enjoying her mock reproof.

The door opened. "Thought I saw your back, Dev. Didn't know you would have a lovely lady with you." The newcomer, a short man with a cherubic face, was Hubert Grace, the son of Sir Patrick and Lady Grace. He smiled at Wenna.

"Let me intro—"

"Move along." Luke Worthing, a lawyer who'd studied at Cambridge, too, pushed Hubert into the room. "We'll have two bottles of that French claret you showed me last week, Mason," he said to the maître d'hôtel. His severe brown-eyed gaze turned to Wenna. "Good Lord. Another redhead. Welcome to the club." Wry lines formed beside his thin-lipped mouth. He'd always been overly conscious of his own red hair.

Dev moved to his wife's side, again preparing to introduce her, as Mason opened the door to leave. Before he could, tall, dark, and handsome James Hawthorn entered. "Hubert invited me," he said defensively. Younger than the others, he was often referred to as the pup. "He thinks I have the makings of a member of this exclusive band after playing cards with me last night."

"You're that bad?" Dev turned to Wenna. "We don't take card-playing seriously. We ignore anyone who can win two games in a row."

"James can't win one game in a row." Hubert, a friend of James's older brother as were the others, had teasing rights, which the even-tempered Pup never took amiss.

"Unlike you, I don't cheat," James said loftily. "Will Nick be here tonight?"

"Is that some sort of follow-on? Are you implying Nick cheats?"

"Certainly not. He doesn't need to. Damn man. Drunk or sober, he can win whenever he wants. Excuse my language." James glanced in Wenna's direction. "I didn't know we had a lady among us."

Wenna stared straight at him. "I'm auditioning for the cricket match. If I pass muster, I shall be able to attend tomorrow." She gave the lad one of her wide beautiful smiles.

James looked momentarily stunned. "You pass my muster. Are we to be introduced?"

Dev stepped forward. "May I introduce Wenna—" The door opened again.

"Wenna!" Ivor Penrith strode into the room. Slim, fair-haired, and too sophisticated to look like the heir to the largest copper holding in the colony, he lowered his eyebrows with disapproval. "My God, Wenna. What on earth are you doing here?" He reached for her arm.

She moved, evading his grip. "Mr. Penrith. How do you do?"

"How do I do? Who brought you here?" His expression angry, he gazed at each of the men in the room. "Which one of you?"

"T'was I," Dev said, not knowing whether to be insulted or amused.

"What would your mother say?" Ivor continued, not about to be stopped mid-questioning. "You were always a very scrupulous girl. I'm shocked to see you have come to this."

Wenna raised her fine red eyebrows. Apparently, Ivor couldn't intimidate her. Dev knew he should have mentioned his marriage, but the devil in him wanted to see Ivor put nicely in his place. "I was shocked by you a number of times," she said in a honeyed voice. "The first time was when you broke the rector's window, and you let me take the blame."

"That's hardly an excuse to take up a life of sin." Ivor folded his arms across his manly chest.

Wenna turned to the other chaps, her face a picture of hurt innocence. "I haven't seen him for at least ten years, and yet he thinks he has the right to admonish me."

"So, you were childhood friends?" Dev asked, puzzled. Ivor's very wealthy family lived on a sprawling acreage in Clare. Wenna's family, on the other hand, had mined—in Clare. "Clare. That's the connection."

"That's the connection, but we were hardly friends. My mother did his mother's laundry."

"As a matter of fact, we knew each other for years before that. Her father was the manager of our mines. And her mother might have had to earn a living during the last year of her life but..." Ivor looked embarrassed. "Wenna was more Nell's friend than mine, in any event."

"Nell? Tony's wife?" James raised his eyebrows at Wenna. "Nell is my new sister-in-law. I'm James Hawthorn."

"And...." Dev left a dramatic pause. "Wenna's my wife."

James gave him a hearty congratulatory thump on the back.

"Hubert Grace, at your service, Mrs. Courtney. Well done, Dev."

"Luke Worthing. Delighted to meet you. Are you back in your sanctimonious box now, Penrith?"

Ivor shot his cuffs and had the grace to look embarrassed. "Nell will be pleased to see you again. She misses all her friends in Clare."

"And I will be pleased to see her. It's been many years. I hope she will recognize me."

"Your hair," Luke said, relaxed and looking slightly amused. "No one ever forgets redheads."

Dev allowed himself a smile. "Now we're all settled, let's order a meal. I've been working all day, and I need sustenance."

Hubert pulled out the chair at the head of the table. "This is the place for you, Mrs. Courtney. The only place. We can worship you from here without our vision being impeded."

"Call me 'Wenna.' That's what I'm most used to." With a glowing smile, she sat. While Ivor seated himself on her right, and Luke on her left, she fussed with the arrangement of her skirts. Although having the complete attention of a roomful of gentlemen might be a first for her, Dev didn't doubt she could handle them the same way she'd handled him when they'd met, with her forthright speech and inability to suffer fools.

For a moment, he wished he'd seated himself beside her. He had the need to protect her despite knowing firsthand how well she could protect herself. As he took his place at the table, the inevitability of this night hit him. He'd finally made a real commitment. Introducing Wenna into society as his wife meant he could no longer keep his marriage a secret. He could no longer put off his return to Cornwall. Finally he had to do the job he hadn't been born to do. A sigh pushed out of his chest. The duty he had to the Courtney family had conjoined with his duty to his wife.

"Married, eh? Time you bought a house then, isn't it, Dev?" Luke twirled the stem of his empty glass.

Dev suppressed a wry smile, knowing he had, and knowing he would never live in the almost-completed sturdy gatehouse of the gracious mansion he had hoped to build in the foothills. "City living is for me. I meet very interesting people on Rundle Street."

"Was it you who found the hat on the footpath last year?" James's mouth curved. "And when you picked it up, the man beneath asked if you would help dig out the horse beneath *him*?"

Dev raised his eyebrows. "I believe that is a story from some twenty years ago, James. If you would care to visit your carriage-building business in town more often, you would notice we now have footpaths and gas-lighting."

"That's right, Dev. Time someone reminded Pup that life isn't all pleasure. Some of us have to work for a living."

"Speaking of working," Hubert said, unfolding his table napkin. "How are things in Clare, Ivor?"

"None too good." Ivor crossed his forearms on the table. "The copper is still puttering along, but the gold's finished. And what with the drought, I hear that no farmer has more than a quarter of his stock left. Fortunately, beef is on the hoof and they can keep moving the stock. They can probably go on for another year without rain, but after that I don't know."

"It's a mistake to put your money in stock. The weather's too uncertain in this colony." James sounded satisfied. He could, since, with his brother, he had inherited a fortune from his father.

"Diversification is the answer," Ivor said morosely. He raised his head and stared straight at Dev. "I'm sorry, Dev. I've money worries and woman trouble, and I don't know which is worse. Probably women," he added after a quick glance at Wenna.

"Any woman in particular?" Dev asked, interested.

"Yes. Has anyone see Nick lately?"

Luke laughed. "That's a *real* word association for you. I saw him last week at the races with, as usual, a woman hanging onto him. He didn't particularly want to know me."

"He's keeping a low profile," Dev said as the menus arrived.

The waiter edged in beside Wenna, about to fill her glass, but Dev caught his attention and indicated the water jug. She glanced up.

"You're drinking watered wine, remember?" he said. She nodded, watching as the waiter leveled off her glass with water.

"It's quite refreshing."

"Most of us drink watered wine on Saturday night." Hubert held his glass out for the waiter to fill his with water, too. "Cricket on Sunday, you know. Can't play with a muzzy head."

James chortled. "So you can't use that as your excuse for being the worst cricketer in the colony. Your youngest sister plays better than you."

"I know, dear fellow, I know," Hubert said mournfully. "She's a constant embarrassment to me."

The waiter took the meal orders while Ivor spoke under his breath to Wenna. Dev didn't trust him. Ivor had a reputation for "romancing" women below him in class. But as Dev had fallen in love with a milkmaid himself, he'd never had the patience to listen to the gossip or to join in. However, he doubted Ivor would attempt to inveigle a woman married to one of his friends, and so he tried to tamp down his new possessiveness.

The food was as good as always, and the conversation didn't seem stifled by a woman's presence. Quite the opposite, in fact, with each of the chaps trying to outdo each other in competing for Wenna's attention. The conversation about the stock market interested her the most, which he found interesting but possibly not surprising. She hoarded the money he gave her like a miser, plotting the spending of every penny.

The meal finished, and the chaps rose to their collective feet. "Is Wenna going upstairs, too?" Hubert asked, looking slightly worried.

"Of course. If she loses too much of my money, I'll take her home."

Wenna caught his glance. "I can't lose something I don't have."

He fished in his pocket, and his hand came out with a one-pound note. "Try to make this last."

"You do know I have never gambled, don't you?"

"Wenna would probably prefer to go home now that it's dark." Ivor gave her a confident smile.

She shook her head. "I'd prefer to go upstairs."

"You can't take her upstairs, Dev." Ivor drew his eyebrows together. "Be a gentleman and take her home."

"Upstairs or home?" Dev waited for her answer, watching her gaze waver between Ivor and him. Although she was his wife, she clearly thought Ivor didn't want her exposed to an unsuitable environment. This, of course, would tempt her to flout him. Dev needed to suppress a laugh when she tried to read the expressions on the other chaps' faces. None had an agenda and each waited politely.

"Upstairs."

In a line, Wenna and his friends trooped toward the stairs.

"I'll escort you home if you'd prefer it," Ivor said to her, apparently still intent on guarding her.

"No, thank you, Ivor." She offered him a firm smile. "If the rest of you can afford to play badly, I can't do any worse."

Ivor shrugged, and she was escorted into the gambling rooms. Dev doubted she would be shocked by the women present. She seemed to fit in with any class, and not only women of the night frequented the rooms, but also avid gamblers of either sex. Most of the women stuck to the expected standards of dress, though Wenna's, as a former lady's maid, looked better than most.

Hubert, who had three younger sisters, took her off to explain the intricacies of the games, and Dev lost sight of her while he tried the roulette wheel for a while. "Where did you meet her, Dev?" Ivor asked, rocking on the balls of his feet.

"She was Dora Brook's maid. She caught my eye."

"She always was noticeable. That wild hair! And she had a motherly streak, which attracted Nell, being a couple of years younger." Ivor's fingers worried the tip of his chin. "But you know what women are. They might take against her because she worked as a maid. I think it's a territorial thing—they don't like female servants being noticed by their male relatives."

"She doesn't look like a servant." Dev met his friend's gaze. "And she doesn't act like one. I don't think she'll have a problem as my wife."

"At least she knows Nell."

"Are you going to put those coins on the wheel or keep rattling them in your pocket?"

"I'm going to help your wife win some money." Ivor stalked off.

Dev stared after him. He'd never seen Ivor so restless. Knowing Wenna could look after herself, he drifted into a game of cards and realized that these idle pursuits bored him. He would rather be doing something constructive—though winning money was mildly constructive. He won a little, lost a little, and began to understand why Tony Hawthorn would rather be at home with Nell.

Drumming his fingers, he glanced around the crowded room, trying to spot Wenna. After stalking around the room, he found her in a card game with Ivor, Hubert, and a couple of men whose faces he knew, though he couldn't put a name to them. He said he would wait for the end of the hand before he spirited Wenna away.

She frowned at him. "I was just starting to learn the game."

"We'll want to be up early for the cricket match tomorrow."

"We don't begin until ten." Ivor placed his next card.

Dev raised his chin. He didn't appreciate being seen as a disgruntled husband. "Our day begins before that."

After some fiddling with the gloves on her lap, Wenna scraped to her feet. The gentlemen stood. Although she continued to assess the expression on Dev's face, he put a firm arm around her waist and guided her to the stairs. "It seemed to me that I could win some money for us," she said in a peeved voice.

"Please rid yourself of the idea that I need money."

She stared at him. "So, you gamble simply for the intellectual exercise?"

"I know when to stop."

"Oh, good lord. You assume I'm a fool."

"I think you've spent enough time with your old friend Ivor," he said grimly. "And I'd rather you spent more time with me."

"We've been married six weeks, and in that time I've spent every Saturday, morning and night, alone. And now we're finally out meeting other people, you want to rush me home to spend time with you." Chin raised, she turned to him after marching down the stairs. "If you're worried about Ivor paying so much attention to me, don't be. I can handle him. When you've washed someone's underwear, you have some sort of advantage, which I always used."

"I'm sure you did, but you mistake me. I'm not at all jealous. I don't have the sort of friends who try to snatch each other's wives."

Her face stiffened. "You may well have a wife who wouldn't flirt with her husband's friends?"

"That, too."

"We had some catching up to do."

He wouldn't be wise to begin questioning her about her younger dealings with Ivor, who had been quick to deny a relationship but even quicker to get Wenna to himself. Although not completely at ease, he scooped his arm around her neat waist. Tonight, Wenna had done him as proud with her table manners as with her forthright, educated speech.

He opened the main door to the warm dark night. The gaslights flickered and the moon sat just above the Adelaide hills in the distance. Tomorrow, Wenna would need more than forthright speech and nice table manners. She had to fit in with the female members of Adelaide's society.

He thought she could, especially if he explained his father's title to her. His own he wasn't ready to admit to yet.

The only fly in the ointment might be the presence of the Brooks.

Chapter 12

Dev undressed for bed. Wenna, still surprisingly modest, always changed into her nightgown in the room she now used as her dressing room, already showing the poise of the Viscountess she was. Although this amused him, he would much rather see her step out of her gown. His imagination made him smile as he plopped onto the bed and pulled up the cover to his waist.

She arrived, dressed in her usual pristine white nightgown with her hair a bright haze across her shoulders. He wanted to bury his face into the lush softness. Undoubtedly, she noticed his desire for her, which he had harbored since this morning, for she shook her head. "Not tonight. I'm tired."

"I thought I had you on a promise?"

"Do you want me to be dutiful, or enthusiastic?"

He rubbed the back of his neck. "I could change your mind."

"I know, but I don't want you to."

Sighing, he lifted the sheet so that she could wriggle in beside him. "You've had a long day. I understand. I don't know if indicated this, Wenna, but tonight I was proud to be your husband."

She lay beside him, her face a picture of astonishment. Her mouth curved into a delighted smile. "Proud?" She stroked his cheek in a way he found placating. "That's a lovely thing to say. I don't think I've ever heard that word before in my life—or perhaps my mother once told me she was sure I would make her proud."

He covered her hand with his palm. If she didn't want him tonight, he would settle for affection, for he'd begun to feel a great amount for her, too much perhaps. "I didn't know you at all when I married you. I could see you weren't afraid of anyone, and you wouldn't let anyone run roughshod over you. But I didn't know then that you would be yourself on every occasion. You have no pretense about you. My friends appreciated this. They scooped you up like one of their own. We might have a business relationship rather than a real marriage, but every day I'm realizing what a perfect choice I made in you."

"I had a dreadful moment when Ivor arrived." Her breath tickled across his neck as she laughed softly. Every time she smiled, something inside him relaxed and warmed. He wished he could make her laugh more often.

"You handled him perfectly by reminding him of his childhood."

"How amazing that he didn't marry Nell. She used to be his shadow. She always assumed she would marry him. I always knew *I* wouldn't." She laughed again. "He needed admirers. Even as the daughter of working people, I didn't admire him. He was always so judgmental."

"He certainly judged you when he first entered the room. You got him onside quickly. I think my father would approve of you. He doesn't tolerate ninnies." He rolled onto his side, smiling into her eyes. Her soft hair, as always, drew him, and he sifted his fingers through her wild curls. Only a few weeks ago, he wouldn't have imagined enjoying this simple pleasure. When he pulled her into his arms, she snuggled her head under his chin and promptly fell asleep. Surprisingly, he did, too. The daylight shone through the window by the time he awoke, and he lay alone.

On Sundays, he didn't run. Cricket substituted on his day of rest. He arose, dealt with the hot water for the baths, and Wenna made the usual breakfast, though this morning she hummed. After they ate, she went upstairs to choose an outfit, and he dressed in his cricket whites. He hoped she wouldn't be bored today. None of the female staff employed by the Brooks had taken time off to watch when he'd played in the hills. Therefore, he had no idea what she thought about the game of cricket, which some thought of as very slow.

Every Sunday before the match, he had The Pig and Whistle make him up a picnic basket. As usual, he stepped out of the gateway onto Rundle Street, meaning to order the food. A smart green gig with gold scrollwork along the sides pulled up in front of him. He might have crossed behind, but a familiar voice said, "They're still laying these gas pipes?"

Shading his eyes from the sun peering over the rooftops, he glanced up at Ivor Penrith. "They've finished, but they keep springing leaks. Well met. You can give us a ride to the field."

"Such was my intention." Ivor brushed a speck of dirt from his white cricket trousers. "I come bearing gifts since I missed the wedding, though nothing very substantial at this stage. My father's housekeeper made up a picnic basket, in which she has included everything she can think of to tempt Wenna's taste."

"That's very generous of her. Step inside."

Ivor tied the leading rein to the gaslight post. Restrained, the horse made a show of head-tossing.

"Wenna should be ready soon, though she's fussing a little today."

Ivor followed Dev up the path. "Par for the course. Women always fuss when they're dumped in the middle of a pack of strangers for the very first time, and then deserted." Ivor glanced at the dingy wooden staircase. "Time you bought a house," he said as he followed Dev up to the landing.

"So everyone seems to think."

Wenna shot out of the bedroom, her face alarmed. "Oh," she said, spotting Ivor. "The rear guard."

Ivor laughed. "You can't have too many escorts. Aside from that, Dev usually walks to the field. I didn't expect his wife to do the same."

"You can advise me about my hat, too, then. What do you think?" With her flattering russet gown, she wore a low-crowned straw hat at a smart angle. She twirled.

"Very nice," Dev said with a frown. She never twirled for him.

Ivor examined her and narrowed his eyes. "You'll want gloves and a parasol."

She nodded, shifted back into her dressing room, and returned with the required items. Dev collected his cricket bat. During the short drive to the north parklands, Wenna didn't participate in the conversation. Instead, she stared at the passing view, the native-stone wall of the Botanic Gardens, the grove of small fig trees around the corner, and the expanse of native shrubs. The suburbs on the other side were beginning to sprawl into the hills. The way she kept stretching her gloves over her wrists showed uncharacteristic tension, which worried Dev.

He picked up her hand, and she clutched his tightly. He glanced at her, but her expression was as cool and self-possessed as ever. He hoped she could maintain her façade, because the moment the game began, she would be left to converse with the mothers, wives, and sisters of his friends—people she'd not met socially before.

"Don't worry. You'll be with Adelaide's nicest women," he said, swinging her down from the gig. "They'll take good care of you." He handed her parasol to her.

"I don't doubt they're nice to you. But if they recognize me as Mrs. Brook's maid, I don't know how nicely they'll treat *me*." Unfurling her parasol, she glanced toward the variously grouped spectators.

The grass had been neatly scythed, and canvas chairs were set out along the boundaries. In the distance, the North Adelaide buildings stuttered along the skyline, a clear blue scattered with wispy puffs of cloud. Glass clinked, conversations murmured, and light laughter rang out. No one glanced over.

Ivor collected his picnic basket, leaving his gig to a young lad hired to mind the transport. "Come along, and I'll introduce you to everyone." He began to stroll across the ground.

Dev followed, his hand clasped with Wenna's. "Lady Grace is over there. Remember? The lady from whom we borrowed a parasol?"

"I hope we remembered to return it."

"Ernie delivered it to their townhouse weeks ago."

James Hawthorn, his smile welcoming, had spotted them, and he turned, waiting for them to join the group. "I arrived home too late last night to speak to Nell about you," he said to Wenna. He lived with his brother in the family home. "And it seems she and Tony left for the country again, yesterday. As soon as they return, I'll have them call on you."

Dev hoped not. He couldn't imagine young Mrs. Hawthorn in his pokey little sitting room. The woman lived in a mansion filled with imported furniture and lush carpets. She would be shocked by his living conditions.

He introduced Wenna to his other team members, who in turn introduced her to their sisters, their cousins, and their aunts. Ivor put his picnic basket with the others, and he and Dev, who knew Wenna was in safe company, grouped with the other men ready to start the match.

* * * *

Lady Grace had very kindly remembered meeting Wenna, who stood drowning in the hordes of pretty young women who crowded around her after Devon's departure. She couldn't spot a single sincere smile hidden among the pastel gowns and flowery hats. "So...sudden." "Quite a love match." "Where did you meet?" "Are you from England?" "What was your maiden name?" "Married in the registrar's office?"

Miss Daphne Grace tucked a dark curl under a hat overloaded with pink peonies. "Devon's people are in England, which probably explains his need for a private wedding," she said prosaically.

"We're all very jealous because you've snatched up Mr. Courtney," said Miss Zanthe Grace, the middle of the three Grace sisters and probably not a day over seventeen years old. "He's so divine. Isn't he?" She elbowed her shorter and older sister, who had turned to watch the approach of Patricia Brook and her parents.

Wenna stood, not breathing, hoping the expression on her face was one of polite indifference. She doubted this would be the worst day of her life. Many more would surely follow now she had to be introduced into Adelaide's society.

"Mrs. Courtney, I'd like you to meet Miss Patricia Brook," Miss Grace said, dragging her stony-faced friend forward. "Mrs. Courtney is Devon's very new bride and this will be her first cricket match."

"Mrs. Courtney?" Miss Patricia's lips curled with cynicism. "I certainly haven't heard about a marriage and, of course I know Devon. I also know this woman as Miss Chenoweth. Until a month or so ago, she was my mother's maid." She took a moment to breathe heavily. Her fingers whitened on the ebony handle of her parasol. Like the other ladies, she wore an elaborate morning gown and a brimmed hat. Green didn't suit her, a fact that Wenna had hinted at a number of times. "Such a dear little gown, Miss Chenoweth. Did you make it on your days off?"

Wenna stared straight at Miss Patricia. "All my days are free since I married, but I still wouldn't have the time to make gowns. Men, you know. Always wanting their wives' attention." She gave what she hoped might more resemble a satisfied smirk than a terrified smile.

"I don't know men as well as you do." Miss Patricia's nostrils flared. "Clearly. But I'm sure Devon couldn't have found himself a better servant if he searched the whole of Adelaide," she finished with a nasty stretching of her lips.

Daphne's brow creased. "Um," she said in a faint voice. "Women are men's helpmates, and all that sort of thing." She couldn't meet anyone's eye. "Strictly not servants."

"Devon's new helpmate *was* a maid." Miss Patricia shoved the point of her parasol into the grass, clearly prepared to stay and spread her mean little message.

Mrs. Brook put her hand on Miss Patricia's arm. "That's enough, Patricia, and congratulations, Mrs. Courtney. Or, should I say best wishes? You married a very honorable gentleman. As for your former position with me, I was very sorry to lose you, because not only did you dress my hair like none other, you made sure I wore the right gown for every occasion...as I must say you have certainly done for yourself today. How nice to see a simple cotton on a hot day like this. So much more suitable than silk," she said glancing pointedly at her daughter's elaborate arsenic green gown.

"Thank you, Mrs. Brook." Wenna stared straight at her former employer. Her husband moved beside her. His collar looked too tight, and he sweated. "I believe we owe you money."

Wenna nodded. "You do." Her lips firmed.

Patricia tittered. She let her mouth curve and said in the most poisonous of voices, "We wouldn't want to be beholden to you."

"We'll call it even." Wenna's cheeks froze. "But for you, I wouldn't be married to Devon now."

"Oh, I think your own talents—"

"I said no more from you." Mrs. Brook jerked her daughter backward. "You've done yourself enough damage." The Brooks left a dead silence in their wake.

After staring at Wenna, especially her hat, Miss Zanthe Grace asked, "Were you really a maid? How romantic, except for having to fetch and carry for rude people. Did Devon fall in love with you while you were sweeping the cinders?"

Wenna smiled at the tall, fair-haired, awkward Zanthe. "It's been many years since I swept cinders. I was a lady's maid."

"The Brooks made their fortune out of building. Mr. Brook started out as a tradesman. I expect Patricia forgot that. None of us are anyone, really. Even my father, well, he was knighted for military service. Our money came from farming, but here, only money counts."

Wenna's throat thickened. She would earn money, and she would somehow push Devon into earning money himself, instead of wasting all he had on gambling and keeping up with his rich friends. No one had the right to look down on someone who had the wit and the will to work. "Miss Brook is a brat, born and bred. Don't worry about me. I'm used to her. I expect she wanted Devon for herself, and she is very disappointed."

"She did," Miss Grace said in low voice. "And she is—disappointed. Come over and sit with us. You must meet my friend, Charlotte Davies. The gentlemen only play for a short time before they're wanting a tea break, and we must be sure of having everything ready for them."

"Do you enjoy cricket, Mrs. Courtney?" Zanthe took long strides beside her.

"Please call me Wenna. And no, I don't know a thing about cricket."

"I'll tell you all about it."

Unfortunately, Zanthe did.

* * * *

Devon imprisoned Jenny's hand between his chin and shoulder. He opened his eyes, blinked, and focused not on Jenny, his love, but on Wenna, his wife, who lay on her side facing him. "Good morning."

She pushed her hair back from her face. "I was wondering what Nell would be like now. She used to be a sweet little poppet, always running after Ivor. I wish she'd been at the cricket yesterday."

He stretched and eased out of bed.

Wenna rolled onto her back to watch him dress in his running clothes. "I like the Graces."

"I see you got on well with Daphne."

"Not so very well. She's a friend of Patricia Brook."

"I didn't see the Brooks."

"They left before the tea break."

"Did they speak to you?"

"Briefly. Mr. Brook offered to give me the money they owe me."

"Oh, good. I'm finally married to a wealthy woman."

"Unfortunately, you're married to a maid. Patricia Brook couldn't wait to tell everyone."

He shrugged. "No one will care. It's what you do in this country, not who your parents are."

She gave him disbelieving smile. "Not so, but money helps. Are you that way every morning?" she asked. He noted the downward direction of her gaze.

He gave her a suggestive glance. She knew he was. "You've had me on rations lately."

"You were starting to be too greedy."

"Wenna," he said, trying to sound authoritative when he really wanted to laugh. Wenna was the most complex woman he had ever met. "I can't make a baby by myself. We had an agreement that you would do your share."

She gave a flip of her wrist, waving his words away. "Ivor said Nell would call on us. We can't have callers here. We don't want people to know how poor we are."

He shrugged. "I don't care about that, because I don't want people to call on us."

"If Mr. Finn found another office, we could use the shop front as a sitting room."

"If we used the shop front as a sitting room, I would lose an amount of my income."

Her eyes widened. "I had no idea you rented the place to Mr. Finn. I assumed you rented from him."

He ignored the opening, preferring her to think he made his money from laboring, as he had never mentioned his private income. Not yet. She had more than enough preconceptions about the wealthy without him adding the load of a title and the further responsibilities that came with his family name. First, she needed to be comfortable in society. "If I got rid of him, we would have less money." No amount of enlarging the premises could make his lodgings into a gracious home, and the one thing his wife craved was money. "You wouldn't want less, now, would you?"

She looked as if she might be preparing to argue, which put a hopeful grin on his face. "Oh, no. I mean to have much more."

"You will have, in time." He laughed and made a dive onto the bed, grabbing her and kissing her under her ear. After dreaming of Jenny all night, he wanted Wenna. "Let's make love."

"You don't want to make love." She pushed at him. "You want to make babies."

"Not always. Let's just do this for fun."

She stared right into his eyes. "I'll believe you mean that if you...you know."

He nibbled at the soft white skin of her throat. "I'll pull out in time. I promise."

Her fingers slid around the back of his neck and combed through the hair on his nape. "If you did, you would prove we're just having fun. I quite enjoy trying to make babies, but I would enjoy the act far more if we were simply pleasuring each other and had no ulterior motive. But men often make your particular promise without intending to keep it."

"When a man is lying on a bed with a woman, he will promise anything, so you have to trust me." He slid his hand down to her delightful behind and lifted her onto him.

She nipped her teeth against his ear lobe. "If you betray me once, I'll never trust you again, you know."

"Trust me." The idea of modifying their original bargain and leaving off baby-making for a year or so entered his mind. Her trip back home would be more pleasant without the burden of a pregnancy, aside from the problem of seasickness combining with her condition. Saying so might gain him points, but she would think he wasn't as enthusiastic about his heir as she might have thought. She would certainly rail against a change of plans, as eager as she was to leave the colony. His lips curled ruefully as he settled her against him.

She ran a hand up his arm. "One good thing about the building you do is that it makes your body so hard." Her palm pressed against his chest, and she began a slow route down to his abdomen.

His stomach muscles tightened under the pure torment of her teasing. His flesh quivered as her hand moved to his hip and wandered to his thigh. He breathed heavily and concentrated on his toes while he suffered her wrist brushing over the place that had hardened before he'd covered her on the bed. Not for the world would he stop her exploring his body. He'd craved this from the start. A muscle in his leg twitched.

"Am I annoying you?"

"Mmf."

"Roll onto your back, and I can touch you all over."

He moved so quickly that the bed shook, and he had the idea that he might be a half-witted idiot. Touching would mean teasing and not relief. He groaned with the first experience of her hand on his scrotum. She cupped and squeezed him gently. When her fingers hesitated, he tried to relax.

"Do you like this?"

He thought he made a positive sound and obviously she did, too, because she grew bolder. Her hand examined his rod, tested, and with any luck gave him full marks. "You feel beautiful, so hard and manly. Am I depraved to be excited by touching you like this?"

"No, no, not at all. It's done in the best of families." He covered her hand with his, surging into the full length of her palm. She seemed not to mind, for she opened her mouth over the point of his shoulder and licked him. Relief no longer seemed paramount; a heightening of the senses beckoned. "Take off your gown, my love. I want to touch you, too."

He read no hesitation into her movements. Soon enough, she lay pressed against him with the spread of her fingers splayed against his back and her soft breasts flattened on his chest. He took her mouth and her tongue, while shaping her breasts to his palms. His heart thudded while caressing the hard little points. Her fingers dug into his buttocks. Forgetting everything but his desire, he rolled her over and dropped on top of her. His hardness sought between her legs.

She lifted her knees. His mouth slanted over hers, angling to take the kiss deeper, and she crossed her ankles over his back. With a groan he slid inside her, expanding her slickness. Plunging deeper, he breathed unevenly, as one with Wenna, an integral being with the woman who would bear his child. He savored every thrust, every one of her upward surges, holding back, enjoying the heat of her flesh, her quiet gasps—

until she dug her fingers into his straining buttocks and ran one heel down the back of his thigh.

With a terrifying lack of control, he began to climax. Just before he came, he kept his promise and spent his seed onto the sheet. He collapsed, soaked with perspiration.

"I suppose you've made a terrible mess," she said indulgently.

His languor left. He sat up and swung out of bed. After cleaning himself, he gave her the washcloth from the bowl. "I proved you can trust me, at least. A little too visibly."

"It is much nicer when we're not just doing a job."

* * * *

He shaved, ran, bathed, dressed, and slung bricks all day, his flesh tingling, his mind plotting his next encounter with his wife, which he hoped might be minutes after he walked in the door that evening. He wanted her more than he'd ever wanted another woman. Perhaps being her husband and knowing he didn't have to hurry with her and that he could have her again and again made the difference. Certainly his cobbled-together marriage suited him in every single way.

Wenna had managed well yesterday. Sitting with the ladies at the cricket match hadn't been easy for her, but he'd not noticed any awkwardness during the lunch break or at the tea break. She had at least as much class as any of the other ladies, but she would need plenty to deal with his father, who would treat her like dirt, given the chance.

Dev didn't want to give the earl that chance until Wenna knew the ins and outs of society and could assuredly give his father a run for his money. Then she would be treated with the respect she'd already earned from Dev, who regretted his initial plan to use her simply as the package in which to present the heir. He winced. Had he really been so small- minded?

By now, he was sure he didn't want a baby yet. He wanted to stay here as long as possible, at least until his house was finished, his vines were planted, and his cow was ready to lay eggs. That long.

He prayed that his ship would be delayed. Pretending to himself he could stay as long as he liked, he explained the situation to Finn, who thought he could move to the vacant premises next door within the next couple of days.

Chapter 13

Wenna popped into The Pig and Whistle the next morning and asked Maisie to do the early hairstyles. Toying with the skin on her neck, Maisie said, "I can do the simple styles, but you'll need to be there for the others. I'm a good copier, but I can't think of different hairstyles the way you do."

"You'll soon learn, Maisie. Practice makes perfect. I'll stay until you are sure you can manage, and then I'll run home. My husband has decided to absorb the shop front into our lodgings." She smiled, almost helpless with delight. Should she have a visitor, and she didn't expect any but Nell, she wouldn't be shamed by having to seat a lady in her tiny kitchen at her tiny table. "I have a few things I need to work on."

As soon as the first customer's hair was washed and dried, she discussed the style required and left Maisie to manage. "If you need me, you know where I'll be," she said as she left, confident that Maisie could cope with the basic styles for the next three customers. After that, Wenna would go back and work herself. Her organizing wouldn't take all day.

She mentally totaled the money she had saved. Since Devon would be losing part of his income, she would need to use her own money to furnish the new space. Fortunately, she still had the two pounds she'd won at The Castle, his one-pound stake, and his initial two pounds that she'd kept. At this stage, she didn't need to spend her earnings, nor tell him about her business.

With Maisie taking her place, she spent the morning drawing the more complicated hairdos she planned on teaching her apprentice. Finn moved out over the weekend. Devon worked on Saturday, played cricket on Sunday, and she sat with the ladies again. Although she made sure of being agreeable and pleasant, her company was suffered rather than sought. Nell still did not appear. Perhaps she did not want to revisit her connection with Wenna. Wenna had expected more of her childhood friend, but accepted the rebuff with only a modicum of disappointment. Nell had married the richest man in the colony. She couldn't be expected to take up with an ex-maid simply because she had known her as a child.

The next morning, almost with pleasure, Wenna cleaned the front office meticulously. After lunch, she hauled the carpet square from the study down the stairs and bumped the armchairs down after. She left the desk upstairs, assuming Devon would still want to keep that small room as his, though she also used the desk for her drawings. During the afternoon, she took over from Maisie again, trying new styles on customers and showing off the latest shapes in hats. Mrs. Busby was very pleased with her extra sales, pleased enough to hire a new assistant herself.

Wenna would need to buy curtains before the downstairs space could take over as the sitting room, but she could afford the fabric, and when she had a spare moment, she could have lengths cut and sewn at Seymour's. First, she had a big box of paintings to sort through. Devon hadn't yet hung a single one, but given her choice for the sitting room, she would use the rural scenes, which would remind Devon of home.

In the meantime, she wanted to tackle Devon's mother's boxes, which still filled the store cupboard. Wenna dragged the boxes out and opened the one she knew contained the precious china. She lifted out the first gold-edged cup, so fragile that when she held the bowl to the light streaming through the window, she could see her hand through the porcelain.

Wenna unpacked the whole box of treasures carefully, also revealing a silver tea service, complete with an elaborate serving tray. In the very bottom of the box sat a small parcel wrapped in tissue. The paper had disintegrated, and when she blew off the fragments, a tiny portrait of a lady with pale blonde ringlets around her face dressed high in the style of yesteryear stared up at her. Wenna noted a likeness to Devon in the lady's blue eyes. She fingered the gold frame into which brilliants had been set, before putting aside the delicate portrait.

Then she washed every piece of the setting for twenty and stacked the china on the shelf in the storeroom. Now, if any of Devon's friends should happen to call, at least she could offer an armchair, a dainty cup for tea, and a portrait to admire, though she certainly hoped none would arrive before she had furnished the room. When she could, she planned to buy a dining table and chairs, as the area now doubled the size of the lodgings. Wenna had great plans, which before dinner that evening she began to explain to Devon. "A table and chairs, and curtains. I should also like to buy a larger carpet. Will you trust me as to the colors?"

He glanced around the largely empty space, his expression noncommittal. "You're working far too hard, my love. I think...yes, tomorrow I will take a day off and we'll go to the hills for a picnic."

She glanced down, disappointed. She wanted him to care about his accommodation. He had said he was proud of her. She wanted him to be even prouder. "I don't have time for picnics."

"As I said, you're working too hard. I'll order a basket from Snow in the morning, and we'll have a nice relaxing day."

She swallowed, her mind searching around for a way to cancel her appointments. If she raced down to Madame Fleur's now... No, she would have to explain to Devon, and she didn't like lying to him. She also didn't like letting her customers down and if she didn't appear, two ladies would be put out. That wasn't a way to run a good business. Aside from that, she had already changed out of her working black gown for dinner.

She decided she could at least let Maisie know, and Maisie could in turn let Mrs. Busby know, and relay Wenna's apologies. She sat with Devon in The Pig and Whistle in an agony of anticipation, waiting for Maisie to attend the table. Finally, while ordering the roast pork from her apprentice, she said, "Mr. Courtney and I are going on a picnic tomorrow."

"Oh. Where?" Maisie's eyebrows lifted in query.

"In the Beaumont area." Devon smiled at the waitress as charmingly as always. "My wife works too hard. She needs a day off."

"Really." Maisie sounded dour. "Must be nice to take off time whenever you choose. Didn't you have *somethink* else to do?"

"Such a lot, but I couldn't disappoint Mr. Courtney. I wouldn't want to disappoint *anyone else* either." Wenna waggled her eyebrows at Maisie. The waitress knew Devon wasn't to know about Wenna's business.

Maisie stood staring at her. "No. That would be bad." She wrinkled her brow. "Nor would I, but I was thinkin' of telling Mr. Snow that I might go down to part-time work here. Got meself—*myself*—another part-time job, and I might be needed there more often."

Wenna nodded frantically. "That sounds like such a good idea, Maisie."

"What other job do you have, Maisie?" Devon looked curious.

"I've got work in a hat shop. I'd rather be there than here, that's for sure."

"A hat shop. Ah." Devon took a long sip of his ale. "I'm pleased for you, but Snow will be disappointed to be losing you."

"He won't be losing me for a while yet." Maisie sailed off.

Wenna heaved a sigh of relief. If Maisie could do the afternoon hairdos, all would be well. Unfortunately, Wenna would have to put off going through the other boxes until another day.

* * * *

Devon slept like a hibernating bear, knowing he didn't need to leap out of bed early. He enjoyed not dressing in his old working clothes. Instead, he had the pleasure of watching Wenna put on a pretty morning gown in place of the black she donned each day, obviously for her housework duties. Why she insisted on cleaning all day he couldn't imagine. The place was already spotless after weeks of her tending. And he didn't want her to make his lodgings into a home. He was building a home, which they could both occupy very comfortably if he didn't have to return to Cornwall. If he didn't give her a baby, perhaps he could put off leaving for an extra month.

He heaved a breath. Today he intended showing her the land he had bought and his almost-completed house in the foothills. If she liked the place, if she approved, perhaps she would want to stay in the colony for a year longer. Another year would give him a chance to see if his vines flourished, if his fruit trees took, and if he could collect enough water for his household. If not, he would have to drill a bore. He would like to know that before he left.

While Wenna tidied the kitchen, he went to the hotel and collected his picnic basket, which he dropped off in the lodgings. Next, he hiked off to the livery, where he hired a two-wheeled gig and an even-tempered piebald.

The sun shone on the city rooftops, glinting on the slate, beaming in the cloudless blue sky. He'd chosen a perfect autumn day, a little on the hot side, but a person got used to the dry heat in this southern land. Wenna's smart little hat did nothing to shade her face, but she now owned a parasol, which she held upright as he traversed the busy streets on his way to the road that twisted up into the foothills.

As he passed through streets of houses, he noted once again the clever planning of the city, with single houses built on plots of all shapes and sizes. A variety of stonework had been used. Slate roofs had begun to dot the landscape now that the mines were up and running. These days, the old natives stone was rarely used other than as sidings. Now that the brickworks had been established, red brick had become more popular although the bluestone was still prevalent.

"In the box of porcelain, I found a portrait of a young lady," Wenna said, interrupting his musing.

He turned to her. "Oh. Who is she?"

"I've no idea. I forgot to show her to you last night. The painting is about the size of my palm, and the lady has blond ringlets and blue eyes. The frame is very pretty."

"I'll have to see it when we get back, but it might be my mother." He smiled, pleased. "I thought my father had sent me enough to set up a small place of my own. I can't imagine him doing such a strangely sentimental thing as sending me a reminder of my mother."

"I think he must have meant all the paintings to be a reminder of home. They'll make our new combination dining-drawing room look very gracious."

He nodded. "I'm not expecting to entertain, you know."

"If you're worried about furnishing the room, don't. I can pay for almost everything we need."

"I don't think Waldo Brook will give you a fortune. His two pounds might buy a few chairs or a table, but not much more."

"I wasn't thinking of that money, which he hasn't sent yet. I have the money you gave me to waste on gambling, plus the money I won."

"You won money?" He stared at her. "I thought you'd lost the lot."

"Any man silly enough to give a woman money to lose deserves to have her lose it for him. This is why I have decided the money is mine. So, I have three pounds from gambling and the two you owed me because Mr. Brook didn't pay me. That should be enough to buy a whole suite of furniture."

"I have never priced furniture, but I expect you are right." Whatever she bought could be transferred to the gatehouse after they left. He flicked the reins and turned the horse onto the street before the tollgate. Silver had been mined here in the early days, but the mine had played out long since. "Hold on to the side of the gig, because the road is bumpy here."

She lowered her parasol and glanced around. "This doesn't look like a picnic spot."

"It's a beautiful place with a full view of the city and the sea. I'm going to show you the house I've been building."

"The house you work on every day?"

"See the trees? See how thickly they grow here? And the birds, thousands of them. The native parakeets feast on the she-oaks and those little lorikeets eat all the fruit and seeds. The place is a paradise. My house is at the end of this road." The horse began to pull up the steep incline through the trees, but soon enough the makeshift road leveled out. Dev's ten acres came into view. "There, ahead of you. See? All the walls are built. We'll be putting on the roof next."

She shaded her eyes with her hand. "Someone appears to be hauling up the beams. Do you plan to stop?"

"What? And be caught slacking with you when I ought to be working? Not on your life. I'm taking you farther up the hill to the vineyard."

She laughed. "You are shameless. You don't feel a scrap of guilt about taking time off and don't pretend you do. Oh, look. We can see the whole of the city from here."

"And the sea. You can even see the port over there. Where else but Adelaide would you find a view like this?"

"I don't know. I've never been anywhere but in this colony." In the morning sunshine, her beauty stood stark and clear, her profile elegant with her straight nose and determined jaw. For a moment, she looked bereft, but the moment passed so quickly that he might have imagined the regret on her face. "But I'm sure the views in England are much prettier."

He shrugged. "Maybe. The eye of the beholder, and all that. Let me show you around." After pulling the horse to a stop, he eased on the brake. The sun sat at midday, directly overhead. The trees rustled with birds. Pine and eucalyptus fragrance, released by the sun, hovered in the air, and the freshly lifted soil added a fresh aroma. He could look over the rooftops of the houses below. This was the place to build, where he could see the whole of the capital city and watch the suburbs expand. Here he could grow his vines and his trees and nestle with his woman, breeding happy, healthy, confident, loved children.

He put his arm around her waist and surveyed all he owned. "See these furrows? The terraces will be grape vines, grown in commercial numbers. Over there is where the olive trees will grow. Around the house, apples, pears, oranges, and lemons. The weather will sustain the Mediterranean plants. Nearer to the house will be the vegetable patch and the chickens, and maybe a goat or two, or a cow. How does that sound to you?"

"Very rural. Though, I think the owner has planned a lovely, simple sort of life. I envy him, being so self-sufficient. He can mix country living while being no more than twenty minutes from the city."

"We could spread the blanket down over there and eat lunch while we are lords of all we survey. I'll get the basket."

The horse was grazing happily when he removed the basket from the gig, placing the food where Wenna indicated, on a nest of low-growing native ground cover under a large she-oak. She settled herself on the blanket and peered into the basket. "This looks like a feast."

"I left Snow to decide on our menu. He seems to have added a couple of plates and two glasses. Here, I'll cut that pie. What size piece do you want?"

"Half that. What's in these bottles?"

"Ginger beer."

"How do I take the stopper out?"

"Pass the bottle over, and I'll do it." Dev loosened the wire. The glass stopper shot out, and the ginger beer exploded, drenching his shirt and wetting his hair. "Wretch. You knew that would happen, didn't you?"

She returned his smile. "Better you than me. I can wash your shirts, but washing my gowns is a little harder." She kneeled over him, leaned down, and kissed his lips.

"What was that for?"

"You're happy. I love to see it."

"No more of that." He rested his hand on the side of her neck. "I'm too impressionable."

"Oh, I doubt it."

He laughed. "One thing I like about you is you're not gullible." To disguise the fact that he did, indeed, appreciate her, he picked a native dandelion flower and joined the stem to another by splitting a hole in the stem of the first.

She watched his fingers. "What are you doing?" she asked.

"I'm making a necklace of sunshine for you."

He picked another and another. She helped, scrambling around on her hands and knees to find every flower she could. When he untied her hat and dropped his prickly creation onto her braided head, she glowed. He'd never felt so guilty in his life. She received a circlet of flowers as another woman might have accepted diamonds.

Blinking rapidly, she raised her eyes to his. "It's the most beautiful thing anyone's ever given me." Slowly, she rose to her knees and put her arms around his neck.

"Save your thanks for something real."

"What could be more real than you making a gift especially for me?" Her mouth curved into a smile, but the downward tilt of her head showed a touch of sadness. "Once, long ago, I made a plaited grass bracelet for Mumma. In the end when she was dying, she reminded me about the bracelet and a chopping board Da made for her. She didn't mention a gown she owned, or a piece of lace, not a single thing that'd been bought. I doubt that even a gold brooch or a hundred pounds would have given her the same memories. We made those things for her because we loved her."

"Such a romantic nature you have hidden under that practical streak of yours." He cupped the sides of her face, examining her earnest expression and realized that he certainly had feelings for her, a combination of respect and desire.

Her innate strength, her eagerness to move ahead, her willingness to work, her uncomplaining acceptance of the appalling living conditions he had presented her with, and her utter enjoyment of his body gave him the heart to keep pushing on, despite his shifting goals. Hers had never moved. He had no illusions about her feelings for him, numbering none—other than a healthy tolerance mixed with a desire to shake his complacence. Not bothered by either, he succumbed to the lure of her mouth, taking the kiss far deeper than he meant.

Every reason to put aside his emotional attachment to her flashed through his mind while she accepted and returned his kiss. Never had he appreciated a woman quite as much in bed. Her hand crept over his abdomen, and her tongue played with his. He tried to remember where he was, but he heated and hardened anyway. Unable to help himself, while supporting himself on an outstretched palm, he shifted his other hand to the outer side of her breast.

She turned her triumphant eyes to his. "I believe I could tempt you into coupling with me right here."

"I'm more than tempted, but we don't want the workers down there to get an eyeful," he murmured into the clean fragrance of her beautiful hair.

She leaned back, glanced at his house below, heaved a sigh, and slid her hands into her lap. "I didn't plan to make an exhibition of myself, which reminds me of your mother's plates."

He grinned. Women's minds could never be unraveled, but at least she gave him a chance to subside.

She looked offended. "I might use some of the vases I've unpacked. Do you mind having your family's possessions on display?"

He stared for a moment, considering. "They would be my mother's family's possessions. At home we used the Courtney plates, which naturally my father wouldn't send out here, since everything belongs to the estate. I imagine those dishes were part of my mother's dowry."

"Does that explain the crest? The letter 'M' entwined with vines?"

"Her family would have had that done for her wedding."

"And nothing was ever used?"

He shrugged. "I have no idea, but I'm her only heir, so it's mine now."

"All her linen is initialed, too. Do you think she did the embroidery?"

"In my memories, she worked at that sort of thing all the time." He lifted his knee, where he rested one elbow. "In my study, I have another box of old things, mainly personal papers. I think I might have other possessions of hers there, too, but don't worry about unpacking it. I'll get that done now that the study is not a sitting room, too."

She sighed. "We almost have a real house."

"Speaking of real houses..." He glanced sideways at her. "Would you like to see the house we're building below?"

"Of course. That was a lovely lunch. Thank you."

He introduced his wife to his builders with an amount of trepidation, afraid one might mention the place was his. Perhaps his face warned them off. He managed to show her every room without any of the men saying a word. "What do you think?" he asked her in the gig on the way back to the city, after she'd also said nothing at all.

"Someone will be very happy there. The rooms are a good size."

"If you had a house like that, would you change your mind about living in Cornwall?" He held his breath.

"If I planned to live here for the rest of my life, that house would suit me. If I thought the garden would grow the way the owner has planned, the garden would suit me. But I plan to live in Cornwall, and I know that in this hot dry country, finding enough water to keep fruit trees alive is difficult. Having a having a lush green garden here is impossible."

"Plenty of people here have lush green gardens."

"Only the rich. And with a husband who works only when he wants to, I'll never be rich."

Miffed, he stared straight ahead. She saw him as a slacker. He would like to tell her who he was and that he would never want for money, but he would rather she valued him for himself, for the hard work he put into this property. He had meant to, today. He had hoped she would admire the place and he had expected to proudly confess that the planning and a part of the building had been done by him. His mouth curved ruefully.

His dream to live here would never be fulfilled. She planned to live in Cornwall, and he couldn't break his promise to her.

* * * *

Devon slept with his back to Wenna that night, but she didn't mind. Lately he had seemed more interested in congress in unexpected places, which suited her. By his own rule, congress other than in bed was for pleasure, and she didn't have to worry about her sponge.

With no teas to deliver in the morning, she hummed as she dragged out the second of Devon's mother's boxes. Curiosity drew her on. The more she could learn about her husband and his family, the better, if she had to spend the rest of her life in England. She had given herself an hour, for today she planned to start work at Mrs. Busby's shop as soon as the doors opened. Heaven knew Wenna had increased her own customer base threefold. Even with Maisie's help, she could barely keep up. Almost six weeks ago, she'd picked through this box, looking for tablecloths and fabric she could use for curtains. She had also found the lace for her evening gown in here, but she hadn't yet gone past the tissue-packed top layer yet. On her knees, she lifted out a series of monogrammed pillowcases edged with exquisite lace, matching sheets she would need to freshen in the sun, more table linen, and a paisley shawl, which she arranged around her shoulders. She could certainly use this.

In the very bottom of the box, she found a leather case. Inside were three hairbrushes, a set of tortoiseshell combs, six glass bottles with silver tops, and an ivory fan. Likely she could use all these, too.

She slid the case back into place and noticed a paper lodged in the corner of the box. Pulling, she discovered a scruffy, stamped, unopened letter addressed to The Honorable D. Courtney of Rundle Street, Adelaide. A letter with a Rundle Street address among his mother's things? On the day she had collected his mail, she had left the pile on the top of this box. The letter must have fallen through.

She rose to her feet, her forehead creased. The postal clerk had called him the Honorable Mr. Courtney. Wenna thought that had been the clerk's joke. She had no idea why any man would be addressed as "honorable."

Puzzled, she put the letter aside, draped the sheets and pillowcases on the clothesline outside to air, and came back to her mess. All the spare linens would be better stored in the second bedroom. She took as much as she could carry upstairs, and jammed on her hat. Devon's clock informed her that she needed to leave for the hat shop.

When she had finished her hairstyles for the day, she carried the rest of the linens upstairs, remembering the misplaced letter this time. Guiltily, she placed the envelope among a few others, sitting on top of the box of papers he had stored in his study. He would find this fast enough without her having to explain her blunder.

Chapter 14

"Bec, look over here. This peony pink is just your color."

Wenna's back stiffened. Frozen in place, she stared at the doorway into the hat shop, where the loud, over-privileged voice of Miss Patricia continued extolling the virtues of a hat. Wenna's seated customer, a well-corseted, gray-haired grandmother, glanced up at her from the mirror.

Wenna saw her own panicked reaction reflected back at her and realized that she still held a hairpin mid-air. "Dear me," she said, her voice a wobbly semblance of her usual tone. "The woman's voice so close startled me, and now I've lost my train of thought." As she pushed a curl into place, she made an effort to control the tremble of her hand.

If Miss Patricia walked through to have her own hair done, she would doubtless name Wenna as "Mrs. Courtney," not "Miss Chenoweth." She would doubtless make a song and dance about Wenna working in the back of a hat shop. By the next cricket match, Devon would be snidely mentioned as a man who needed his wife's income to maintain his lifestyle.

Eventually, Miss Patricia's voice retreated, and the doorbell tinkled. Wenna breathed again. For the first time, she had to face the fact that any of the wealthier hat shop customers might be tempted to avail themselves of the services of the hat shop's hair stylist, despite having maids of their own—an unlikely event, but still possible.

Her day earned her six shillings, two of which she paid to Maisie, who grew more proficient by the day. Wenna arrived home by four, in time to change for dinner and redeem her mistake with Devon's letter by sorting out his untidy box of papers in the study.

As he had said, the box mainly held papers and old letters, but in the bottom, she found parts of a horse's bridle, a leather-bound Bible, three illustrated books about plants, a pair of canvas gaiters, and a tobacco box. She sat on the floor beside his mess. On her haunches, she sorted the mail into one pile and his invoices into another.

Most of his mail came from a London solicitor, A. M. Merriwether, addressed to The Honorable Devon Courtney. She presumed "The Honorable" was a title, perhaps granted because of his services to the governor. This warmed her cheeks with pleasure for herself as well as him. Apparently she'd married a man out of the ordinary, which was confirmed when one of his letters had been so roughly jammed back into the envelope that she could read "Marchester" monogrammed on the thick expensive paper.

Mumma had served Lady Ann, the Earl of Marchester's countess. A proper wife would simply refold this correspondence and place the message more neatly back into the envelope, but Cornwall seemed so close when Devon had correspondence with her mother's mistress' family. She smoothed out the paper and read. Marchester himself had wanted to discuss farming matters with Devon, whom he addressed informally, which would have been interesting if she understood the half of it. Meanwhile, Devon would be home soon.

She found a place in the bedroom for his gaiters, and lined up the Bible and the books on his desk, using the tobacco box as a book end. The broken bridle, apparently a keepsake, went back into the box, and his papers sat neatly on his desk, with his letters on top. The study now looked more like a purposed room than an empty space that needed filling. Pleased with herself, she sat on Devon's desk chair and swiveled the seat around, planning a set of bookshelves beside the desk in the very least, if not some sort of filing cabinet.

Footsteps pounded up the stairs. Devon appeared in the doorway, his hardy work shirt sweat-stained and his trousers dirty on the knees.

"I've sorted out your papers, but I had to leave them on the desk because your drawers are crammed already."

He nodded. "What a treasure you have turned out to be." Since the picnic, she hadn't seen his smile. He'd been grim ever since.

"I see you know the Earl of Marchester."

He stood stock still, an expression of shock on his face. "Have you been going through my letters?" Reaching across her, snatched his papers up.

"No, of course not. You hadn't put that letter back in the envelope and when I caught sight of the name... Well, I read that one." Her cheeks slightly warm, she offered a placating smile.

"Which one?" His eyes turned icy blue.

"Something about stocking cattle in one of his fields."

"Cattle." He sounded indifferent. "Then you would have been thoroughly bored." He tossed his papers and envelopes back onto his desk. The looser pages continued the impetus, flying in a cascade onto the floor.

"Extremely." She bent from the chair seat to pick up the sheets. Using the flat of his desk, she evened the edges and set the lot back on his desk again, glancing at topmost gold-embossed card. Her eyes read a few words and her breath halted.

"What?"

"Nothing."

"What did you see?"

She straightened her spine. "Nothing important." Her palm sat flat over the invitation, as if the words didn't exist if she couldn't see them.

Devon moved her hand, read, and examined her face. "I planned to refuse this invitation."

Her jaw tensed. "Of course."

"I'm invited to many balls. I rarely go."

"Oh." The back of her neck ached.

"You wouldn't want to go to a formal function."

"Of course not." She raised her chin. "Not when I wasn't invited."

"I received the invitation before I met you," he said, his forehead creased.

"That's convenient." Her mouth twisted into an uncomfortable smile. She knew a polite excuse when she heard one.

He sighed. "Lady Grace has met you. I haven't answered yet. I'll accept."

"It's a week away." She drew an agonized breath. "You can't answer now. It's far too late. Anyway, I don't want to go to a ball. I don't know how to dance. And I don't have a ball gown." Nevertheless, her eyes prickled.

He had hoped not to take her. She embarrassed him.

"Easily fixed. Use the money you held back for furniture, and you can buy yourself one." With a lordly tilt of his eyebrows, he stalked off into the bedroom. His autocracy seemed to be inborn.

Mightily annoyed by his attitude, she waited for him to change for dinner, arms crossed and staring at the folded invitation. Sighing, she decided that she *could* socialize with Adelaide's richest, if only because she'd married an honorable gentleman.

With this in mind, and utterly terrified, before she went to work the next morning, she entered Millie's Mode, Adelaide's most exclusive dress shop.

"Good morning, Miss Chenoweth." The owner herself, Mrs. Miller, smiled at her. The lady, dark haired and somewhere in her middle thirties, wore a blue gown of impeccable cut, which few people would recognize as deliberately plain. "I've been hearing about you and the great turnaround in Madam Fleur's."

Wenna put a hand on her chest to still the nervous quickening of her heartbeat. She had expected to be recognized as Mrs. Brook's maid, rather than as the local hairstylist. The rate that gossip travelled up and down the street was enough to make a person's head spin. "She's made some changes, and her business is evolving."

"Evolving." Mrs. Miller laughed. "I could do with a bit of evolving around here too. Not that business is bad—no, indeed. What can I do for you?"

"I'm here to buy a ball gown for myself," Wenna said, not willing to meet Mrs. Miller's gaze. Should her hopes be upset, she could appear blasé rather than crushed. "I need one for next Saturday."

"Lady Grace's ball? That's only five days away." Mrs. Miller's face creased. "I don't know...we have so many orders..." The discreet little doorbell tinkled.

"Good gracious, Daphne. Do you see who I see?"

Wenna's shoulders stiffened. Patricia Brook. Again.

"It's *Mrs.* Courtney. You know, the redheaded maid that Devon Courtney has some interest in."

"Good morning, Wenna," Daphne Grace said, dropping Patricia's arm.

Wenna could see the girl's dilemma. She didn't know how to be rude. "Good morning. I'm buying a gown for your mother's ball."

"I'm here to pick up my mother's dress and mine," Patricia told Mrs. Miller, ignoring Wenna. Clearly she expected the dressmaker to tend to her before Wenna, leaving Mrs. Miller with a dilemma, too.

Mrs. Miller drew a long breath. "Miss Grace, Miss Brook," she said politely. "I'll call Miss Bunter to attend you."

"We'll wait. We don't want one of your minions."

The approaching minion stopped in her tracks. She moistened her lips. "If you don't mind, Mrs. Miller, I'll attend to Miss Chenoweth."

"Thank you," Wenna said, her smile wry. Since these two dressmakers remembered her as Mrs. Brook's unmarried maid and clearly knew she had turned her hand to hair styling as "Miss Chenoweth," she needed to remain "Miss Chenoweth." As "Miss Chenoweth," her job didn't compromise Devon. However, her single name compromised her in the eyes of her new social contacts. Time stood still. She had no idea how to get out of this mess of her own making.

Patricia gave a derisive laugh. "Oh, so you are Miss Chenoweth now, are you? Not Mrs. Courtney? Your wedded status changes daily. But we know the truth of it, don't we, Daphne?"

"I'm not sure," Daphne said with a funny little blink. She could possibly see that sneering at Wenna would win her no points with Mrs. Miller, nor her blue-gowned minion, who both stood watching the byplay.

"Now, Millie dear." Patricia turned her back on Wenna. "I am desperate, positively desperate, to have a new shawl for the ball. Green silk. Tell me, please, that you have a green silk shawl."

"I do." Letting out a breath, Mrs. Miller glanced apologetically at Wenna. "Miss Bunter, please escort Miss Chenoweth into the dressing room and take her measurements."

Wenna, holding her breath, followed Miss Bunter into the back room.

"Would you like a cup of tea? You look rather pale, Miss Chenoweth."

"Patricia looks foul in green," Wenna muttered. "Oh, I hope Mrs. Miller has a yellowish green because that would look perfectly unhealthy on her."

Miss Bunter's mouth turned up at the corners. "Green is a difficult color. I'm sure Mrs. Miller will find the right shade. Now, let me run the tape measure over you. Though, a week... It'll be a rush job. What on earth do those two have against you?" she asked in a whisper.

"You mean, other than I was Mrs. Brook's maid?"

"Ooh." Miss Bunter nodded sagely. "I suppose Miss Brook would rather have you pattering hither and thither for her than making a fortune for yourself." She began to race her tape over Wenna. "I say be darned to the lot of them."

"Be darned to the lot of them," Wenna repeated in dire voice.

"That's the way." Miss Bunter's tape swooped and her pencil jotted down figures efficiently.

"They've gone." Mrs. Miller's neat little frame appeared in the doorway. "They didn't really want anything. They just came in to give Miss Chenoweth a hard time. How are you getting on with that, Bunny?"

"Finished. We haven't discussed styles or materials yet."

"Most of my ladies are very nice. You won't meet with that sort of treatment often, I'll be bound." Mrs. Miller folded her hands across her waist. "This isn't the old country. A man is as good as his master here. And your hard-earned money talks loudly."

Wenna shrugged. "I'm going to Lady Grace's ball with Mr. Courtney. That put Patricia Brook's nose out of joint."

"I should say so." Mrs. Miller's bright eyes twinkled. "Mr. Courtney from the surveyor's office? My. You've done well for yourself. How did you meet him?"

"Through Mrs. Brook."

"I see." Mrs. Miller nodded sagely. "Miss Brook had an interest in him. That would explain her attitude. Now, what style were you thinking of?"

Wenna spread her hands and shrugged.

"What about color?"

"Red." Wenna compressed her lips. "Bright red for a scarlet woman."

"Pastels are in this year," Miss Bunter said, smiling hopefully.

Mrs. Miller narrowed her eyes. "I've got just the thing out the back. Old stock, but I'll give you a discount." She bustled off.

"You don't want red, Miss Chenoweth. Not with your hair. Have a pretty cream."

"No." Mrs. Miller huffed into the room and set down a bolt of shining red satin. "Miss Chenoweth wants to cause a stir. She will in this color and personally, I think it'll be stunning. We'll make it up real plain, low cut, and a heavy full skirt, pleating perhaps. Cap sleeves, no ruffles, no frills, nothing. What do you think?" She looked into Wenna's eyes.

"Will I look like a lady?"

"That's up to you," Mrs. Miller answered severely. "My gowns are made for ladies, but how they act in them is their business. I often wondered how you'd look if you took off that nasty black gown of yours. I guess Mr. Courtney had the same idea, that is to say..." Mrs. Miller blushed.

Wenna laughed. "Don't apologize. He might be a gentleman, but really, he's all man, too." And then *she* blushed.

Until Miss Bunter had the presence of mind to prick her finger, none of the ladies' eyes met. However, her yelp brought on a solicitous conversation, which led to Wenna's appointment for her first fitting in two days' time.

She moved out of the dressing room, stopped to gaze at a little frilled cape, and heard Miss Bunter say in a low voice, "So, it's true. She's Mr. Courtney's mistress."

"Word is, he married her."

"Whose word? She didn't say so."

"Mr. Snow. And she's going with Mr. Courtney to Lady Grace's ball."

"The rich get up to all sorts of shenanigans. They don't roll up their noses at mistresses the way us ordinary folk do."

Confounded, Wenna left the premises. She'd done this to herself, but she couldn't see a way of working without using her single name. On the street, she was known as Devon's mistress. In society, she was his wife—unless Patricia's poison spread. Only she knew where she belonged—in both places. She laughed bitterly. Only she knew she couldn't belong in two places. At some stage, she would have to make a choice.

* * * *

The seam between the two velvet curtains allowed a vertical gleam of moonlight into the room. Her vision clear and her purpose uncertain, Wenna rolled against Devon's broad naked back and touched her lips to his shoulder. From "Miss Chenoweth" to "Mrs. Courtney" and back again, Wenna knew her duty, but her heart was another matter. She knew almost nothing about her husband other than the bare essentials, most of which seemed shady at best. Yet he had never broken his word to her, he had never let her down, and even the mere sight of him caused her heart to skip a beat. He didn't move, but she lost the sound of his deep regular breathing. Knowing she'd disturbed him, she opened her mouth over his skin. "Are you asleep?"

"Not now."

"The first time you had a woman...were you in love?"

"It's midnight. Is this an important conversation?"

She pushed herself away from him and rolled onto her back. "I suppose you don't want to answer because you were and she wasn't." She tried not to sound snappish. "If the woman loved you, too, you would be married to her."

He rubbed his hand through his hair. "It wasn't possible. She married someone else."

"Then she didn't love you."

"She married another to prove she loved me, I think."

Wenna rolled onto her other side. "Good night."

"Was there a point to this?"

"A woman who loved you wouldn't marry someone else," she said into her pillow. "Not in a lifetime."

"Why the hell are we arguing about Jenny? I haven't seen her for years."

Wenna squeezed her nose. Jenny. She hadn't wanted to hear a name, but now she had. "Gone, but not forgotten."

"No, not forgotten. She'll always have a place in my heart. A man never forgets his first love."

"What about his first wife?"

He didn't answer. A hollow formed inside her chest. She knew he had married her, but she didn't have a marriage license. She didn't have a wedding ring. If he hadn't really married her, she didn't want to know. If he hadn't, she knew she wouldn't leave him. Aside from the fact that she wanted to be near him every second of the day, if he didn't love her now, if he hadn't made a lasting commitment to her, she would have to stay to earn his love, to force his commitment.

Rolling over, she cupped him between the legs and hated herself. He might always love Jenny, but he responded to lust. "Touch another woman with this, and I'll leave."

"Promise?"

"I promise." Her voice sounded louder than she had meant, and far more vehement. If he hadn't laughed at that moment she might have shed a genuine tear or two, but the sound of his chuckling infuriated her. "What's so funny?"

"You're admitting to jealousy."

"I'm admitting to selfishness."

Grateful that the darkness hid the sulky tightening of her jaw, she caressed him, determined to prove that he belonged to her. Under her palm, his male part expanded, lengthened, and hardened. He rolled onto his back. "I don't object to either." He covered her hand with his.

Her heart thudded. She could excite him whenever she chose. She loved him showing her how to pleasure him. He wouldn't get rid of a woman whose touch he craved.

"You know that I haven't thought of anyone but you since I met you. The only trouble is that you're so darned perfect for me that it's unlikely I will."

She let out her breath slowly. "Perfect?" she said, burying her surprise in his chest.

"Perfect." He sat up, leaned over her, and pressed his mouth to the curls at the apex of her legs. Angling his head so that his cheek rested on her stomach, he circled his arms around her hips.

Almost overwhelmed, she didn't move. However, the weight of his head on her abdomen seemed a comforting thing. She ran her fingers through his hair, loving him, now almost certain he felt as possessive as she did. With her touch, he turned his head and kissed her at the juncture of her thighs again.

From the first time they'd made love, she had realized she would never want anyone but him. That night, she belonged to him in a slow, gentle way, all the more precious because of its intimacy. They pleasured each other deliberately, carefully and with groaning delight. Strangely, he made sure he didn't impregnate her.

* * * *

The slate roof on the lodgings held the heat during the long spell of unseasonable weather, not that Wenna, born in South Australia, expected winter early. Autumn was usually warm and winter usually came almost as a surprise. In the mugginess of the hat shop, she worked, clammy with sweat. Her rigid black uniform didn't help cool her skin. When she went for her fitting on Wednesday with Mrs. Miller, she almost couldn't bear to try on her gown.

"This red looks so hot," she said to Miss Bunter. Regretting her ridiculous decision to dress in scarlet was about as useful as a toothless comb.

"There'll be a change in the weather soon," Miss Bunter answered through a mouthful of pins.

"The fit's good." Mrs. Miller stood in the doorway of the dressing room, her eyes narrowed on the gown.

Sticky, and with her face red from the heat, Wenna knew she looked far from glamorous. "If this weather keeps up, I doubt I'll be able to go to the ball." She hoped she sounded casually unconcerned. Both Miss Bunter and Mrs. Miller stared at her. "They'll ban me in this red. I'll look like a fire in the room."

"Don't you go worrying about anyone else," Mrs. Miller replied in a severe tone. "You'll be credit to my dressmaking and that's the truth."

Silenced, Wenna stood while Miss Bunter eased the gown off her. "Pick it up on Friday."

Wenna sighed and paid, although her hands shook when she parted with the three pounds. The furniture she had planned for the downstairs sitting room would now not be forthcoming, all for the sake of her vanity. When she told Devon and he didn't turn a hair, she decided that if he didn't care about not having a respectable place to entertain guests, she didn't either, and she spent ten shillings on silk stockings and black velvet dancing shoes, not because she expected to cavort all night, but because she had never owned elegant shoes. Her economical habits of a lifetime had simply vanished, all for the sake of trying to impress the gentleman she had married.

She despaired of their future together, each as irresponsible as the other.

* * * *

Saturday dawned with a perfect pink sky, the day only moderately warm. Dev left to work on his house, as usual. He could now see the end of the building. The slate would go on the roof next week and he could start on the inside. The Baltic pine for the floorboards had arrived by steamer last week. He couldn't stop himself from standing back and admiring the first house he'd had a hand in building. The stonework on the front face added a grander look.

He finished up at four thirty, as usual. When he arrived home, Wenna had hot water waiting for him. "Did you wash your hair?" he asked, gazing at the frizzy mass she rubbed with a towel. She wore a paisley shawl over her chemise.

"Don't worry. It won't look like this when I've finished." She watched him unbutton his filthy work shirt. His clothes had been prepared for him, as usual, and lay neatly across the bed.

He was glad he'd told her he worked as a laborer. Leaving daily dressed neatly and having to change when he arrived at the site had been a time waster. Now, when he arrived home, he only had to strip off his working clothes with the suspicious redhead watching him, no chore, because she was always amenable to daytime dalliances should her interest be caught. She was not quite so willing at night when he had to pretend he was trying to impregnate her. Twice he'd faked completion, and she hadn't noticed either time.

She disappeared into her dressing room while he washed and changed. He expected her to take longer tonight, and she didn't disappoint him. He had time to total most of his bills before she appeared in the doorway of the study. His jaw dropped. Why on earth he hadn't queried her choice of a gown was anyone's guess. Perhaps he trusted her taste. "Hell!"

"The gown is too loud. You don't want me to go with you."

"The red screams for attention, and I definitely want you to go with me. You look..." He lifted his hands, lost for words for a moment. "That red with your hair. The effect is...amazing."

She glanced down at her unadorned skirts, which filled the doorway. Her neckline curved from the tip of each shoulder to just above her cleavage where a line of fabric buttons ran to her tiny waist. Someone else in that gown might look like a brassy tart, but Wenna's magnificent hair had been carefully styled back from the elegant bones of her face.

"Turn around." He admired the simple lines of the gown and the thick arrangement of plaits she wore shaped into her nape just behind her ears. "Very nice."

She looked wary, but she smiled. "I'll get my shawl."

When he escorted her into The Pig and Whistle, Maisie gaped and seated her very carefully. "You look gorgeous, Mrs. Courtney," she said in a whisper before dashing out to the kitchen.

Within seconds, Mr. Snow appeared at the table. "Blow me down. You look a fair treat. Don't she, Mr. Courtney?"

"She does indeed." Dev leaned back. "I'm introducing a flare of heat into Adelaide's society."

She pulled her white lace shawl across her shoulders. "That was the idea." Her chin lifted.

He noticed the sheer perfection of her jaw line. He also noticed the tremble of her hand, which he took in his. Braving society as a former lady's maid was not an act of a coward, but he would take care of her. She had, after all, married him.

Chapter 15

Although the Graces' double fronted townhouse looked modest from the outside, the single-story house sprawled back along the acre block. The straight slate path, lined with rose bushes, gleamed in the light of the planted torch flares, which lit the imported palms in the lawns from beneath. The sound of a hundred voices all speaking at once pelted through the open front door where Sir Patrick and Lady Grace stood greeting each new guest.

The couple, satisfied parents of an eligible son and three pretty daughters, had repurposed their very fine reception area into a ballroom and a supper room. Dev patted the tentative hand Wenna had latched around his arm. Although outwardly confident, her fingers gripped tightly. Despite the fact that no gossip about her former position as a maid had come to his ears, he didn't doubt Patricia Brook had done her utmost to discredit the woman, who was, after all, if he ever mentioned his birth, Viscountess Dellacourt, wife to the heir to the title and estates of the Earl of Marchester.

She smiled while greeting their hosts, she formally shook hands, and she held Dev's arm as he moved her into the green painted main room. His friends stood together, gossiping casually. Ivor turned and beckoned them.

"See now. You had no need to be nervous." Dev strolled toward to the welcoming group.

"I'm wearing red. I'm terrified," she said barely moving her lips.

He glanced at her again. The red might call attention to her, but the color showed up the milky whiteness of her skin and the perfect styling of her glorious hair. Being a former lady's maid had advantages. She knew how to dress to an inch. On his way, he stopped to introduce her to the new governor. "Sir Domonick, I'd like you to meet L—" He came to his senses. He'd near as hell introduced her as Lady Dellacourt.

The smile hardened on her face. Her chin lifted and her eyes glinted a chilly green.

"My dear delight, Wenna." To gloss over his embarrassing gaff, he moved into a comfortable conversation with Sir Domonick Daley while keeping Wenna tucked close by his side.

As soon as he joined his friends, Wenna's dance card filled, though he insisted on the first waltz with her. She didn't melt against him, but kept her body rigid and trod on his toes. "Relax, my dear. You seem to know the steps."

"I've never danced with a man before. Only with maids like me who wanted to ape our betters." Her voice sounded stiff.

"You have no betters."

She gave him an impatient glance. Tonight, clearly, would not be the cheery social event he had expected. Nerves made her edgy and hard to please. When James drifted over and claimed his dance, Devon was glad to escape from his prickly wife. He began honoring his commitments, taking his first dance with the Grace's oldest daughter, Daphne, a short young lady. He could easily peer over her head and watch Wenna entertaining the enthralled men who surrounded her.

"Your wife is very popular," Daphne said, staring at his jacket buttons.

"Don't worry," he said, sighing. "I'll make sure she is not too popular."

Daphne looked at him as if he spoke a foreign language. Wenna would have bitten back, which was one of the many things he enjoyed about her. His smart, independent wife was never lost for words. Apparently some time would elapse before she was lost for new dancing partners. Not keen to line up on the end of the never-ending queue, he joined Hubert and Luke in the card room. For reasons he didn't want to explore, he couldn't watch his wife charming other men.

* * * *

Wenna now knew the meaning of the word "gentleman." She could apply the description to every male whose toes she tripped over during the dances. Not one of them as much as winced.

She couldn't find a meaning to the word "lady." Not one had spoken to her, other than Lady Grace at the door. As far as the women were concerned, she didn't exist. A former maid would never be accepted into Adelaide's society, not unless she was very rich, and she wasn't yet rich enough and never would be.

Faces averted as she made her way to the garden outside. Her head ached, her feet hurt, and she had been deserted by the only man in the room with whom she wanted to be. Once through the French doors, she stopped. Staring at the massed stars in the sky, she twisted her gloved fingers together until her bones ached, trying to build up the nerve to seek out Devon and ask him to take her home—if he could remember who she was. He'd forgotten her name when he introduced her to the governor, and he'd been careful not to identify her as his wife. Was she his wife? He'd only said so to his friends. Other than that, he'd introduced her as Wenna or referred to her as his precious angel or his dear delight.

"Did you see that redhead in the red dress?" The female voice, a decibel or two louder than the piano and the violins, came from just inside the doorway.

"Did I? One couldn't miss her, my dear. You know who she is, of course?"

"She's Devon Courtney's mistress, I believe. This happens every year. Some young man decides to shock society by introducing his light skirt. If the foolish man has to spend a fortune on her gowns, wouldn't you think he'd have the sense to tell her that she should never wear red with that hair of hers?"

The first lady laughed indulgently. "If he's besotted enough to bring her here, he's besotted enough to let her wear anything she likes. I hear she was a lady's maid. Patricia Brook says that the sharp little creature is spreading around the story of a marriage."

"Those foxy-faced females are always sly. I believe Patricia had thoughts of marrying our Mr. Courtney herself, but she couldn't now that he's entangled himself so unsuitably elsewhere."

"The match would have been so perfect, too. Patricia's such a pretty girl and... ahem...the *younger* ladies find Mr. Courtney very charming. Our former governor thought the world of him. If you want my opinion..."

Perhaps the second lady did. Wenna had heard enough. Gathering her full skirts in one hand, she dashed across the lawn to the shelter of a large palm in sight of the main gate. Her throat had closed over, completely, and ached so badly she might have swallowed the stone that had lodged in her chest. Before marching home without "our Mr. Courtney," she stopped to compose herself, swiping impatiently at the tears that streamed down her cheeks. Wishing she'd had the sense to bring a handkerchief, she lifted her topmost petticoat to her face.

When a snowy white, freshly pressed handkerchief appeared through her blurred glance, she reared back in shock. A handsome man some inches over six feet tall stood beside her.

"How did you manage to sneak up on me?" she asked in a constricted voice.

"Take it. I won't be crying myself tonight, and so I don't need it."

Too angry with herself to accept sympathy, she pushed his arm away.

Unoffended, he lifted her chin, carefully blotted her face, and gave a smile the angels would envy. "I've never been so offended in my life." His eyelashes looked as thick as a girl's, and he had a deep modulated voice that would melt a heart of granite. "Until about three minutes ago, I thought I was the answer to Adelaide's dancing-partner problem, but now I know that you saw me make a mistake in that last polka."

"I've never seen you before in my life." Wenna eyed him in the moonlight. No one who had seen this glorious creature would ever forget him.

"How embarrassing." His beautiful lips curved ruefully. "We were introduced about an hour ago. I'm Nick Alden. I think you'll find that my name is on your dance card for this waltz."

"You must have me confused with someone else."

"I don't think so. You're Dev's wife, aren't you?"

"No. I'm not Devon's wife. I'm his light skirt." She waited for him to show disgust, or too much interest, but instead he shook his head.

"You're no one's light skirt. Only a fool would think so."

"Ask anyone in that room. They'll all tell you that I'm a sly looking female in a tasteless gown who has trapped *our Mr. Courtney* into an indecent liaison." She grabbed his handkerchief and blew her nose loudly.

He winced. "And what does Dev have to say about this?"

"How would I know? He disappeared some time ago."

"My dear, I think I ought to take you back into that ballroom and make your marital situation quite clear to everyone."

"My situation is so clear now, even to me, that..." Her voice cracked, "I'm going home."

Nick stared at her and crossed his arms. "Very well. I'll come with you."

"I imagine I'm supposed to be bowled over by that disgusting offer. Just take your pretty face back inside that ballroom."

His perfect eyebrows drew together. "I'm one of your husband's best friends. If you can't trust this *pretty face* of mine, I'll arrange to have my nose broken. I don't imagine that'll be too hard. Since I'm intending to take you home without telling Dev, I'm sure he'll break it for me."

"Oh, I doubt it," she said, eyeing him sideways. "He's almost impossible to rile."

"I have the ability to test the patience of saints. It's my one true skill."

She narrowed her eyes. "No good friend of his would take me home without telling him."

Nick spread his hands. "We were at Cambridge together. No one could have been kinder to a hayseed from the colonies than Dev was in those days. Now, Mrs. Courtney, I'm going to escort you home because I am unutterably bored here. Shall we take a carriage?"

She glanced at her feet. Should he turn out to be a person other than he seemed...she didn't care. "My shoes say *yes.* They're new."

"I don't think you can go past shoes when you want good advice."

Despite her desperation, she laughed.

With a hand under her arm, he guided her to the gates. A line of carriages stood in the street. "Which one would you choose?"

"Isn't one yours?"

"No. I came from the club with Luke Worthing. We took a cab. There, that one. It belongs to James Hawthorn. Hi, you," he called to the nearest idling jarvey. "Find the driver for this coach. We've a mind to go home."

Fascinated, Wenna watched the man doing Nick's bidding. In a trice, without Nick being questioned, though undoubtedly the driver knew his own master, Wenna was sitting in a comfortably appointed brougham being driven to Rundle Street.

"If I hadn't bought new shoes, I could have walked. Alone. I've walked all my life. I'm the daughter of a washer woman." She didn't glance at his expression. She didn't care what he thought.

"I'm the son of a carpenter and my mother was a maid until she married," he said, crossing his legs at the ankle. "But I've never seen the need to brag about it."

Again she laughed. She had let herself be carried off into the dark night with a handsome stranger, and she didn't care. Everything he'd said to her could have been a lie, and she had certainly judged him by his looks, but being a responsible citizen had earned her nothing so far.

"I was a maid, too, until I met Devon."

He rubbed his hand over his chin. "He's a good man. One of the best."

When the carriage stopped outside Devon's lodgings without her giving a hint as to the address, she believed Nick knew Devon. She spent less than three seconds wondering what she might have done if the two hadn't been friends, and gave a mental shrug.

She and Nick stepped out of the conveyance, which moved off as Nick opened the side gate for her. Wenna stood on the doorstep and glanced at him. "I can't get in. I don't have a key for the latch."

"No problem." He wrapped his wet and crumpled handkerchief around his hand, swung back with his fist, and broke the glass on the door.

She gasped and covered her mouth with both her hands. "In for a penny, in for a pound," she muttered to herself, and she squared her shoulders. She had gone along with him so far, and backing out now would clearly be too late.

After he reached inside for the latch, he waited for her to pass inside ahead of him. "I'm going to stay with you until Dev comes home."

After lighting the lamp, Wenna took him to the front room, the sparsely furnished former surveyor's office. She drew a deep breath. "Would you be interested in a cup of tea? I can fire up the stove in an instant."

He glanced at the two chairs, the bare walls, and the carpet square. "Do you have any brandy?"

"I'm afraid not. We don't do much more in these lodging than sleep and bathe."

"I'll duck across the road and buy a bottle."

She stripped off her gloves, placed them neatly over the arm of a chair, and went off to find two cut crystal glasses on the shelves in the kitchen. She couldn't be ashamed of these fragile and very precious offerings.

He returned almost instantly, with the bottle uncorked. "Ah, good, glasses. Very civilized. Please sit." After pouring a bare inch into one of the glasses she held, he took the other from her and filled the bowl to the rim. Then he settled into an armchair, the bottle on the floor beside him, and carefully hooked one ankle over one knee while sipping. He emptied half his glass in a couple of swallows.

He shouldn't need drink to sustain him. A man with his looks had the world at his feet. Somewhat disappointed in him, she said, "You should go back to the ball. I imagine someone is waiting there for you."

His gaze left the contents of his glass. "No, I'm not married, if that's what you're asking. I'm not a marrying man. Dev is. He is not the sort of person to take a tart to a respectable establishment. Anyone would be a fool to imagine otherwise."

She stared at him. "Are you saying *I've* confused the fools?"

"I think you have. I heard the gossip about you the moment I entered the room. It's your gown, of course. It's outrageous, it's beautiful, and it's clearly not bought from the rack. With that hair of yours, you look stunning. You look like a lady, but no one knows who you are, hence the speculation. I don't know why Dev didn't end it. He could have, easily."

"Yes, he could have, but perhaps he has an aversion to lying about his marital status."

He lifted his eyebrows. "As soon as he arrives, we'll find out."

"We could have a good long wait until the ball has ended." She took a tentative sip of her brandy.

"I don't think we'll need wait longer than half an hour." He tossed off his drink with an upward tilt of his head. "Only two armchairs, though. Either he or I will have to stand."

"The room is not yet reader for callers. I've only just begun the furnishing. If I had the money, I would put a table over there...sorry. I'm being a boring housewife, aren't I?"

"Not at all, though I don't think you should waste your time. Dev should have set you up in a proper house." Audible footsteps beat down the path outside, and he glanced toward the lobby entrance. "I imagine that's him right now." Rising to his feet without another word, he strolled into the lobby and raced up the stairs two by two.

She stood, blinking in confusion that quickly turned to trepidation when the lobby door crashed open, the office door slammed into the wall, and Devon appeared in the doorway.

With his fists on his hips, and his lips compressed, he stared hard at Wenna. She'd never seen him angry before, and she gasped in a nervous breath while butterflies smashed themselves against her rib cage. She cleared her throat, unable to speak a word, but Nick walked down the stairs and into the room, concentrating on the front of his shirt.

In a voice of overdone relief, he said, "Thank the Lord I found my shirt stud before Dev came home." He raised his gaze to Devon. "Oh, you *are* home."

Wenna watched him take his time replacing the stud.

Devon's face compressed with fury. He stepped forward and grabbed Nick by his jacket lapels. "If you've touched my wife, I'll kill you, Nick."

"Your wife?" Nick drew down his eyebrows, looking confused or sozzled, or both. "She's not your wife. Everyone knows she's your fancy piece. Don't be so damn possessive."

"*She's my wife.*" For the first time, Devon looked straight at Wenna. "Tell the bastard you're my wife," he said, his lips barely moving.

Wenna swallowed.

Nick laughed and shot his cuffs. "She's already told me she's not. Let's be civilized about this."

"Civilized?" Devon said in a dire tone. "I won't accept anyone touching my wife, and that includes you, Nick. You're the last person I thought would do this to me."

"You've both had your fun." Wenna rose to her feet. "I'm not your wife, and Nick didn't touch me."

Nick found his glass and the bottle where he'd left both on the floor. "Do you want a drink, Dev? I've left a few drops. My, this is an interesting situation. You say she's your wife, and she says she isn't. Who's speaking the truth, I wonder?"

"Why are you denying it?" Devon shot a flaming glance at Wenna.

"I'm not a fool, Devon. Men like you don't marry women like me, even for the sake of an heir."

Nick refilled his glass. "Everyone knows you're together, but no one was invited to your wedding. No one saw a mention in the paper. Besides, you wouldn't live in a place like this if you'd married." He passed a scathing gaze around the room. "No, you can't fool me. You haven't married this little flame, which you made quite obvious tonight. At least three people told me you had trouble remembering her name."

Devon ignored Nick. "*He's* the friend who applied to the courts for our wedding license. He knows we're married. You *are* my wife, Wenna, and you can't shame me by leaving a ball with one of my *former* friends."

"Former?" Nick inspected the edges of his jacket sleeves. "I'm one of the few people who knew she was your wife, but I couldn't convince *her*. You'd think everyone else would realize that you're such a toff that unless she was your wife, you wouldn't be seen with her at the governor's ball. But you're so bloody arrogant that you expected everyone to accept her with no explanation from you."

"I didn't forget her name." Devon shot a sidelong glance at Nick. "I almost used her rightful name, which is irrelevant in this country."

"I saw The Honorable written on an envelope. But I'm sure I wouldn't be Mrs. Honorable." She queried Devon with lowered eyebrows.

Both men stared at her.

Looking nonplussed, Devon said, "No." His shoulders relaxed.

Nick said, "Unfortunately, because to hear that would make my life complete. However, that doesn't excuse what happened. You should have stayed by her side tonight, Dev. You'll have to make amends."

Devon shoved his fists into his pocket. "Who asked your opinion?"

"She shouldn't be living in this place." Nick threw back his head and tossed off his second glassful. "You can afford a real house, and a cook, and a couple of maids."

Devon clamped his lips.

"Or do you want to carry on like a bachelor?"

"I still don't know why you were coming out of my bedroom, and I still don't know what you were doing with my wife. Are you attacking me to disguise your actions? I ought to break your nose, you bastard."

"See?" Nick said with an amused glance at Wenna. "I told you it would be easy."

Wenna drew a long deep breath. "He didn't touch me. He's been an absolute gentleman."

"It's an interesting bed you have," Nick said, glancing at his fingernails.

His face tight, Devon stepped toward Nick, grasping his lapels. "It's time someone dealt with you."

Wenna pushed between the two, one hand on Devon's chest. "I've known Nick less than an hour, and even I can see he's having a lend of you."

Nick grinned nastily. "No need to protect me, sweetheart. He couldn't hit me if I had both my arms tied."

"And you couldn't run to the end of the street," Devon said, his jaw jutted. "You're not going to explain yourself, are you?"

"No," Nick smoothed the front of his evening jacket. "I think you ought to get rid of that bed before you have children because when they see it, *you're* going to have to explain yourself. I'm going back to the ball. Coming?" He raised his eyebrows at Wenna.

She found her dance card tucked into her gloves on the chair and she tilted the cardboard to read. "Nicholas Alden, you disgusting liar. Your name is not on my dance card."

Nick grasped hold of her card, picked up the attached pencil, quickly added his name, and said in a satisfied voice, "It is now."

"You both think this is damned funny, don't you?" Devon placed his fists on his hips. "James's driver alerted me to the fact that my wife had gone home with you. He drove me here to protect her honor and neither of you will answer any of my questions."

"You shouldn't need to ask. I didn't have a chance to find you at the ball. The moment I arrived, I heard the gossip about your wife and, as she was pointed out to me, I saw her rush outside. After she soaked my handkerchief, I didn't want to talk to you. I'm easily swayed by tears. I think we need to go back and make the situation between you and your wife clear. As well, I don't want to miss my dance with the beautiful Mrs. Courtney."

"I hope it's not a polka." Wenna took her evening gloves from the arm of her chair.

"Surely you didn't believe that story." Nick stared at his empty glass and the bottle, and sighed. "I've never made a mistake in a polka in my life."

Purposely, Wenna didn't tell Nick about her lack of dancing skill. He would find out.

Chapter 16

"Let me introduce Wenna to a couple of influential people and then you can dance with her," Dev said to Nick. Nick rarely attended balls and, if he did, he only stayed long enough to walk through the supper room to pick up a drink.

Nick nodded. The alcohol appeared to be catching up to him, and his cynical smile had taken on a fixed gloss. He searched out a brandy while Dev glanced around the ballroom. Near the French doors that led into the garden, he spotted two women staring his way. He gave them a wide smile and, with his hand keeping Wenna's on his arm, he escorted her toward them.

"No," Wenna muttered under her breath, trying to pull back. "They're the ones who were talking about me. They'll never believe you married a maid."

"They're the biggest gossips in Adelaide. A direct approach will save time."

The ladies stayed frozen in place, clearly aware he meant to bring Wenna over.

"Mrs. Latimer," he said as he reached the two. "I don't believe you've met my new treasure, Wenna."

Mrs. Latimer, tall and thin, raised her pointed chin and her eyebrows. "I don't believe I have."

"And Mrs. Albright. This is my wife, Wenna, formerly Mrs. Brook's personal maid. It took me some time to gain her attention, but once I did, I snatched her up and married her instantly."

Dev let his gaze roam tenderly over Wenna's face. Wenna gave him a melting, doting smile. Her smile almost ruined his act, because he wanted to hold that expression and gaze into her eyes all night. For a while, he'd thought he might have lost her. He hauled in a breath. "But I couldn't keep her to myself any longer."

"Your *wife?*" Mrs. Latimer frowned, and she took her time to answer. "So, you plan to introduce her into society. This is her debut, as it were." She looked puzzled and uncertain.

Dev nodded casually. "Sir Patrick and Lady Grace have met her, of course, and my friends. But to be welcomed into the inner circle, she needs formal acknowledgement. My godmother, the former governor's wife, would have paved the way for Wenna, had she remained in the colony, but failing vice-regal sanction, I chose you two ladies because of your influence."

The ladies stared at each other. Mrs. Albright, a pigeon-chested woman in her fifties, ordinarily rather poised, moistened her lips with her tongue. "It should be Lady Grace's place, but I, for one, am delighted to meet your lovely wife. Wenna, you said?" She drew a deep breath. "A maid."

"Yes." Wenna stood, her smile unutterably gracious. "And now wife to a courteous and very noble gentleman." Her second hand moved to clasp her first on his arm.

At her best, Wenna could confuse any man, or woman, too, and she was doing this right now. Dev didn't have to fake pride in her. She amazed him. Barely an hour ago, she'd left the ball in a flurry. Now, even he would have assumed she had associated with aristocrats her whole life. "As you can see, I chose wisely."

Mrs. Albright gave his words another moment's thought before nodding. "Quite a romance."

"I take it, it is now our job to spread the word." Mrs. Latimer narrowed her eyes at him, although a reluctant smile lurked on her lips.

"If you would." Dev pulled his ear lobe. "I believe the word has already been spread, but not the truth. You two ladies now have it. And so I can dance with my wife, safe in the knowledge that I will hear no more gossip about her." He took Wenna's hand and moved her onto the dance floor.

"The truth," Wenna said, crunching the toes on his left foot as he tried to waltz her into a turn. "You're such a good liar that I almost believed you myself. But I find I don't really care what they think. You defended me and that's all that matters. Oops, sorry. I thought you would do a right turn there."

"Let me lead. Relax. You only need practice, my dear. You're graceful, and you've been comparatively light on my feet."

She gave a reluctant laugh. "Pass me on to Nick. I should think by now that all the brandy he's consumed would have numbed *his* toes."

Watching while she danced with Nick, Dev finally understood the totality of his commitment to her. For her, he would spend his days wandering around an echoing mansion in a cool, dank country with little to do but carry forward the idleness of ancestors who might not even be his. He would be the heir who didn't look like the others, the spare who should not have been born, but without whom the estate would be lost to a minor branch of the family. The savior, but the cuckoo in the nest.

He folded his arms, smiling ruefully, watching Nick expertly guide Wenna through the complicated moves of the dance. This country he loved was now lost to him. He couldn't stay here, and he couldn't leave Wenna in Cornwall with his father and come back.

His dream would never be his because no matter how much he loved this land, he now realized that he had fallen completely in love with his wife. He loved her more.

* * * *

Wenna stared at the shards of glass remaining in the door. She let out a breath, mentally estimating the cost of a replacement pane.

"Presumably Nick did this?" Devon kicked the few splinters out of the way; most had landed inside and crackled beneath as he swung the door open.

"I didn't have a key."

"I don't suppose anyone will notice the hole, since no one visits us. Tomorrow I'll nail a piece of wood over it. How did he do it? With his fist?"

"Yes. The glass must be very fragile."

"He could do the same with wood. His punches are lethal. He learned to fight at school and later he trained with a professional. He seems to be in good shape, which is surprising considering the way he drinks."

"I don't know why men have to fight. He doesn't look like the type, somehow."

Devon shrugged. "That's why he learned to fight. He told me years ago that when he started at school, some of the other boys were a little too interested in him and it was a matter of either learning to fight or giving in gracefully."

"What do you mean, interested?"

"It was a boys' school. You've seen how handsome he is. I imagine he was even prettier when he was younger. There would have been plenty of boys who would have been happy to use him as a girl. I don't suppose I missed much by not going to school."

"You didn't go to school?"

"I had a tutor at home. You go up and get into bed while I clean up the mess. No need to leave the lamp on for me. I'll undress in the dark."

"Good gracious, Mr. Courtney." She stood with her hands on her hips. "I'm wearing stays. They were hard enough to hook up by myself. I'll never manage to unhook without your help."

"In that case," he said, his face losing expression. His eyes fixed on hers. "I'll clean up the glass in the morning. My dear lady wife mustn't be left to undress alone."

She smiled at him. Tonight would be their real wedding night. She would love him, caress him, hold him in her arms, and run her fingers through his soft hair.

Yet even though she didn't use her sponge and even though relations with him tonight should be for baby making, he must have forgotten, for again he didn't release inside her. Instead, he'd fastened his lips across hers as he'd moved off her.

After he'd cleaned himself, he fell asleep. Sleep didn't come so easily to her. Once, her life had been simple. She saved her money so that she could go back to Cornwall and be of some use to her elderly grandparents. Before she met Devon, her trip to England had been some years away. Now she had begun her longer-term plan instead, meant to be facilitated in Cornwall: the starting up of a business, which would support her into her old age.

Here, she had two lives, one as a businesswoman and another as a wife to a gentleman. In fact, she lived a lie. No amount of acceptance at a ball could change that. And tomorrow morning, she would attend his cricket match again and see if her success at the ball had altered how the other ladies reacted to her. If they fully accepted her now, she would have to give up her job and join them in their morning calls, sewing bees, tea drinking, and gossiping. She wouldn't be able to keep working, or they would despise her all over again. And yet she *had* to work. Devon needed her income if he meant to keep playing his role as an idle gentleman.

Her mind stuck somewhere between social and business success, she slid out of bed and drew back one of the velvet curtains. In the light of the full moon, Devon lay on his side, his face relaxed, his body naked and beautiful. Together, surely they could make something of themselves.

If he cobbled together a team of men, he could have others building for him. He was a natural leader. Anyone could see that by the way he played on the cricket team. When he wished, he could rally the others, who played in a less competitive way than he did. He could be a major influence in this colony with his connections back in England, governors and such like. Why, oh, why was he content to be a laborer?

Why, oh, why did she want him to have everything he wanted? Tonight she would have given in to his wish to have a child to take back home, when she didn't want to go to England, not any more, not while she could see job opportunities here for him as well as her. She could imagine building a lovely home, perhaps near the house he had shown her, a place where she could see the ships arrive and all across the city plains.

She sat on the windowsill, watching Devon sleep. As if he noted her scrutiny, he stirred, his palm moving to the spot in the bed she had vacated. Sighing, she slipped back beside him, smoothed his soft hair back from his face, and snuggled his rough hand into the safe space between her shoulder and her chin.

* * * *

Dev awoke to a pure bright sunlight. Sunday. Cricket day. He turned his head and watched Wenna sleep. With her hand flat under her cheek, she looked vulnerable, young, and very sweet. Wenna. The smartest, prickliest, most self-sufficient woman he had ever met. He swung out of bed, slung a towel around his neck, and went downstairs to light the stove. The hot water came to the boil just before Wenna joined him.

"Do you think we'll be invited to another ball?" Her expression dubious, she sat at the kitchen table. She wore her nightgown with a shawl, and she carried her towel.

"It's still the ball season. Now that people know we're married, I expect so."

She set her elbow on the table, cupped her chin in her hand, and watched him carry the pot of hot water into the bathroom. "The ball season is only interrupted by the rain in winter and the worst of the heat in summer." She sounded glum.

"It's certainly longer than the season back home. You go first in the bath, but don't be too long." He filled the pan with cold water. "While I'm waiting, I'll try to clear up some of my paperwork before the match."

"I should never have chosen red for my ball gown." She sighed deeply.

"I thought it was an inspired choice."

Their gazes met, and she slowly shook her head. "No one could wear a bright red, very memorable gown more than a few times. If I'd chosen white or cream, I could wear that forever without anyone remembering."

"I expect we could afford to buy you more than one ball gown." He grinned.

"I really ought to be more discreet in future."

He laughed.

She dressed in her plain black-and-white gown for the cricket match, but he noticed she wore a new hat, a front-brimmed straw packed with red ribbons and roses. She had no idea how to merge with the crowd. With her style, she would always stand out, as befitted the future Lady Dellacourt.

Perfectly satisfied with her appearance, he walked her over to the group of ladies he had been associated with since his friends in the colony had introduced them. His food basket was added to the others, but instead of moving off with his team, he lingered, ready to support Wenna if she needed support, a task he should have done from the first, knowing she was nervous and sadly out of place with frivolous, empty-headed young females.

"Oh, good morning, Wenna," Patricia Brook said, turning with a saintly smile on her face. "Such a lovely gown you wore last night. So brave of you. No one else would touch that red Mrs. Miller has been trying to sell forever, but you did."

Wenna's grip on Dev's arm tightened.

"Her superb coloring carried it off." Dev gave his wife an indulgent smile. "But I agree. She has an unusual amount of courage, if I may say so as her proud husband."

"We're all so jealous," Daphne Grace said, lowering her gaze. "We have to wear pastels as unmarried ladies, but I can't wait to be able to wear something brighter than pink."

"I would wear any color in the world if I could dance with Nick Alden," young Zanthe Grace said. "How on earth did you do it, Wenna? He forgets my name every time he sees me, and he has known me since I was born."

"I hope he has recovered from the cricket ball hit at Stirling?" The extraordinarily beautiful Miss Davies, dressed in the gray of half-mourning, watched Dev's face as if awaiting his reassurance.

He smiled at her. Most men would, and then smile again. The lady's demure vulnerability called men to her like ants to a picnic. "Barely a bruise on his saintly face."

She nodded and moved back behind her friends, as if trying not to be noticed— not easy for a woman with her looks. Like Wenna, she would always be noticeable.

Unlike Wenna, Patricia vied for attention. She gave her particularly annoying smile again. "It's not kind of you to dance with the single men, Wenna. So few of them have the right backgrounds, and so many single young ladies are available. You should be more generous."

"Nick isn't hanging out for a wife, Patricia." Daphne turned to her friend. "He told my mother he planned to remain single all his life."

Dev laughed. He hadn't realized that Wenna dancing with Nick would overshadow her wearing red. "I'm sure he'll change his mind when he meets the right woman— as I did."

"Now, why would you have married Wenna, I wonder?" Patricia's eyes glittered with spite. "For love? Or the other?"

"What other?" Daphne frowned.

"The 'other' no lady would discuss. Frankly, I would rather rely on my moral rectitude and honesty to attract the man of my dreams."

Dev's gaze met Wenna's. "No. I wouldn't touch that line if I were you."

Wenna raised her chin. "I was only going to say that I would presume that most couples marry for love, and I pray Patricia will find it someday." The smugness of her tone was certain to irritate the other woman.

Dev patted his wife's hand, determined not to be amused.

The cricketers began shouting, "Out, out."

James appeared at his shoulder. "Luke's out and Sir Patrick has just gone in to bat. Be ready, Dev, because he rarely makes a single run before being caught."

"That's my father you're insulting," Zanthe said, poking James on the shoulder with one finger.

"He swears he's not." James laughed and grabbed her hand in his. "You're the child of Satan, I've heard him say."

"I'm needed by my team, if you'll all excuse me?" Dev took a step back, querying Wenna with his eyes.

She nodded. "We'll see you for lunch." She took Zanthe over to Lady Grace.

Dev wished Nell Hawthorn would return from the country. Wenna didn't require the company of the unmarried young ladies. She needed a friend, probably married, and with interests other than trapping a husband.

However, by the time the match finished, she'd seemed to have found a friend in Lady Grace, who invited her and Dev to eat dinner with her extended family that night.

"Leftovers," Lady Grace said, but the menu was an extensive cold collation of rare roast beef, breast of chicken, and pressed duck, as well as the delicacies ladies seemed to prefer, like vegetables in aspic and stuffed mushroom caps. James and Luke had been invited as well as Miss Davies. The company was so entertaining that Dev wished he had introduced Wenna into society sooner.

"Why is Patricia antagonistic toward you?" Zanthe asked Wenna across a dinner table dressed with seasonal flowers.

"I was her mother's maid and I married Devon. That would be reason enough, but it's so pointless. It does work in my favor, however. She gave me the red ball gown when I seemed to have no hope of it." Wenna delicately lifted a spoon quivering with red jelly.

"The ball gown? You had it made, I thought." Dev glanced at her.

"In a week, which is unheard of. Most people have to wait a month for a gown from Mrs. Miller, and she said she wouldn't be able to fill a rushed order. She sped up the process when Patricia was so unbelieving about our marriage." Wenna's face lit with mischief.

"I'm sorry I couldn't stop her." Daphne looked guilty. "I'm trying to ease off our friendship. She's not the person I thought she was."

"She is a little harsh in her opinions," the beautiful Miss Davies said mildly. "This apricot preserve is particularly delicious, Lady Grace."

While the ladies talked about recipes, Dev watched Wenna, who appeared to have found her niche while discussing sugar quantities and cooking times. He wished he could set her up in her own house where she could reign supreme, but that would be a waste of time. They would be departing for England within the month.

Chapter 17

Wenna thought Devon would never leave for work, though eventually he came out of his study.

"The building is almost finished, you know," he'd said as he opened the lobby door. "I don't need to work full time now."

She suspected that meant he would be unemployed soon. To keep up her hairstyling with him underfoot would be a strain. Doubtless, she would have to confess to running a business, but she planned to keep her secret for as long as possible. The more money she made, the better, for not only would the trip back to England be expensive, but her plan to have a sitting room was already costing Devon his lost rent. She didn't imagine they would starve because he was always so confident that he could find money, but she'd had to look after herself for most of her life, and she couldn't stop now.

A normal family could be supported on a man's average wage of a little over a pound a week. Currently, she earned more than two pounds per week and from that, after wages and outgoings, she took home about the same as the average man, sometimes more. A part she saved; another part she used for normal living expenses. She couldn't say her husband was a kept man, because she had never given him money. But she assumed she would have to eventually, if only to maintain him in his gentlemanly lifestyle.

She also assumed she could. Despite the fact that she had begun her salon a little less than two months ago, her customers increased daily and were already beginning to crowd out the hat shop. She planned to employ an additional apprentice if another could be squeezed into the tiny space. Had she not been about to leave for England, she might have considered expanding into a shop of her own. This would mean spending most of her earnings on rent and fittings.

For a moment, her spirits sagged. Then she buried her selfish thoughts. Decorating the lodging's sitting room should be her first priority, since she really ought to maintain her husband's position in society by attempting to befriend the wives and sisters of his wealthy friends.

* * * *

Shading his eyes from the wavering sun, Dev watched the cut-slate shingles pass from man to man along the line from the wagon bed, tossed to the tiler on the roof, and then neatly laid. The speed of his laborers and their work ethic impressed him. At this rate, the roof would be finished in another two days. He stepped inside the empty house, gazing out the window at the tall buildings of the city and the sea beyond.

At this stage of the construction, only skilled tradesmen were needed. The floors had been laid and currently the walls were being plastered. He could help, and had. Along the way he'd learned enough about the various trades to be able to build at least a shed on his own. Not that he would ever need a trade, but learning couldn't ever be a waste of a man's time. At this stage, however, he had nothing to do but "supervise"— his term for getting in everyone's way. He sighed. Boredom had set in. He preferred being occupied.

Socializing with the Grace family last night had been most enjoyable. Not having a place of his own to entertain friends hadn't bothered him until recently, but now he saw himself as a parasite, watching others work, sharing other people's families, and offering nothing in return. Wenna wanted a sitting room, or so she had said, but a sitting room would lead to a dining room, which would lead to meals at home. Since she didn't have a cook/maid, she would do the work herself. He couldn't approve of that, not when he could afford a cook/maid. This meant finding one for her at the labor exchange, which would be unfair to the cook who would barely begin work before her employers left for England.

The plasterer, Jem, a thin pale man in his early thirties, interrupted his contemplations. "You'll want to decide on the colors for the inside walls soon." He stirred his bucket of lime near his bare wet feet.

Late May, the weather had cooled which meant the plaster took longer to dry. Only another month until the rain and the bluster of winter…if the rain arrived, that was. The vines had been planted and by August would need to be pruned, but not by him. He would be long gone. Only another few weeks, and he could move into his house…should he want to move into his house. He sighed. He did, but he wouldn't. He couldn't get Wenna settled, only to leave within a month. Either that or wait another full year. He didn't plan to be rounding the Cape in dangerous weather.

"We'll stick to white plaster for the time being. I see the garden as a priority." He still was not able to admit to anyone that he would never live in this house. Until the words were uttered, he could dream.

"Best time to plant is now, before the real cold comes." Jem wiped the back of his hand under his nose. "I don't get much work in winter. The lime plaster slips off the walls. I'm handy in the garden if you want a worker there."

Dev rubbed the back of his neck. "I do. But first I'll want a front path. Are you handy with paving?"

The man grinned. "Even in the rain."

"You can use the leftover red bricks and start whenever you're ready."

"Next week, I expect." Jem straightened his shoulders.

Dev smiled and tramped up the hill to inspect his vines, which hadn't changed since his last inspection a week ago. He expected to begin on the post and wire supports for the grapes as soon as the wire arrived in a few days. While he gazed around his property, he mentally marked out a place for his citrus trees. Apples and pears might do well here, but olives should be in their element. Acres and acres of olives, and down below a crusher where he could produce the much-needed oil for the colony.

He stuffed his hands in his pockets and measuring his steps with his gaze, he strode back down the hill to his hired wagon, not yet willing to let go of his plan.

When he arrived back in the city, dusk had settled. He stopped for a moment by the side gate of his lodgings, watching the gas workers bury the last of their pipes in the street. The sooner the rains came, the better. The billowing dust had become such a nuisance that passers-by covered their noses and mouths with handkerchiefs.

He opened the door and spotted Wenna, scrupulously dressed for dinner at The Pig and Whistle. The warmth of the stove wafted through the doorway. Rubbing his hands, he glanced at the hob. "Do you have water heating?"

She rose to her feet. "Of course. Cold water is all very well for washing in the heat of summer, but not now."

He washed in the sink, conscious of his efficient wife's gaze on his back. "They've almost finished with the pipes outside. We'll be glad to see the end of it."

"The engineer said that one day we'll have hot water piped in every house as well."

He nodded. "Why not? If we can supply the gas through copper pipes, we can supply hot water through a boiler."

"Ivor will make his fortune, since his family owns a copper mine."

"It might be a good idea to buy shares." He turned and raised his eyebrows at her. "Copper is being used more and more for gas piping—not only here in the colony, but all over the world. Gold is all very well, but gold is merely a luxury. Copper is fast becoming a necessity."

Wenna lowered her chin and looked up at him, a skeptical glance if ever he saw one. "It's been a necessity since men began making tools more than six thousand years ago."

"A regular little fount of all knowledge, aren't you?" he said, drying his face and hands.

"You forget. My father ran a copper-smelting plant. He lived and breathed copper. But you're right. Necessities are far more important than luxuries." Her gaze lingered on his bare chest.

He left off his shirt because the sensation of his wife staring at him with a softened expression prickled at his nipples and warmed him to the bone. Spiked with sexual anticipation, he strode up the stairs, and dressed for dinner, too. Having a wife who enjoyed the pleasures of the flesh was a bonus, but he could maintain his manners long enough to wait until after the meal.

However, as he ate his steak pie, he realized he still had a great amount of paper work to catch up on. As soon as they arrived back home, he reluctantly settled down to work. Wenna sewed for a while, and he didn't notice when she went off to bed. Too many bills still sat in a pile on his desk awaiting his attention.

Perhaps she awaited him, too, but he didn't know. He would take her when he could, which had been implicit in their original arrangement. Too much thinking about her, too much concentration of the pleasures of her willing flesh, and he would be putty in her hands. A man had to lead a woman, not follow behind her. He allowed himself a faint rueful smile, and began totaling the costs of his building supplies.

As for leading her, he already knew he couldn't change their agreement. Her goal had always been to live in Cornwall—her lifetime goal. She had married him for no other reason. Although he wished otherwise, he couldn't take her dream from her to gain his own. She had abided by their original terms, giving him no choice but to abide by them, too.

His inevitable future depressed him. He had not been brought up to think of himself as the earl, not with two brothers ahead of him in line of succession. Nothing in his education had prepared him to stroll around a large estate with little more on his mind than the hunting season or his horses' bloodlines. Instead, he had been trained to look around for an opportunity. In the south land, he had found his opportunity.

His costs now in order, he glanced over the tradesmen's accounts, deciding to have his unneeded painter begin on the downstairs area. Wenna would want another color on the walls before she began her furnishing. The floor needed varnishing, too. He would like her to be comfortable while she worked at that everlasting sewing of hers. Perhaps when she had finished primping herself up with new hats and gowns, she would find a life for herself. She now knew enough ladies to be able to pay morning calls, join sewing circles, plan arbors in her garden—no, she had no garden.

Frustrated by his thoughts, he combed his fingers through his hair. He had given her nothing but a few rooms to live in and the time to make her own clothes. In return, she had given him a comfortable homecoming daily, bright, interesting conversation, and her welcoming body. Even when he tried to work, he could picture lying naked with her on that obscene bed, kissing her beautiful white skin, teasing her and being teased by her, lifting on top of her, lying beneath her, having her mouth nipping at him, licking him, sucking him, giving him everything she hadn't yet given him. He knotted his fist on the desk, admitting to himself that she was everything he wanted and needed, in his life and in his bed.

He tried to concentrate on the figures in front of him instead of his longing to remain in this country with her, his perfect wife. The oil lamp spluttered by the time he had totaled a list of amounts to be paid. He folded his accounts into envelopes, ready to have money added when he went to the bank tomorrow. The untended pile in front of him had greatly diminished, but had not by any means disappeared.

Ready to leave the rest until tomorrow, he did one last skimming through his remaining correspondence, most of which appeared to be estimates, brochures, or sales pitches.

His gaze stopped on a letter addressed to him in a hand he knew, that of his brother, John, who had died a year or more ago. He frowned, at first assuming he must be mistaken. Others might have the same ragged hand as John. Lifting the tatty envelope, he examined the grime, the dog-eared corners. He couldn't possibly have overlooked this letter the whole time John had been lying in his foreign grave. No. Not foreign. A British stamp sat clearly on the outside. He flicked the envelope across his knee, once, twice, frowning. To read his brother's last thoughts would be painful. Foreboding held his breath.

He slit the thickly padded envelope. John, a man of few words, had apparently used most of them to write his last letter. But, not so. John had written a single page. The Earl of Marchester, his father, had filled the other three.

Dev didn't wake Wenna when he finally crawled into bed. Instead, he stared at the grimy ceiling, his thoughts racing from grief to guilt and finally to self-recrimination. To have all his dreams come to fruition, he merely had to sacrifice Wenna's.

* * * *

The day dawned cool and gray. Wenna pattered into the warm kitchen, pleased to see her husband had the hot water ready.

"You will be a credit to me when we arrive in England," he said, his back to her.

"What brought this on?"

"Much thought. My family assumes everyone born in the colonies is no better than a barbarian, but I'd like to show that I made a wise choice, which no one would expect based on my previous history."

"Do you think you did?"

"I think I did. You haven't conceived yet, have you?"

She stared at him. "And what if I don't, ever?"

"It's only been a few months. You can't assume you're infertile."

"I don't." Her cheeks heated. "Perhaps you're infertile," she said, annoyed.

"There's no such thing as male infertility."

"I think various women who've had babies by one man and don't by another might have something to say about that."

He laughed, but sourly. "Yet another myth exploded by the indomitable Wenna. I'm having the front room painted tomorrow."

"Just like that?"

He nodded. "Just like that. You are taking your time about making the decision, and I thought I would help. When the paint is dry, we'll have the floor varnished."

She clamped her lips. The early morning was no time to quarrel about money. While he left for his usual run, she gulped down her breakfast, and when he returned he disappeared again. She'd never experienced her husband in such a mood, but she decided to wallow in her own, that of muttering to herself about men who might have scrupulous manners, but no idea about how far a few pounds would go. By the time he arrived home that night, she had mulled long and hard about being married to a man whose rich friends sponsored his way through life, giving him no idea of reality.

Willing to be magnanimous, she tried a normal conversation with him over dinner at the hotel, but he seemed preoccupied during the meal. Having lost patience, she stalked ahead of him across the road to the lodgings and waited for him to unlock the front door.

Once inside, she stopped and faced him. "And where do you think you will you get the money?"

"What money?"

"To refurbish the sitting room. I'm not giving you my savings."

"Calm down." He put out his hand to touch her shoulder, and she smacked him away.

"Calm down! That's just like a man. How do you expect me to calm down when you tell me to calm down?"

He laughed.

She hit out at him, missed because he stepped back, and she stood, breathing with fury. "I don't want a painted sitting room in a cheap and nasty lodging. I want a house, a real house. I'm sick of trying to look as if I'm perfectly comfortable. If I can't have what I want here, I'd rather leave. The sooner we get out of this country, the better."

He stared at her, his face frozen. His chin lifted to a new haughty angle. "We will leave as soon as possible."

She ran up the stairs and into the bedroom where she sat, nervously awaiting him, wishing she hadn't said she wanted to leave when she didn't want to leave. Her temper had gotten the best of her again. She rose to her feet, knowing she owed him an apology. Not wanting to share her money when he shared his was truly ungracious and she didn't want him to think...

The door downstairs slammed.

She ran to the window, watched him stride down the path, open and slam shut the gate, and disappear. Flurries of wind kicked up in the street. The evening sky filled with threatening clouds. Thunder rumbled. The black weather echoed her mood.

Miserable, she began to undress. She would apologize to him in the morning.

* * * *

Determined to keep out of Wenna's way until he could come to terms with leaving the south land, Dev decided his best course would be to drink himself into oblivion with cheap plonk. He strode toward The Stag hotel near the east end markets where Wenna shopped. Outside the hotel, a merry band of roisterers sang *Greensleeves* in a tuneless caterwaul. Ignoring them, he pushed open the set of doors that normally closed by seven at night.

He paused when he spotted Nick Alden sitting at a window table ringed with beer slops and decorated by two rather inebriated women of the night. "Ah," he said, strolling over, wearing a snarl of a smile. "You must be spending a fortune to have attracted two such pretty young ladies."

Nick pushed his hair out of his eyes. "If you're here for the wedding celebrations, I fear the bride and groom have left. And no, I don't know who they were. What's the time?" He lifted his handsome face, looking not half as bleary as he sounded, damn him.

Dev glanced at his fob watch. "Seven thirty."

"Off you go, my lovelies. My friend is very much married and won't approve of you."

"On the contrary." Dev sat beside the nearest whore who grinned delightedly at him. He settled in for the night. His dear lady wife had no time for him. She had decided long ago that he was a fool who couldn't be parted from his money, and she wanted to go halfway around the world to find his family who could be.

Being introduced into society had shown her for what she was—an avaricious female who wanted nothing but the best—not the woman who would work by his side, have his babies, entertain his friends, and keep his home in the colony well run and happy. She wanted to leave, which fact of course he knew. He'd married her because he knew, but he could arrange for her grandparents' support and should have months ago. Then she might not have been in such a rush. "A man needs home comfort once in a while," he said sourly.

"You're confused. Fucking a whore isn't home comfort. It's a paid service."

"You pay one way or the other," Dev said with heartfelt bitterness, slinging an arm over the shoulders of the nearest woman. "Why not treat the transaction honestly?"

"It's too early in the night to have a philosophical conversation about prostitution. These lovelies are here merely to keep me company. They don't want my body or yours, only the money."

"Well, yes," the thin woman who had snuggled into Dev said. "Money's good. It pays for food and lodging. But youse two gents aren't our usual sort. I wouldn't mind a go with one of you." She put her palm over Dev's fly and groped.

His hand covered hers. "Not in public, my pet. It's not polite."

"You're not up for it." She looked from his face to Nick's and groaned. "You're here for him. Not that I blame you. Man or woman, anyone would want him. C'mon, Connie. We'll find a couple a'men who are interested in females." Her mouth a sloppy pout, she rose unsteadily to her feet.

The other looked puzzled for a moment and then she inexpertly gathered the knot of her hair back into a bunch. "Daisies," she said disgustedly. "Wouldn'ta guessed, though."

Nick watched them leave with a resigned tilt of his eyebrows. "That ever happened to you before?"

"There's a first time for everything." Dev sighed and motioned to a barmaid who bustled over and took his order. "It'd be easier though, if we *didn't* want women."

Nick made a sound like a snort that Dev took to be assent. He proceeded to get sodden with his friend; so soaked, in fact, that Nick offered to walk him home a few hours later, which involved singing. Only a tenant above the chandler objected.

Either Dev or Nick stumbled over the doorsill and either Dev or Nick ended up crawling into the two-chaired sitting room. "Two chairs," Dev said in disgust as he tried to haul himself onto the seat. He remembered. He was the one who had crawled. Seemed an easier way to travel when a man's head didn't know up from down. "I said I would buy more furniture, but 'no' she said. She controls the money and she wants to go to England."

"Why should that bother you?" Nick said as he lowered himself into a chair. "You never meant to stay here."

"Many a man has had second thoughts." Dev hit the tender part of his shin on the chair leg as he turned to sit. "Pass that bottle."

Chapter 18

If the slamming of the outside door hadn't woken Wenna, the voices downstairs would have; would have probably woken most of the tenants in the street as well. Instantly alert, she arose, snagged the paisley shawl from the end of the bed, and covered her shoulders. The night had cooled. Drawing in a resigned breath, she padded barefoot down the stairs. The murmur of at least two voices almost stopped her. She hadn't expected Devon to bring his friend inside, but the least she could do for her apparently drunk husband would be to haul him upstairs to bed. She proceeded to the angle of light visible between the sitting room door and the jamb. Not dressed for company, she hesitated for a moment.

Devon, his voice slurred and hesitant, said, "My plan, you understand, was to take her to Cornwall—said that's where she wanted to go." Clearly he spoke of Wenna.

Her heart began to pound.

"Which sounds convenient." Nick's voice, the usual low cynical tone. "Your family lives there and so will you."

Devon gave an uneven laugh. "Could you imagine my father's face, though? A redheaded servant married to his son?" Scathing, not like Devon, but his voice all the same.

"She's a smart woman. He would be a fool not to see that."

"Know who he wouldn't let me marry? The love of my life, Jenny, a redheaded dairymaid. I was sent to France because of her, and then out here. I would see sense, my lord thought, and find a lady he could approve of one day." Devon's voice cracked. "I showed him."

The love of his life? Yet he could make love to Wenna like a man dedicated to bed-sport. Her face hardened.

"Likely he has your best interests at heart."

"So he said, but I didn't know that then. I found Wenna. She wanted to go to Cornwall. Suited me. I wanted to bed her. Didn't matter if I got her pregnant. Good idea, as it turned out."

"It must have been torture for you." Nick, cynical, drawling.

Devon made a sound like a grunt.

"You could have persuaded any one of a number of colonial hopefuls to do the same thing. You know how impressed the females here are by the British gentry."

"Not a redhead among them." Devon, flippant.

"Nothing but a redheaded maid would do for you. I understand revenge, unfortunately."

"Should never have considered it." Silence from Devon.

Wenna couldn't move either back or forward. Every joint in her body had locked into place. Her heart sprung a hole right in the center, a great cavernous hole. She had died, but her body remained upright, stiff, and cold.

Devon had married her to avenge himself on his father.

She had red hair and Devon saw her as a servant, no more than that to him. Not the woman of his dreams, not the woman who tried hard to save him money, to make him comfortable, to push him ahead in life. Not the woman who thought she would love him until she died.

"She would have been able to handle m'father, despite that red hair of hers." A shoe scraped on the floor as if one of the gentlemen had moved.

"Would have? You think she can't now?"

Silence again. Another shifting of feet. "Don't need her to do so. My plan was puerile, but, Lord, I wanted her. And Courtneys always get what they want no matter what they have to promise." Said sourly by her dishonorable husband. He had married her to gain a bed-warmer, no more, no less, and now greatly regretted his haste. Lust didn't last forever, not as long as a need for revenge. "And Courtneys don't break promises."

"So, now what?"

The silence lingered. Wenna swallowed to ease her dry throat. He wanted her because his father wouldn't approve of his son marrying a servant, and certainly not one with red hair. Unwillingly, ignobly, he would be a redheaded servant's escort to England, *because he had promised*, all the while trying to put a baby in the servant's belly so that he could complete his vengeance by giving his father an underling's child as his heir. Perhaps she *ought* to let Dev impregnate her. Then they could be done with each other.

Shivering, she groped her way back to the bedroom, led by the moonlight beckoning through the upstairs windows. Strange rasps forced through her throat and tears flooded out of her eyes, blinding her, too fast to be blotted, gushing too heavily to stop. Her crying became weeping, noisy and ugly, betrayed, unstoppable, seeping out of her in a volume she couldn't imagine or control. She had mourned before, but she had never been betrayed before, not like this, not by a man she completely trusted. She thought she would never feel warm again.

She crawled under the sheet, the linen around her soaked with her distress until the deluge stopped, leaving her drained of all emotion except an aching cynicism about herself and her foolish expectations. Her husband hadn't betrayed her, hadn't lied to her. When he had asked her to marry him, she had heard his honest explanation. He hadn't tricked her. Redheaded maid that she was, she'd had no problem tricking herself. Knowing her attraction to him, she'd hoped he might learn to love her.

At some stage through the muddle of her flickering thoughts, she heard Devon stumble up the stairs. She turned her back to the door, refusing to acknowledge him. He didn't enter. He had enough sense to snore the rest of the night away in the dressing room.

In the morning, she slowly dressed in her servant's black, not sure of her next step. She thought of her beautiful red dress and ached. A redheaded servant in a red dress at an exclusive ball. Without a doubt that had delighted Devon as much as he said. By wearing that color she played right into his hands. She couldn't have been more out of place, more noticeable, or more the sort of woman with whom to taunt his father.

She'd been told often enough that she didn't know her place and, literally, she didn't. As a child, she'd had status of a sort as the daughter of a mine manager. In those days she had associated with children of the wealthier settlers, including Nell and Ivor. After her father's death, she had moved way down the ladder when her mother could only support her as a washerwoman.

However, as soon as Wenna reached the age to take her first job as a scullery maid, she had pushed her old friends to the back of her mind and fought her way up again, until she'd reached the highest position a woman servant could attain. Though for her, being a lady's maid was not enough. Being as good as anyone was her aim; as good as the boy her father had craved.

Then she had married Devon. Even then, she continued being humiliated and ridiculed because of her hair and her lowly status. To cap that, Devon had married her only to avenge himself on his father. She couldn't even force a self-derisive snort. But she managed to curl her lip and harden her heart as she tramped down the stairs to the kitchen.

Ignoring the cold stove, she left the husband sleeping upstairs to heat his own water and prepare his own breakfast, and proceeded to her job in the back of Madame Fleur's. Her persistence meant nothing at all if, throughout her life, she never rose above being a *redheaded maid*. As she walked through the doorway of the hat shop, she lifted her chin.

From this day and forevermore, she intended be more than the sum of her hair color and her gender.

* * * *

The daylight poured into the window as Dev tried to get his bearings. He lay in a small bed, barely a cot, and he wore his suit and shoes. His head thumped. He tried to sit up, but the anvil pounding in his skull kept him supine. Apparently he'd slept the night in Wenna's dressing room. Memories came back to him of drinking with Nick. If he had kept up with his friend, his head could be explained. And then he remembered why he had been drinking. He groaned.

Wenna wanted a life in England. Later he would process this. Right now he needed to wash and shave—as soon as he could stand. Since he had booked to leave Adelaide on the next passenger ship, he needed to get his affairs in order. After groping his way up the wall, he stood up and, with agonizing slowness, he fumbled to his bedroom. Wenna had gone.

He saw no sign of her in the kitchen. The stove sat gray with last night's ashes. Moving slowly, he had a cold-water wash before he dressed for a day's labor. After a large cold glass of water, he puttered down the street to discuss the management of his properties with Tom Finn.

After that, he bought a glass of ale, which somewhat dulled the thumping hammer in the cavernous black space of his head, and he jammed a meat pie into the cesspit of his mouth on the way up to his almost-completed house.

His mind couldn't process his immediate future. He could do nothing but sit for a while on the hill, wrists dangling from his knees, contemplating the view that would soon be replaced by the stark boredom of idling in Cornwall.

Finally, he rose to his feet and walked down to the house he would never occupy, unless Wenna tired of Cornwall, or unless she grew to love him and wanted to live with him at the end of the earth. He couldn't expect love from her, though. He had done not a thing for her except *tup* her day and night, and expect her to be content in society, although she'd not been born there. He had expected her to be comfortable in the company of his friends, though she likely had her own elsewhere.

Not once in the past few months had he given a thought to the life she might have wanted. He had expected her to live his. Without a doubt, he had been a graceless, inconsiderate husband who would now do his duty by his wife, who had always done her duty by him.

* * * *

If Wenna did nothing else in her life, she would make a lasting success of her business. She finished washing and drying her customers' hair; she showed off the prettiest hats, she booked her time for the next day and the next; she finished for the day at the same time as usual. Then, after tying her hat firmly under her chin, she dropped into The Pig and Whistle to talk to Mr. Snow. From there, she walked to the land agent's office.

The portly red-faced man, of course, didn't want to deal with a mere female. "Who do you have as surety if I let you rent out a place?" he said, hooking his nicotine-stained thumbs into the pockets of his tweed waistcoat and rocking back on his heels. His belly looked important enough to have its own office.

She glanced down her nose at him. "I have myself, Mr. Bainbridge, and cash. My business is very profitable, and I'm expecting to hire more staff if I have larger premises. You are advertising a vacant shop. Do you want to let it, or not?" She waited, tapping her foot impatiently.

He ran his tongue over his teeth as he stared at her. Then, with a hearty sigh, he took down the advertisement from his window and scanned his wording, as if making sure he could let a woman with her own money hire the place. Finally, he buttoned his jacket and took his dusty hat from the peg by the door. "If you'll give me a moment to lock up here, Miss Chenoweth, we can see if it's suitable for you."

Clouds hovered low in the gray sky. The walk down the wind-blown street would have been more pleasant alone. The man almost creaked while he huffed and puffed beside her. She didn't have any respect for a man who let himself get so out of condition that walking at a smart pace along a street could cause trails of sweat to drip from under his hat.

Devon could run for miles, and he did so every day. She had never asked why, but the exercise showed on his big, healthy, beautiful body. Lifting bricks also didn't hurt his physique one bit. But dreaming about the perfection she had married was a waste of her time when he had no affection for her. She tightened her face and continued on with the small-minded man beside her.

The building that interested her had been vacant for a week. The last tenant, a shoemaker, had moved to a side street with cheaper rent. Wenna thought she would do well in the space, which was attached to the pastry shop where Devon had taken her the day she had arrived. The proprietress, a widow with three children who lived above the premises, employed smartly uniformed waitresses, a ploy that attracted the well-heeled customers who could also use Wenna's services. As a bonus, Wenna's clients would likely purchase pastries or cakes so conveniently placed.

After a short amount of haggling, she hired two very suitable rooms, the large front room and the smaller back room on the ground floor. She planned to use her main area for her customers and her back area, which housed the wood stove, as her utility room. The tenants upstairs had the same arrangement as she and Devon had in their lodgings, a lobby and staircase, and would be no trouble, or so Mr. Bainbridge said.

Her first task completed, Wenna took a detour and strode along the back lanes to Frome Street, planning her shop's decor. The walls needed to be painted a color that would show up the ladies' hairdos in the most flattering way. A dark cream would be suitable. She stopped outside Alden and Company where she could find the chairs she wanted for her customers, briefly wondering if Nick Alden's family ran the place. His surname was unusual.

Forewarned being forearmed, she carefully glanced around the showroom before entering, but she didn't see Nick. This didn't really surprise her. His drinking habit wasn't compatible with the early rising required to work in a shop, and his hands showed no signs of being used for physical labor—not like Dev's with his cuts and scratches and hardened palms. She breathed in the hot aroma of boiling glue, wood dust, and shellac while listening to the hidden murmur of conversation behind a partition, a sudden shout of mirth, and the regular bite of a saw.

The chairs could be delivered within the next few days. The painter shouldn't take longer than that, once she found one. She estimated that in a weeks' time, she would no longer be visible to society matrons who shopped for expensive hats. Only women who needed an occasional lift to their spirits would see her.

The relief she experienced in moving to her own space lightened her steps. The thought of defying her husband tightened her lips and stiffened her spine.

* * * *

Dusk had settled before Dev had finished supervising the property. During the next few weeks, he would hurry up setting out the area. Finn knew his long-term plans and would hire a couple to live in the house to maintain the home farm and the gardens. Dev would not be able to return. He didn't want to sell, though a small part of him hoped his wife might not find the life she had dreamed of in England, and would agree to settle back into the land of her birth.

He arrived home that night, weary, chastened, and contrite about his appalling loss of composure the night before. As soon as he opened the door, he spotted Wenna sitting in the kitchen as usual, awaiting his arrival. The stove warmed the place. He smiled at her, his beautiful, patient, redheaded wife.

"Does your head ache?" she asked politely.

He smiled ruefully. "Like the devil."

"It serves you right." She indicated the water on the stove awaiting his wash.

He began unbuttoning his shirt. "I won't be drinking to excess again in a hurry." At least he hadn't annoyed her with his drunken attentions the night before. "You're right. We should have moved into a house the day we married. I simply thought... Well, we expected to go to England." He shrugged.

"At least we have a date to leave now." She turned her back.

He sighed. Likely he deserved an amount of punishment, but he'd grown used to the intimacy of her watching him while he washed. He changed upstairs as usual, and they ate across the street as usual, but the conversation no longer had the give and take he so much enjoyed with her. The remote expression on her face warned him off, though he couldn't fault her manner. He had apologized. He could do no more than wait out her displeasure.

The worst was her sleeping with her back to him. Apparently wives withheld their favors when husbands went astray for a couple of hours. If she thought that would remind him not to do so in future, she was likely right. But a wise husband would keep out of her sights until she relented.

* * * *

Two days later, Wenna stood in the doorway of her new shop, still a mere nameless space, although very much planned in her mind. Today the walls would be painted pale ochre. She imagined a set of shelves behind an entrance counter, and on the other side, two comfortable armchairs where customers would wait for the next operative.

Hidden behind the reception area would be a long slice of red gum made up by one of Alden's carpenters to serve as a bench that ran from the back of the shelves to the far wall. A basin would be set in at the end for washing customers' hair. Upright padded chairs could sit under the bench, and four big framed mirrors above. She had seen a smart new dark green floor-cloth painted with yellow and red flowers on the corners, which she intended to buy.

She pattered her fingers on her chin. She couldn't afford to buy pictures for the walls, but the flower seller might agree to leave a bunch of her flowers on the side table between the two armchairs if offered a pasteboard card in the window as an acknowledgement. Wenna had already discussed forming a conglomerate with the women shopkeepers in the street. She would show her drawings of Mrs. Busby's hats with the right hairdos, and depictions of Mrs. Miller's gowns either on the walls or spread along the main working bench. The other traders would advertise for the whole group as well.

Looking over the space, Wenna decided to hire a third apprentice. Certain customers didn't have the time or money for a complicated hairstyle, but appreciated a good washing, which meant more time taken to towel-dry the hair. The newest apprentice would also need to tend to the heating of the water and the curling tongs on the wood stove in the back room.

Grinning like a paperboy spotting a dropped penny, she shut the door on her new premises and hurried off to her old location. No customers had yet appeared, leaving Mrs. Busby and Maisie admiring the newest creations on the hat stand in the window. "If you know a bright sixteen-year-old who wants to learn a trade, send her to me for an interview," Wenna said to Maisie as she breezed through to the back of the shop. Maisie and Mrs. Busby followed.

"I have a cousin." Maisie smiled hopefully. "She's working in the jam factory as of now, but she's bright and pretty and deserves better. Plus, she has four younger sisters and a pa who is out of work, though that's his choice. Loafer," she said with disgust.

"There's plenty of men around here who expect their women to support them." Mrs. Busby leaned against the doorway. "Mrs. Miller, though I shouldn't say so, has a husband who helps her by buying her fabrics. He has made visiting the sales rooms into a full-time job, but they don't open more than once a week, if that. My Stan used to work on the docks, a hard heavy job." She shrugged. "Died young, though."

"Do you have children?" Wenna asked, shaking out the dressing capes.

"A son and a daughter. My son is apprenticed at Alden's and my daughter makes the flowers for my hats. She's only fourteen and she does a lovely job. She wants to be a schoolteacher." The bell in the shop tinkled, and she hastened away.

"I'll get my cousin to see you tomorrow." Maisie packed the stove with kindling. The towels had dried overnight, but hair would need washing as soon as the first customer arrived. "They say we'll have gas stoves one day. I don't know how that will work."

"Probably about the same as gas lights, though I expect stoves will be too expensive for everyone to own." Wenna heard the front door open and smiled a welcome to her new customer.

* * * *

Almost exactly one week later, Wenna moved into her new business premises, *Wenna's Place*, a name chosen after intensive thought. Wenna wouldn't let herself be shamed by her beginnings as a servant any longer. From the time of her mother's death, she had fought her way up into the job as a lady's maid, no mean feat from a position of utter penury. Now, she employed others, who were also not servants, in her own business.

She gazed around her rooms, which during the day would be lit with the flickering light of four gas lamps. Thus far her husband hadn't asked her what she did all day, why she left early, or why she wore black. He had barely been home since the night a week ago when he had told her how short the time was before they left for Cornwall. She ate with him and slept with him, but he didn't touch her. Apparently, since he'd told all to Nick about their marriage, he'd come to his senses. A redheaded servant wasn't good enough for his father and not good enough for him. If he wanted to be ashamed of her, so be it. She didn't feel at all humble, not now, not when she knew she had the ability to change her life and the lives of others as well.

She had begun an extensive training of Maisie so that the other woman could take over as the main hairstylist when Wenna left. Mr. Snow had agreed to run the business side until Maisie was ready to take over. Wenna trusted him, but he had insisted on a legal agreement that she would sign this afternoon. She had also hired a youngster who, for the time being, would simply wash and dry hair. This idea was proving enormously profitable. Later, after Wenna had left, Maisie could train the apprentices as she wished.

In the meantime, *Wenna's Place* was exactly that. She had found her role in training others, in listening to new ideas, and implementing them. The women shop owners in the street now fully supported each other, referred customers to each other, and discussed their latest business ideas in the pastry shop, owned by another woman who had been left in the lurch by a man.

In South Australia, women could vote in council elections. Soon, women would be able to vote in government elections. The day would come. Women didn't need men to tell them what to do, how to work, or how to run their lives. The women traders on Rundle Street were every bit as successful as the men. And not a single woman on the street wanted to go back to the old country.

Wenna explained her projected trip to England as family duty. She said she would return if at all possible. One day Devon's father would die. Devon had good friends here. He might not be too averse to the idea. Hope kept her spirits up, hope that Devon's father would despise her on sight and insist on banishing Devon all over again. She knew Devon wouldn't stick up for her. He was too used to running with the stream.

Chapter 19

"I hope you intend to forgive me sooner or later." Devon turned from the water heating on the stove, his handsome face tense and drawn.

Wenna stood, wrapped in her shawl, waiting to fill her jug for a wash. "And for what do you need forgiveness?" Although she waited, hoping for one moment that he would say he loved her and that he hadn't meant a word he said to Nick, he had no idea that she had overheard the conversation. To tell him and risk showing that he had hurt her would be impossible. She knew that her husband didn't think of her as anything but a servant, when she was so very proud of her accomplishments.

He drew a deep breath. "I'm ashamed that I drank too much, Wenna. Consider me contrite and not about to repeat that particular, painful error." His repentant smile came too easily to be anything but a tried-and-true ploy.

She hardened her resolve, not about to fall for his easy charm again. He had called her a redheaded servant. And so she would likely remain in his eyes. A woman who could manage on her own should not need the praise of a man who relied on others for his support. "My temper burns out quickly," she said with a shrug. "We could have settled the argument the same night, but you ran off and drank yourself into a stupor." She backed toward the stove, her spine rigid, but her heart far too willing to listen to an explanation.

"A male solution that rarely works." He made a rueful mouth. "I thought you wanted a sitting room, and I thought I would please you by offering to have the work done quickly."

She shook her head, almost shocked by his irresponsibility. "You don't understand our situation. I couldn't afford to spend money on painting and furnishing. As it is, I make my own clothes."

"But you had no need." He sounded frustrated. His forehead creased and he spread his hands. "I told you I would buy you all the gowns you wanted. I made the offer to refurbish the sitting room. I intended to pay."

"And then where would you be when you wanted to look as rich as all your fine friends?" she said, her throat aching.

"I would be where I am now, financially. I have money, Wenna. I can afford to look as rich as my *fine* friends. I simply don't spend for show."

"I've yet to see a fistful of money other than that you hand over every night for our meal." She blinked hard.

"I keep most of my money in the bank."

"How much is *most*?" She met his gaze, hoping against hope that he really did have enough money to support himself.

His shoulders lifted. "Currently, I have no idea, but I have an income of five thousand a year. I don't have much call on my pocket other than the costs for the house."

"Five thousand?" Her heart gave one big thump and then went into a pitter-patter that shortened her breath. She didn't know a person in the world who had that much money—but yearly? She shook her head, her mouth curled with disbelief.

He looked defensive. "I'm quite rich, you know. You *should* know. How else would I have been able to buy these rooms and the house?"

"What house?"

"I showed you my house. You thought it would be very nice for someone else to live in."

"You own the house you are building? And you have five thousand a year?" She took another step back, turned, and with her back to him, very carefully placed her empty jug in the sink. "No family would pay a younger son so much to stay away," she said in a definite voice that hid her fading doubts.

"I'm not paid to stay away. I'm wanted at home and have been this past year. You know this. I told you from the very beginning."

She couldn't make herself turn back to him. "You're the son of a gentleman farmer and you have five thousand a year? What is your father farming? Gold?" Her laugh sounded derisive, but she knew deep inside that he told her the truth. He had always had the sort of confidence that seemed to be inborn, the sort that came with money and security.

"In a way. He did own acres of land. In terms of rentals, that's gold, but my main income comes from my mother's estate. I told you before that I'm her only heir."

"So, your mother was rich, too?" Her gaze lowered with her voice. Part of her died at that moment. Of course his mother was rich. No one in the colony owned plates and dishes as beautiful as those Wenna had stored under the stairs. She had misjudged him, and for no reason other than that he didn't waste a penny. Nor did she, yet in herself she thought being careful with money was a virtue. Although she should be wild with joy, but she could only shrivel with shame. Her hands shook as she slowly turned to face him.

"I was going to have to tell you sooner or later, and as it pans out, I should have told you sooner, but it's not common knowledge. Nick knows, and the lads I met at Cambridge, but no one else."

"Knows what—about your wealth?"

"That my father had a title."

She blinked. "A title? An aristocratic title? Is that why you're called 'honorable?'" Her ignorance warmed her cheeks with embarrassment.

His face relaxed and he stared straight into her eyes. "It's the courtesy title for younger sons of earls, when no other titles are currently available in the family."

"So you're the son of an earl." Moving away from the sink, she groped behind her, found the back of a wooden chair, and sat. "I thought I had married the family wastrel." Even to her, her laugh sounded too high-pitched. "I thought I would be supporting you until I could get you into a decent job."

"Wenna." Shaking his head, his mouth tilted with remorse, he reached for her hands. Somehow he urged her up and she stood against the wall of his chest. "How could you possibly support me?" He touched her neck, then his knuckles rubbed gently across her cheek.

"You're the son of an earl. An earl in Cornwall." She met his gaze. "Which earl?"

"Marchester." His tongue flickered briefly over his lips.

She nodded, her eyes burning with unshed tears. "So, your mother was Lady Ann, a titled lady in her own right. And my mother was her maid." She flattened her palms on his chest, pushing away from him, a weird laugh forcing through her throat. "How utterly perfect. You couldn't have thought of a better way to humiliate your family."

His eyebrows lowered. "What?"

"Don't worry. I'll wear the red dress to show the earl exactly who I am. I made a promise to you, and I'll keep it." She turned, poured her water into her jug, and marched upstairs to wash and dress for work. And then she began to laugh hysterically.

She would be the mother of an heir to the estate of the Earl of Marchester, who had once insisted that her mother leave his employ.

How totally, utterly perfect her husband's plan was to avenge himself on his father.

* * * *

Dev had always known that when Wenna found out that her mother had been his mother's maid she would be taken aback, or possibly even slightly embarrassed. He hadn't realized she would be hurt. Her comment about humiliating his family told him so. She thought she wasn't good enough. Even though his father might have agreed, he would soon have changed his mind once he met her.

However, the situation at home had changed completely now. His reason to keep his title a secret no longer mattered, for he now had no title. The tenth Earl of Marchester, his brother John, would be glad Dev had married a colonial, or he would at least be very careful what he said about Dev's marriage.

Perhaps as a silent protest for Dev assuming she would not need any more new gowns, Wenna bustled about the next morning still dressed in her maid's uniform. The night before he had faced her back again, too guilty to try to make love to her. First he needed to placate her, without knowing how to placate a woman who had a genuine grievance.

"Here," he said, desperate to try anything. He placed the money he kept in his desk on the table, a wad of pound notes and some change. "Buy whatever you want. If you want a gown for every day of the week, buy one."

"I have enough gowns."

"The thing is..." He swallowed. "I thought, assumed really, that you would rather have Paris-made designs. You'll be able to buy the very best when we get to England. Not that we need to save in the meantime, not at all, not if you want a hundred gowns."

Her face expressionless, she stared at him for some seconds. "In that case, you can keep your money. I don't imagine I'll need to be a fashion plate on the high seas."

He rubbed his forehead, certain he hadn't managed to buy her affections. Before he left for his run, he took out his brother's letter and read the words yet again. Perhaps he should have explained his situation to Wenna earlier, despite knowing hers hadn't changed. However, that was the reason why he hadn't said so. He couldn't even hint he wanted to renege on his promise to take her to England. She had married him on the strength of his promise.

Dear Dev, old chap,

As you would realize by reading this, the report of my death in India was too previous. I haven't been taken yet, though I certainly had the devil of an injury. I came near to losing my right arm, which left me unable to write until recently. I am sure you will forgive me for the tardiness of my correspondence. However, the news of our father's demise needed to come from me. He died a month after my return. In his last days he handed over the running of the estate to me.

How it came about I can't say but during a conversation I had with the old man, I told him how Will and I ragged you about your mother. The tutor looked nothing like you. He was a stick with brown hair. You're the image of your mother, as Pater said. Jealousy is a green serpent.

Possibly because of this, Pater was anxious to pen an epistle to you, herein enclosed signed and sealed from prying eyes as you can see. What ho!

As you know, now I'm the earl, you lose the Dellacourt title. I might yet produce a son. Or you might yet inherit all unless I get busy and find myself a wife. Ha ha. In the meantime, I need you to come back, dear chap, and sort out all your personal holdings. It was fitting for Pater to manage this, but not so for me.

Yrs truly, your brother John, Earl of Marchester.

Dev had to go back, but he didn't have to stay. John would marry speedily and produce a brood of children, if only to cut Dev out of the succession. In the meantime, John would treat Wenna with courtesy. She was too proud and beautiful to be despised by anyone and Dev would spend the rest of his life making sure she was honored by all. He laced up his soft shoes and left for his usual run.

For the first mile, he sprinted, his feet pounding, his breath huffing along the deserted paths as the sun rose behind him. The leaves of the surrounding trees warmed, perfuming the air with fresh eucalyptus. Magpies sang, greeting the day with a melodic hymn, and Dev's chest expanded with gusts of air while the muscles of his legs eased and flexed, eased and flexed. The exhilaration of being alive filled him as usual, but finally he steadied his pace into a regular jog.

His marriage would strengthen when he gave Wenna her heart's desire, and he would somehow show his wife that although he might have chosen her without a thought in his mind for her comfort, he had grown to respect and appreciate her, and much more. Although his motives had been ignoble, his choice had been perfect.

No other woman would have had the strength of character to accept being shoved from her comfortable existence into his disorganized world, lodging above a shop with a husband who kept his business to himself. Wenna didn't complain about the living conditions, she didn't insist on servants, and she had waltzed into society as if she *could* waltz.

His lips curved with reluctant amusement as he ran. During her first ball, she had fit in well with society, despite a slight show of stage fright. His father, had he still lived, would have been delighted with Wenna.

My Very Dear Son, his father had written during his last days on earth. *My third born, but by no means my least son. You have always been as dear to me as your mother, my greatest love, my only love, if truth be told. With two brothers ahead of you, you were not born to be the earl after me. I could only give you money and the means to seek a place for yourself, the chance to be your own man, which you have been with great style and dash. I couldn't have been prouder of any son ...* "

Yes, his father, who loved him enough to let him go, would have enjoyed Wenna. John would be guardedly impressed, too. Wenna might be at outs with Dev at the moment, but when she had her heart's desire, her own gracious house in Cornwall, she would see how much he had grown to love her—as he had told Nick—and she might see that Dev was the right husband for her.

He rounded the corner and headed toward the east end markets, still smiling with hope. The night watchman lifted his long hooked pole from one gaslight to the next, a routine he managed with the flair of practice as he steadily doused the street lamps, ducking between the traders as they unloaded their wagons. Cart horses stood by with idly flicking tails and drooping heads, nickering, nuzzling into the water troughs, tossing manes, and adding to the general smell of manure, hay, sweet fruit, and rotting vegetables. A market gardener tossed an apple to Dev as he passed through. "That'll keep up yer energy."

Dev grinned and shoved the apple into his pocket. Other produce growers smiled or waved. Dev had become a morning fixture. Once the camaraderie had amazed him; the acceptance he'd found from all in this colony. No longer. He had grown used to being accepted not for whom his parents were, but because he ran in the morning for no other reason than he liked running.

Wenna would find that same acceptance in England, but because of his birth. As his wife, she would be flattered, deferred to, and invited everywhere. She would have the life his mother had, idle and easy. Wenna would want to stay. He had to accept that.

His jaw clenched as his long, fast strides took him to the Rundle Street corner. He turned into the street, passing the hotels and shops that had not yet opened for the day. Another street lighter moved patiently from one lamp to the next—and the ground rocked with an explosion beneath Dev's feet.

He pulled up, shocked into a stumbling stand-still. Black smoke billowed from the business center. The road ahead, blown up high, began settling in heavy pattering clumps all around. From the middle of the disturbance, flickering flares of red shot into the air, dropped, and faded into an unearthly shade of menacing blue.

"Blimey," the night watchman said, moving close beside him. He shivered. "What 'appened?"

Dev frowned. "Gas, more than likely. Stay back! This might not be the last of the explosions."

"We've got pipes under the whole street." The watchman stood staring at his feet, his two hands gripped hard onto his pole, as if steadying himself for a trip through the air.

Dev squinted at the billowing smoke. "The road has been ripped up. We need to make sure the fire doesn't spread. Run for the fire wagon," he yelled as he sped past his premises toward the explosion.

Within half a block, he saw a line of flame cross the road and lick at the pastry shop. Mrs. Lock, the pie maker, lived above with her three young children. He sprinted faster, leaping over puttering flares and landing in front of the shop. The façade blistered and the flames began to snake up the veranda posts.

He crashed through the front door of the building, calling for Mrs. Lock, but she didn't answer. Thinking of the children, he raced up the stairs, the heavy smoke following him. He opened the first door. Three wide-eyed children dressed in nightwear huddled in a big bed, holding each other for dear life. "What's that noise, Mister?" A girl of about six raised her panicked gray eyes to him.

He drew a breath, willing himself to look authoritative. "That was an explosion in the street. Best not to stay here. Come along with me."

"Mum would want us to wait for her. She's downstairs."

Dev looked around and saw a clothes chest. "Get dressed, and I'll take you downstairs. Coats and shoes will do. Hurry. Put these on. We have to be quick." A fire fueled by gas would travel fast, but he didn't want to scare the children.

"Might be cooking smoke," the biggest said nervously. Her gaze flickered between Dev and her siblings. "Sometimes Mum burns the cakes."

"Well then, we'll go down and see." Dev had never dressed a child in his life and he tried to shove a resisting pair of little arms into a Cardigan sleeve. "If you can't be very fast, you'll need to leave without dressing. And you don't want to stand in the street in your nightclothes."

The oldest very carefully disentangled herself from her other siblings and climbed out of bed. She slipped on a pair of shoes, donned her woolly cardigan, and passed another to the middle-sized child. "Put your shoes on, Sally."

"What's your name?" Dev asked as he kept trying to garb the smallest. Smoke hovered around the window, searching for an entrance. "I'm Devon."

"Molly's m'name. Let's go downstairs and see Mum."

Dev grabbed up the smallest, a boy, and strode to the doorway. "Follow me." Smoke curled into the room behind.

With a frightened yelp, Molly swooped at him and clutched his leg. Sally held onto Molly. Encumbered, he stepped ahead dragging them and carrying the struggling and wailing small boy in his arms. "You go down first," he said to the girls when he reached the stairs, and they hurried down, holding onto a newel at the bottom, their waiting faces stark and anxious. The heat of the fire radiated through the air.

Loaded with the children, he reached the kitchen. The fire of the oven competed with the heat outside. Stew simmered and rounds of pastry waited on the side bench. A saucepan sat upturned on the floor, surrounded by a mess of cooked tomatoes. One leg of the central table had collapsed, trapping a crumpled heap of rags beneath. He took a long look but smoke and dust billowed in through the open back door, and he had no time to waste speculating. He settled the boy on his feet in the laneway outside, gathered the children into a bunch, and noticed a collection of onlookers approaching. "Could you take these children away from the fire," he shouted.

A woman wearing an apron stepped forward. "Where's your mum, Molly?"

"She must have gone down the street."

After a questioning glance at Dev, the woman took Molly's hand and hurried the children away. Dev leapt back into the kitchen. The children would be guarded until order was restored, and he thought he knew where to find Mrs. Lock. Clearly, the pastry shop had taken the brunt of the first blast.

A sudden dust-filled explosion blew out the windows. Dev threw himself to the floor to avoid the flying glass. A tongue of fire licked along the floorboards from the front of the shop, heading for the stairwell. He lifted to his elbows and crawled beneath the table. The rags—petticoats—

resettled to show a black stocking-covered leg. First a moan, an uplifted head, and then, "The children," said in a hoarse voice. "Upstairs."

"I found them. Don't worry, Mrs. Lock. They're safe. Let's get you out of here too. Can you move?"

She rolled to the side. "Slowly. Nothing hurts but my head."

Dev crawled backward, rose to his knees, and hauled her out. He stood, dragging her with him. She subsided in a hoop of skirts. Time was short. The flames would soon begin blistering along the wooden floorboards. He scooped her up and settled her over his shoulder. "We're off. Hold onto me." He made his way to the door as she grasped his belt at the back.

Outside, he sucked in fresh air and then put her on her feet. "Can you stand?"

She swayed for a moment, breathing deeply. "Thank you, thank you. The children. I gotta find them."

He put one arm around her waist, supporting her down the laneway. "They knew the woman who took them." Glancing up, he saw her three children hurtling down the lane.

"Mum, Mum."

Mrs. Lock gathered the three in her arms, patted each little head, and kissed each little face. He waited long enough to smile, hearing the sullen crash of the fire bell. Clearly, the wagon was nearby. The city fire station was only two blocks away. Banging the smoke out of his shirt, he pelted back up the lane to Rundle Street.

The fire-wagon horses stood, tails flicking, eyes showing white. Firemen dressed in heavy canvas ran, pulling out the hose, unraveling the folded length, while volunteers stood helplessly waiting. Dev stood back, assessing the damage. The veranda of the pastry shop was now engulfed in flames, and had begun to drop blackened slat by slat. The other side lurked in smoke, awaiting the same fate.

Dev watched, knowing the adjoining space had been untenanted for a few weeks but as he stared through the smoldering flare, he noticed a sign.

"Wenna's Place," he said to the nearest bystander. "How long has that sign been there? I thought the shop was empty."

"The shoemaker moved out coupla weeks ago. People aren't buying so many good shoes nowadays. That's the new tenant."

"Wenna. My wife's name is Wenna." Dev suddenly lost his breath. "What does the shop sell?"

The man turned to the woman beside him. "Some sort of lady stuff, isn't it?"

The woman nodded. "The owner does lady's hair. She doesn't usually open up until nine, so she won't be in there yet."

Snow arriving, huffing. "Morning, Mr. Courtney. I'm wondering if anyone has seen Maisie." He glanced around at the bystanders.

Dev shook his head, confused. "Here?"

"She works for your wife now."

"My wife." Devon sprang forward. Wenna. His Wenna.

Chapter 20

Ducking under the thick canvas hose, Dev leapt out of the way of a red-faced fireman and raced toward the door of Wenna's Place. Flames leapt from the adjoining shop, eating through the boards lining the veranda. This morning, his wife had dressed in service black. He needed to make sure she hadn't arrived for work yet; the fire had started a wall away. In a bare five minutes, that side of the building had been engulfed. This side, already hot, would burn faster.

He grabbed at the metal door handle and sucked air through his teeth. With no time to experience pain, he kicked in the smoldering wood. The frame crashed against the wall. Inside, smoke curled around the ceiling, an ominous premonition of the devastation to follow. A blast had torn apart a partition near the entrance, exposing splintered lengths of pine. He hurried around a broken chair lying his path, and then another. Shards of glass crunched beneath his feet. The smoke swirled above, sinking to a mere foot above his head.

Breathing through his fingers, he scanned the area behind. One end of a long red gum shelf had crashed onto the floor. Before he could check behind the door that closed off the back of the shop, he heard, "Devon!"

Almost directly behind him, he spotted Wenna, dust-covered and crouched under fractured plaster and lathe. He exhaled in relief, bounding to her, taking her precious face into his hands. He tried to lift her to her feet, but she resisted, clinging to the frame of the partition.

"Maisie's hurt," she said in a dusty, husky voice. Her anxious gaze left him and concentrated on the figure he could barely see under the fractured mess of wood. "I can't get her out by myself."

"Are *you* hurt?" He wanted to snatch her into his arms and never let her go.

She shook her head, her one long plait swinging with the force of her denial. "It's my fault. I asked her to come early."

"It's not your fault, my love. It's the gas supply. Move aside. I'll deal with this."

Eyes glossy with panic, she stared up at him. "You can't manage the weight alone."

"I can as soon as you let me get at the wall." The ceiling above creaked ominously.

Her face pale, she crawled back a few feet.

With strength he hadn't known he possessed, he heaved up the partition, crashing the section back into the middle of the room. The remaining wooden chairs vibrated to the four corners of the room. "Leave now, Wenna." He dropped to his knees beside Maisie, who lay breathing but unconscious.

Wenna stood, her hands cupping her lower face, her eyes wide and glossy, staring at the other woman. "Is she still alive?"

"Yes. Go. We'll be right behind you."

She stood her ground, her expression uncomprehending.

He didn't have time for explanations. Leaning forward, he slid his hands under Maisie's inert body and rose to his feet. While Wenna watched, her face tight, he let Maisie's feet drop to the floor. Then, he bent his knees and flopped her over his shoulder. "Done. Let's go."

Wenna galvanized into action. She moved so fast that the hem of her gown swept up an ember as she disappeared around the front counter. Behind her, smoke rushed down from the ceiling, as if thrown in fistfuls by an angry god.

"The door frame is on fire." She reappeared, her fist over her mouth, and coughing. "We can't get out that way."

"We'll try the back."

"I don't have a key for the door into the side street. If we go into the back room, we'll be trapped. We have to leave by the front."

He prayed silently. "No choice, then. I'll go through first with Maisie. Follow closely behind me. Hold onto my belt." On the way to the door, he kicked at burning furniture, trying to make a safer path for Wenna.

The counter had begun to burn too. The flames crackled insidiously. A crash outside rattled the building. People shouted. Fear and sweat prickled down his spine. His eyes stinging from the ash and dust, he gasped for fresh air. Maisie groaned. He waited, coiled by the entrance, watching for a break in the crackling flares. Wenna stood so close that her breath whispered onto his neck. She believed that he would push through. Her trust made him fireproof.

He glanced through the empty window frame at the eerie pink smoke haze. "Now or never. Crouch as low as you can," he said to her, his voice hoarse. He couldn't crouch because of the weight on his shoulders. He had to get the women outside before the smoke choked them all. "Hold onto me and we'll run together."

"Together," she said in a shaky whisper. Her knuckles pressed into his skin of his back, so tight was her grip.

His arm rigid against the back of Maisie's knees, he took one last glance into Wenna's eyes and leapt through the flames, feeling the drag of her on his belt behind him.

A collective cheer arose from the watching crowd.

He landed upright, leaning forward so that he could ease Maisie off his shoulder. Two men relieved him of her weight. Hands pounded the smoke from his lungs as loud voices sounded in his ears. He snatched up Wenna and hugged her, pressing his cheek against her hot face.

She coughed, pushing at him, but he couldn't let her go.

"Damned woman," he said, nuzzling into her smoky hair. "You scared the devil out of me."

"How did you know I was there?" She struggled against him.

And still he couldn't release her. He stared at every wonderful inch of her soot-smeared face, his heart a puddle in his chest. "I didn't. Snow was worried about Maisie. Then I saw the shop was called Wenna's Place. Two and two. Thank God I found you, my love."

Her expression seemed to flatten, and she nodded. "Wenna's Place. My shop. All my money, gone in an instant. And Maisie ... oh, God, Maisie." Her mouth loose, she glanced toward the stretcher where Maisie had been placed.

A trail of smoke wafted up from the hem of her gown. "You can see Maisie later. First ..." With a determined grip, he dragged her over to the wheeled fire pump, where two volunteers worked up a sweat, alternately pushing on a two-handled bar. Volunteer trained, like every able-bodied male in the street, he called out, "Lads, stop for a moment and spread a little water over here."

The first nudged the second, and both ceased their exertions. The three men holding hoses looked back from Wenna's Place, where the main stream of water currently aimed, to see the problem. In an instant, the rapidly dwindling stream poured over Dev and Wenna instead, dowsing them. "Yo. That's enough, that's enough," he said, his words spluttering from a head doused with water. Relief made him grin. Having his usually neat wife drenched made him laugh with relief.

Wenna stared at him, leaning back, her eyes dark in her pale face. "It is more than enough." Her voice cracked.

"You were afire, Missus. Courtney here got you put out."

"And almost got himself put out, too." Dev glanced down at his soaked clothes, old and thin, and clinging to him like a second skin. Modesty be damned. "But not quite. Now, my love." He took her by her waist and pulled her closer. When she looked into his eyes, he cupped her wonderful face in his hands and gently kissed her. "My love," he repeated. "I almost lost you. I had no idea you were in that shop. Imagine what might have happened if Snow had not told me about your business."

As if on cue, Snow appeared through the smoke and gloom. "Looks like Maisie will recover. She's wakin' up. Thank the Lord you found 'em."

Dev lifted his head. "Thank the Lord you told me what Wenna has been up to. I wouldn't have gone in if I hadn't suspected she might be there."

Snow dropped his gaze. "She didn't want you to know about the shop. Thought a gent like you wouldn't like his woman to work."

"Is that true?" He kept his wife in the circle of his arms.

"No. I opened the shop to show you who I am."

His hands began to shake. Delayed reaction, no doubt. Wenna had been running a business. She thought he needed money. If he had loaded her with the riches she deserved, she wouldn't have been in a shop that was burning down. Her fault, she'd said about Maisie's predicament. No, his fault. The day he had married Wenna, he had made a commitment. He should have told her everything, including the size of his wallet. "I know who you are."

"Yes. A redheaded servant. That's why you married me. Admit it."

He wet his lips, trying to clear a throat that felt as if he had swallowed a hedgehog. Her words hurt, being somewhat related to the truth. "Strictly speaking, I married you because you wanted to go to Cornwall."

"Garn. He's crazy in love with you. Anyone could see that. Ran into a burning building to get you out."

"He didn't know I was in there, Mr. Snow. He told me so himself."

"He thinks the world of you. We all think the world of you. You're a woman in a thousand. You gave Maisie and a few other women the chance of a better life. We need people like you in the colony. People with ideas."

"I almost lost Maisie in that building." She shivered in his arms.

"Tell her you're crazy-mad in love with her."

The shouts in the street, the pall of the smoke, and the pelt of the water retreated to a hazy background as he gazed into his wife's seeking eyes. Her hair hung dark and lank over her face, and her gown streamed with water, but the flare at the hem had died. "I'm crazy-mad in love with you," he said in a voice gruff with tenderness.

"I'm soaked to the bone and I need to see how Maisie is." She dropped her gaze.

Reminded of the other woman, Dev gave Snow a rueful smile, placed his arm around his wife's waist, and took her to the stretcher where Maisie lay holding her head. The two hugged, reassuring each other. Maisie squeezed his fingers for a few moments, and finally Wenna took note of her own appearance. She glanced down at her clinging gown, and looked up at him, her face a picture of desolation.

"It's only a black uniform," he said, wondering if any man had ever learned how to understand a woman. Only the Lord knew if she believed her "redheaded servant" comment. "We can afford to buy you better."

She flared up in an instant, his feisty, indomitable, beautiful wife. "I've just lost everything I own, and you are still talking about new gowns." Turning, she marched off toward the lodgings.

At a loss, he followed.

* * * *

Though Wenna was upset enough to tear her gown to bits if only she could, she needed Devon to unhook the soaked material first. The moment he loosened her stays, she banished him from the bedroom. He took his fresh clothes with him, saying he could dry himself off in the kitchen. And good riddance too. He thought of nothing but getting under her skirts—always had. After those kisses in the street in front of everyone, she knew he had no scruples. She could tell from the expression in his eyes that he would toss her onto the bed as soon as look at her.

He had said he was crazy-mad in love with her on order, all for show. He couldn't love a woman who would rather work than sit at home. He should have left her to die. Then he could marry an aristocratic beauty who would know how to play the role of his wife.

Tears rolled down her face. She could never love anyone but him, no matter how mismatched a couple they were. He was a gentleman, born and bred, and she was decidedly working class. However, though his motives were truly reprehensible, he had married her. In order to honor her vows, such as they were, she hardened her face, blotted her ridiculous tears, patted color into her cheeks, and donned her floral bodice and russet skirt.

After drying her hair, she braided a thick coronet. She knew she presented herself well, having had years of practice at presenting others well. Perhaps she could make herself look like a lady, but the thought of living as a lady in an aristocratic household terrified her. England and humiliation awaited her, but she would never let her fears show.

Despite her intent, her knees wobbled. No one in the aristocracy would accept a miner's daughter as a suitable wife for the son of an earl. If she thought owning a shop would set up the hairs on her husband's neck, her mere existence would prickle him in England, and she had made a commitment to live there. She elevated her chin. If she produced the heir she had promised to her husband, likely he would be happy enough to keep her hidden away in the country. A woman who had not even tried to breed an heir deserved her husband's utter contempt.

With her transgressions heavy on her shoulders, she trod down to the sitting room. Devon rose to his feet as she entered. Those sorts of manners were inbred.

"I used a sponge," she said, clasping her hands behind her. Pride kept her gaze on his.

"Fair enough. If you prefer sponges to washcloths, I will buy you an ocean-full."

She blinked. "So that I wouldn't have a baby. It's a contraceptive device."

"You should have told me. I wouldn't have needed to be so careful."

"Don't you mind?" Eyebrows drawn together, she stared at him.

"Having a baby seemed rather precipitate, bearing in mind the months of sea travel ahead of us. You might be one of those sickly sorts of females for all I know."

She stared at him, at a loss. "We made a bargain. I was supposed to have a child you could present to your father as his heir." A great lump formed in her throat. "Your father, the earl, who would be appalled that you had chosen a former lady's maid for that honor. He would be right. I didn't honor our bargain. You have no choice other than to divorce me." She squeezed her hands into fists, remembering to stand tall.

He rubbed his fingers over his jaw. "I have no grounds. You have never refused your favors."

"Yes, I have."

"You had good reason." He held up his hand to stop her speaking. "I have been the worst of husbands. I deserved to be banished from your bed."

She paused, staring at him, puzzled. "Admittedly, you held your secrets tight."

"As did you," he said smoothly. "I didn't know you were out earning money."

"I thought I had to." Indignant, she placed her hands on her hips, instantly ready to argue.

He grinned. "I have more to tell you, my love, but the fire is still raging and I must go back to help."

"If you are going back, then so am I."

"Firefighting is a man's job."

"And a woman's job is to stay at home, tending to her lord and master. You're right. I should be confined to the home for life. My father had the same idea about a woman's place. I thought I could prove him wrong. Instead, I lost my business and put one of my best workers in danger." Her lips wobbled.

Devon drew a breath, his expression serious. "Firefighting is a matter of strength. You've already seen you couldn't lift the wall off Maisie. If that had required a brain and a will, the wall would have been flung aside. The wall required mere brute strength, such as a man has. If you want to help, put that brain and will of yours to work. For now, I must go back. Promise me you won't do anything to endanger yourself. I love you too much to lose you now."

Wenna's jaw loosened. Words of love came easily to his tongue. Hers had tied. "I'll be careful," she answered, her voice husky. She stood watching as he turned to the door. "Mrs. Lock, the pie maker—did she get out in time?" Her mouth went dry as she thought of the widow's children.

"She and the children are safe," he called in a fading voice as he sped out the lobby. The door smacked shut behind him.

Wenna clapped her hands together in front of her nose and breathed through the spaces between her fingers, thinking. Now that her home and business had gone, Mrs. Lock would need accommodation. Mr. Snow would have a room for her upstairs, and he might let her bake her pies in his kitchen. If not, she could use Wenna's kitchen. She could even have the useless waste of space that was Wenna's sitting room for her shop while she found another.

Her head awhirl with plans, Wenna left for the hotel across the street, wanting to discuss with the waitresses the serving of tea and food to the firefighters.

In a trice, the women sprang into action. Maisie chalked the hotel's board outside with the words "Aid for the Firefighters," and women started pouring into the hotel with offers of help. Mr. Snow was overwhelmed with the largesse, which Wenna organized into plates of food. Before too long, a cart with tea pourers was trundling along Rundle Street toward the fires. While she worked with the volunteers who arrived with bread and cheese and fruit, Wenna's head buzzed with a single thought.

Devon had said, "I love you too much." He risked his life to save a redheaded maid with an uneven temper and a sharp tongue. Her. He loved *her.*

* * * *

Darkness had fallen before the last of the fires were extinguished. Exhausted, Dev opened the lobby door and trod into the lodgings, not expecting to find his wife awaiting him in the kitchen. Tales of her doings had been related to him all day. She had been here, there, and everywhere, making sure each firefighter had been adequately supplied with food and drink. She had also found housing for people whose homes had been lost. He couldn't have been more proud of her.

He had married an outspoken feisty redhead because he had wanted her beautiful body—in more ways than one. Her body was not the whole sum of the woman he now knew and loved. She had a brain, a will of her own, and more than a scrap of ambition.

Her smile beamed at him as she turned. "This would be a day we would never want to repeat." She stood in the kitchen, elegant, self-possessed, and utterly confident. "Could you use another cup of tea?"

"Please." He sat at the table while she poured hot water into the teapot.

"I have some explaining to do." She brought a mug and the teapot over to the table and sat with him. "First, though, I am aware that risked your life for me, and I thank you. If you hadn't, Maisie would be dead too, for I couldn't get her out. And do you know why she was in the shop?" She raised her gaze to his.

"You employ her. Apparently you employ other women, too," he said in a gentle tone. He could see she forced her words. "I'll have to ask you in exactly what capacity. The secret was well hidden from me."

"I was bored." She placed her hands on the table, meshing her fingers together. "I couldn't sit in these lodging with nothing to do when I thought we needed money. I also thought my grandparents needed money. Money controls my life. Yes, I know now it doesn't control yours, but I've been working from a very young age to support myself." Her gaze flickered and fell to her fingers.

He reached out and covered her hands with his. "I wish I had known you were worrying about money. I wish I had asked. I wish I had given you enough. But I hadn't. I wish I had given you a house and servants, but I only saw my own goals."

"And so," she said, stroking his fingers with her thumb, "I'd had an idea years ago of going into business for myself. I worked for rich women who could have their gowns, hats, and hair styled every single day by a personal maid. Poor women can't afford the same service, but in shops they are given advice. For instance, whenever a hat shape changes, a hairstyle needs to change. I set up a salon to style ladies' hair in the back of the hat shop."

"Which explains why you clung to those black gowns of yours. You're very enterprising, Wenna. I knew I had married a woman with pluck. I hope you will forgive me for being such a miserly fool."

She squeezed his hand. "And then, when I heard you tell Nick that you had married me to humiliate your father..."

He frowned. "When did I do that? Not, surely, the night he brought me home?"

"That very night. You said you married me because I was a redheaded servant and your father would be properly paid back for not letting you marry the woman you love."

"I thought I told Nick how very lucky that event was, because I then met you."

"No, you didn't say that. Not in my hearing."

He kissed her hand. "I love you, Wenna. I loved you then and I love you now. I definitely told Nick so. He said I was lucky to have found you; *that* I certainly remember. But if, in my drunken state, I said I married you because you were a redheaded servant...no, I didn't, in fact. I married you because I wanted you. If I couldn't have you without marriage, then—well, then I saw the irony of your hair and position, and that my father would think I had remained true to character."

She glanced away. "I remind you of the woman you love."

"*Loved.* Initially, yes, but you are nothing like Jenny. She accepted marriage to a farmer. You are persistent. If you wanted me, you would fight for me. You are brave and strong."

"Brave." She shook her head. "You've seen how I reacted when confronted with the social set. You've seen how I avoid them. I'll be useless in England. I don't know how to be a countess." Her gaze again lifted to his.

"Oh, you're brave, all right." He met her gaze and smiled. "No woman has ever given me a direct order. I fell for you the moment you told me to distract Patricia. I knew you could handle my father, and he would respect you as much as I do."

"If you had planned to show me off as your wife, you would have given me a wedding ring."

He turned over her hand and kissed her palm. "I'm a fool. I should have given you a token, but my mother's jewelry wasn't sent to me, and I have to retrieve it. When I do, you will have the perfect ring, her family ring. She was the last of her line, but for me. We will be the first of hers."

"And you love me, or so you said."

Leaning back, he tried to read the expression on her face. "But for you, I wouldn't be planning to stay in England. I would come back here as soon as I've settled my affairs. But you want to live in England because of your grandparents."

She shook her head, her smile wry. "You can't come back here if you are the heir."

He scraped his chair out from the table and took her hands. "Sit on my knee. I want you close. I have quite a bit of explaining to do, and I will feel better confessing all if I have you in my arms. Pity me, my love. I've had a wretch of a day, so far."

"I've had an unusual day too." Her expression demure and her mouth soft, she stood, allowing him to pull her onto his lap.

He wrapped her in his arms and rested his chin on her head. His chest expanded with his first deep breath. "My father died last year. I didn't know this until last week. At the same time I found out that my brother didn't die, after all. I'm *his* heir, but as he is only thirty-two, you can bet he'll marry as soon as he can, even if only to cut me out of the succession. The moment he does and produces a child, I'm free." He toyed with her fingers. "I need to go to England to settle my properties—but I love this land, Wenna. I could still support your grandparents if we could come back here."

"I thought we were going because you wanted to be in your own country."

"Are you hinting you might compromise?" He held his breath.

She cupped his cheek with her palm. "My grandparents died last year, too. I found out not long after we married, but because we had a bargain, I didn't see the need to tell you. You might have thought I had changed my mind about going."

"Your grandparents died?" Air whooshed out of his lungs. "So, have you changed your mind about living in England?"

She nodded. "If we could leave very soon and return very soon, that would suit me well. Being plain 'Mrs. Courtney' will also suit me very well. I don't know anyone in England. I would be happier here."

"I wish we could leave tomorrow." Scooping his arm under her knees, he rose to his feet, pressing his sweat-stained face against her soft and fragrant skin. "But first—if we're not making babies, what is my excuse for throwing you into bed right now?"

"I'm sure you can think of one." She circled her arms around his neck. "But you should put me down. I don't want to exhaust you before I've had my way with you."

He let her feet drop to the floor, but kept her body tight against his. "Lord, I'm tired," he said into her neck "I haven't the energy to make babies tonight. We'll just have to make love instead. Well, I will. I don't know if you love me."

Her breath whispered on his cheek as she leaned forward. "You'll know if I do or don't, very soon."

* * * *

Although most of the firefighters had gone home, people still gathered in the street. Murmurs of conversations drifted through the window with the stale smoke. Wenna lay on her side in bed, one arm across Devon's naked chest. "I thought you said you were tired. I thought you would fall asleep straight after, as you usually do."

"I'm waiting for the announcement."

"Take it as said." She leaned over his and kissed his neck.

"I want to hear you say 'I love you.'"

"I love you. There. That's done. Oh, dear God, I love you so much Devon, probably from the first time you laughed at me instead of being offended by my words. I do offend people, I know. When can we see inside your—*our* house? Why don't we move our things there until the ship arrives? I could set up this place for Maisie to run as a business while we are in England—"

"Wenna, Wenna. I appreciate your forward thinking, but let's discuss this in the morning." He loomed over her and dropped a kiss on her lips. "Our ship should be here in a couple of weeks. We can move out of here, but I don't think you will have time to get a new business running before we go."

"If I don't, I'll be leaving too many people in the lurch. If you help me, we can do it."

"You don't need to earn money, sweetheart. We're rich. When we come back, you can busy yourself with charities and sewing circles, like the other ladies."

"I would be hopelessly bored."

"I can find ways to keep you occupied." He gave her an evil grin.

"You'll need to let me out of bed sometime, and it would be a shame to have had a good idea that never comes to fruition."

He touched her face with the pads of his fingers. "I suspect you'll end up training many women to style hair and to dress as well as you do, if only by example."

"What if that's not enough?"

"Perhaps a school, a training place for women who need a trade. We could sponsor some sort of facility like that. Now, go to sleep."

"Devon?"

"What?"

She relaxed in his arms. "I love you." Her eyes closed. He accepted her ideas; he saw her as his equal. She was his wife, not a servant. He was her husband, not an aristocrat.

"I love you."

She didn't need to be as good as a man. Like a man, she only needed to be the best she could be.

EPILOGUE
1866
(Two years later)

Balancing her six-month-old son, Edris, on her hip, Wenna leaned against the ship's railing, gazing at the Adelaide Hills. "As they say, the view is green as far as the eye can see."

Devon smiled. "You were born in the most beautiful country in the world."

She watched the first load of passengers disembarking from the rowboats onto the fine white sands of Glenelg. Later, the ship would unload goods at Port Adelaide, but most people who reached this perfect spot didn't want to wait. "I know that, now I have a comparison. Cornwall was certainly picturesque, though."

"My brother was astonished to hear you say that. He has quite a parochial view of the place, despite living in India for a few years."

"All his views are parochial. Imagine him telling one of the farmers how to repair his wagon? The poor man actually promised to do so. What would an earl know about repairing a wagon? I'll bet he's never held a hammer in his life."

"The farmer might listen to my brother, but he'd go his own way as soon as my brother was out of sight."

"Which he should have said. I'd hate to think myself better than someone because I was an earl. I'd only want to be better because I *was* better."

He turned to her. "I agree that you should earn your way in the world. It's your worth that counts, not the worth of your parents, not the fact that your mother was a washer woman."

"Nor the fact that your father was an earl. I've come as far as you."

"Did I ever take advantage of the fact that my father was an earl?"

"The advantage is inbuilt."

"And now shared with you, too."

"Next you'll have me patronizing the poor backward colonials." She laughed.

He gave an exaggerated shiver. "Your two years away have taught you much. I fear for the colonial society when you start organizing your tea parties."

Wenna laughed. "That was fun, though. Now we're here, it's back to work as usual. I can't wait to see your vines. Producing already, Finn says. And Maisie has a staff of four. I won't know where to begin."

Devon sighed. "Could we unpack first, my precious love?"

See where the South Landers series began...

Charlotte

A marriage most inconvenient...

After losing his first love in childbirth, Nicholas Alden knows with a great certainty that he must never be a father. But to be a husband is a very different matter—mandated by South Australian society, necessary for his family name. So when he meets beautiful social climber Charlotte, he believes he has found a wife he can keep at arm's length. He is terribly wrong.

Born on the wrong side of the sheets, Charlotte hopes Nick can prop up her reputation long enough to secure a suitable match for her beloved cousin. She assumes that is all she can ask of her new husband—until they succumb to a night of uninhibited passion. Her heart is won in his embrace, but he doesn't know the truth of her scandalous parentage. If he did, all would be lost.

Still, somehow, Charlotte dares to hope that her match of convenience could become something more. It is a reckless gamble, but the prize—a marriage of blazing lifelong desire—is one worth any risk...

Prologue

Adelaide, South Australia, 1865

Nicholas Alden wandered down the torch-lit path to the middle of the garden, a stone paved area surrounded by clipped hedges. Glancing around, he chose the only available seat, an uncomfortable looking bench. A piano tinkled in the distance, competing with the overriding voices in the ballroom and a screeching violin or two.

He took a long draught from his wine glass, glancing briefly at the flickering stars before trying to shut out the world. The light clip of footsteps caused him to open his eyes. A hazy shape dressed in white stood in front of him—ah, yes, the beautiful, well-behaved debutante who'd sat beside him during the pre-ball dinner. He lifted his eyebrows in query, again appreciating her lovely figure, her porcelain skin, her huge eyes—and the slender fingers that moved to either side of her neckline grasped her exquisite gown and ripped.

He brought his glass to his lips and quaffed while she stood, her gown asunder and her face expressionless.

"You have my attention," he said, hoping she would pull aside her chemise. A view of her pretty white breasts would likely be enjoyable.

She stared straight at him, opened her lovely mouth, and screamed, almost hitting a high C.

He massaged his forehead. "Was that really necessary?"

Her perfect face softened momentarily. "You know it was. It had to be done, and I'm sorry, but I'm in trouble." She sat beside him, her hands neatly clasped in her lap. "But if you help me, I'll help you. I know about you, you see."

"The whole world knows about me." Giving a long, deep sigh, he stretched out his legs and crossed his ankles. *He* didn't have a reputation to lose. Her attempt to compromise him would do her no good at all.

"If someone doesn't marry me soon, I'll be in dire straits."

He covered a yawn. "I'm afraid you'll have to find someone else. I'm not a marrying man." The next act of her tired scenario would now play out, but not her way.

"I know, but you're just right for me. If only... Oh, I could bear a disgraced life for myself, but not for two of us. Mr. Hawthorn is a cad to have ruined...."

His hazy mind latched on to the name Hawthorn. Footsteps pounded along the slate path. She kept talking, talking, talking, while he concentrated on Tony Hawthorn and his wife. The man had seemed perfectly matched. Who would have guessed?

Nicholas had barely lifted his chin from his chest before the beauty's plain companion, Miss Someone, appeared, making far more noise than the beauty. She grabbed the foolish creature into her arms.

"Your gown, your gown," she wailed, as if more worried about the cost than the reveal.

Her recriminations continued while Nicholas polished off every last drop in his glass. Predictably, others arrived, among them his friend, Luke. Nick's head ached even more. He wanted them all to go away.

Strangely, the beauty didn't make any more fuss, and she kept saying the whole thing had been an accident—not his fault. Before he knew where he was, he was grabbed by the arm and told by Luke he would marry her. Annoyed, he swatted Luke away.

He needed another drink, and he'd already decided the beauty's offer would suit him.

Chapter 1

Charlotte Alden bounded off the central stairway. The morning sun glittered red through the leadlight panels surrounding the main entrance. Bursting with her news, she sped across the hall to the library. Sarah, her only relative, sat sprawled on the lush carpet. Tumbled books surrounded her, and she rubbed her head.

Charlotte stopped. "What happened?"

"Nothing." Sarah glanced up with a frown.

Charlotte breathed out. "I thought the books had toppled off the shelves and hit you."

"I've been moving them around." Sarah pulled a pencil from the knot of her apricot hair and chewed the end. "I was wondering how I ought to sort them."

"You normally do your wondering on a chair."

"The floor's larger than the book table. What do you think? Should I file these by author or subject? I've tried each, and I still don't know which is best."

Charlotte picked up the nearest book and examined the cover. "Don't tell me you're going to read each one first."

"I couldn't possibly. If you wanted to read a story, how would you choose one? Yes, I know. You don't want to read a story."

Charlotte laughed. "When would I find the time?" She watched her cousin pick up a book and scan the contents. "Our visiting cards have been printed," she said, trying to sound casual. Now married into a wealthy family, she could give Sarah her chance to find a husband, one who would love her and give her adorable children for Charlotte to dote upon. "We will be expected to make morning calls soon."

Sarah moved two books to a pile of five. Outside, three squawking rainbow lorikeets fluttered past the window.

Charlotte waited, hoping for interest. "Perhaps in the next few weeks?"

"Perhaps," Sarah said, holding up a book covered with pale orange watered silk and marked with exquisite oriental writing. "Look at this one. I'm keeping it aside for later."

Charlotte took the volume. "It's full of illustrations. Is it Chinese?"

"It's from Japan. Look closely at the pictures."

"They're lovely, Sarah. The ladies are wearing such beautifully patterned fabrics. Look at this clever design. Such intricate...oh." She clapped the pages together.

Sarah giggled. "I'm sure your father-in-law doesn't know he owns this, or he wouldn't have let me catalogue his books."

Charlotte couldn't blink. "I didn't know people printed such things."

"Why not? If people do them."

In the last picture Charlotte had scanned, the sight of the man's naked body had shocked her, let alone the female lying beneath him with her legs apart. "They do?" Her mouth dried.

"You should know."

For a moment, only the ticking of the clock broke the silence in the room. "But I can't discuss that, of course," Charlotte said, a slight constriction in her voice.

Almost two weeks ago, desperate for financial security, she had married Mr. Nicholas Alden, the only son of Mr. Alfred Alden of Alden House, Burnside, and Alden View in Stirling. A careful selection, Nicholas had the requisite income to support Sarah and herself, but Charlotte had chosen him because the façade of their marriage would benefit him as well. He had no interest in females. Adelaide's bustling society, however, didn't know that.

"The luckiest day of your blessed life was the day you met him," Sarah said with envy in her voice. "I wish a man like him would fall into *my* lap. Rich and indulgent. What more could a woman want?"

Charlotte tapped her forefinger onto her chin. "I'll admit the appeal of a man knocked unconscious with a cricket ball is hard to resist, but you know he didn't propose because of my skills with a cold compress."

"Just the opposite." Sarah made a face. "After you were caught with him, half naked."

Charlotte shrugged. "A gentleman would offer marriage, and he did."

But no more than marriage, of course. Nicholas had not, up until now, proved he remembered her name, which didn't bother her a bit. He had never laid one of his misleadingly masculine hands on her. However, not even Sarah, her closest companion, knew Charlotte had to use her knowledge of his secret life before he agreed to marry her. Like the rest of the world, Sarah assumed that Nicholas was simply a too ardent suitor.

"And soon we'll find the perfect husband for you as well."

"One who, I hope, will propose to me in the proper way."

Hearing the reproof in her cousin's tone, Charlotte nodded. "Decorum certainly has its place." She moved to drop the Japanese book on Sarah's pile, but at that moment, a presence loomed in the doorway. Embarrassed by the material she held, she hid the book behind her back instead.

Nicholas Alden was beautiful. Wearing his crisp brown hair fashionably disheveled, he stood propped against the doorjamb. His wide shoulders and lean hips made his unbuttoned evening jacket and his waistcoat of brocaded emerald look especially stylish. Charlotte experienced her usual intake of breath disguised by her carefully oblivious expression.

As if he had all the time in the world, he crossed one elegant ankle with another, aiming a thick-lashed impartial glance at Charlotte. "Are you stealing a book?" His voice was deep, and his tone, as usual, bored.

She breathed out. "Of course not."

"What are you hiding behind your back?"

"A book I was about to give to Sarah."

"But seeing me made you change your mind?" With a suspicious expression on his face, he moved toward her.

She took a step back, trying to pass the palmed pages to Sarah who glanced at her with a look of puzzlement.

Nicholas reached out to take the book. Charlotte swung her arm around, evading him. He grabbed her instead, holding her body against his, reaching for the book, which she lifted high over her head, even farther away from him. Not for the world did she want a man with his bent to think she would scan titillating pictures. Face-to-face with him, she noted his mocking expression.

"Come now." His breath had the aroma of mint. "Let me see."

"Let me go."

His mouth tilted. "No." He settled his body closer to hers. The long length of him fitted against her as intimately as her undergarments. His hand slid to the small of her spine.

Inexplicably, her body relaxed against his, and his eyes changed. The blue-green froze. The moment expanded into a silent challenge, which she realized she shouldn't even try to win.

"Take it." She swallowed. Her whole body thrummed with excitement, and she hoped he couldn't tell that he had such an embarrassing effect on her.

"Oh, that I could, my tempting treasure," he murmured. Sliding his hand along her arm, he reached his objective. Suddenly, he let her go. He opened the book and turned page after page while she watched, her face hot.

"You were about to give this to Sarah?"

"I was about to put it onto the pile." Her voice sounded thready.

"You said you wanted to give it to Sarah. It's hardly suitable for a young female, is it?"

"I, um, no."

He touched the tip of her nose with his finger as if reprimanding her. "I'll be taking luncheon with you today."

Sarah rose to her feet. "That will be nice. If Charlotte wants me to have the book, I'll take it." She stared wide-eyed at him, her hands pressed prayer-like in front of her mouth.

"Certainly not. If my wife needs to amuse herself with these illustrations, I'll keep the collection safe for her in our rooms." He left with the book.

Sarah fanned her hand in front of her face. "That was a little risqué. You shouldn't let him fondle you that way in front of others, though, Lolly, no matter how he feels about you."

"I could hardly stop him without embarrassing us both." Charlotte placed her cool palms on her cheeks.

Sarah gave a resigned shrug. "I expect most women wouldn't want to stop him. He's the catch of the year."

Charlotte nodded. "A landed fish."

"A landed gentleman, which is far more important. You were born lucky."

"I know." Charlotte gave a rueful smile. She was the luckiest woman in the entire colony.

Nicholas could have repudiated her after she'd proposed her bargain. He could have resented her and made a snide remark, but he had resigned himself to marriage with no more than a close inspection of her face and a terse nod. She would never let him regret his generosity. Never.

"I couldn't have done better if I'd tried."

A crease formed between Sarah's eyebrows. "A bad beginning with a good end. But if I had such a handsome husband, I wouldn't let him out of my sight."

"'We think caged birds sing when indeed they cry.'"

"What?"

"It's something I read long ago. It had some meaning for me then, but I've forgotten the context. If Nicholas is staying, I must see the housekeeper and organize a more extensive meal. What would you like?"

Sarah waved a dismissive hand. "A peach. I'm not very hungry today."

"But you'll join us anyway?"

Sarah nodded and resumed sorting through the books, her way to contribute since she'd always talked of herself as a burden. Heaven knew she'd never had Charlotte's advantages—education at an expensive school and an opportunity to take her pick of the eligible bachelors. In a fair world, the cousins would have had an equal upbringing and an equal opportunity in life. Sarah could have that now.

Charlotte left for the housekeeper's room, still surprised by her body's untoward reaction when Nicholas had snatched her into his arms. Perhaps he would have preferred a man, but marriage protected him from accusations of the unimaginable act of *gross indecency*, now only a criminal offence rather than a capital one. She could certainly be loyal to a man who would never claim his husbandly rights, for in exchange she had security, the opportunity to be useful, and the chance one day to be a loving aunt. Since she didn't plan to exploit him again, one day he would like her, too.

Nothing she could do from now on would be as bad as compromising him.

* * * *

Nick changed quickly. He had spent the night with his gloriously infertile mistress and he needed daywear. For the past two weeks since his marriage, he'd spent every night with Beth, not wanting to be tempted by a stunningly beautiful, young wife who he could take if he wished. Judging by today, she would let him, despite her amusingly convenient assumption that he was a daisy.

He had married the most admired debutante of this season. Added to a pair of wide blue eyes was a captivating smile, a charming voice, and the sort of elegant curves that made a man's palms sweat. His body craved the marital rights he wouldn't take, but he couldn't let a devious twenty-year-old tempt him to risk siring a child again.

After attiring himself more suitably in brown striped trousers and a red tie, he walked down to the breakfast room.

One of the maids, bearing a tray full of food, stopped and smiled. "Mistress is having luncheon served in the dining room today, sir."

With a tilt of his eyebrows, he changed direction to the indicated place, a vast area blessed with two sets of multi-paned Georgian windows. The sun beamed in, lighting a room furnished mainly in heavy mahogany furniture and dull pink velvet. For the last few months, he and his father had eaten in the breakfast room, a smaller annex closer to the kitchen. Apparently, his young wife had greater pretensions.

"Good of you join us," his father, Alfred, said, his face set on harsh lines.

Like Nick, Alfred was tall. During the past years, his neatly trimmed beard had begun to fleck with gray, though his hair was still dark. Dressed as a country gentleman, he wore buff trousers and a brown jacket. "Can the racing fraternity spare you?"

Nick moved to the foot of the table. Charlotte, her dark hair perfectly knotted on the nape of her neck and wearing a smart layered crinoline, sat on his father's right. Plainly dressed Sara sat on his left.

"There's no meet today, otherwise, as you know, I wouldn't be here."

"Serve yourself from the side-table." His father eyed him. "There's food aplenty, though this little miss"—he indicated Sarah—"never eats luncheon."

The waif contemplated the empty plate in front of her, her mouth firm. "I'm not hungry. I said I only wanted a peach."

Nick rose to his feet and jerked the bell pull. "We'll have a peach," he said to the maid who answered.

"The peaches is preserved, as Cook told the mistress."

Nick caught Cousin Sarah's catlike glance. "Won't that do for you?"

Sarah nodded and heaved a sigh.

A manservant stepped into the doorway. "Your pardon. The coachman wants a word with Mr. Nicholas."

"Could you relay the message?" Nick shook out his table napkin.

"He says not."

"Send him in, then."

The coachman, Bookmaker Harvey, a stubby knowing fellow with gray side-whiskers, who had apparently been standing just out of sight, smacked his hat on his moleskins as the manservant retreated. "Got this letter here, Mr. Nicholas. And a horse."

"You're not considering bringing a horse into the house." Alfred almost rose to his feet.

"Got the horse outside. Got the letter here in my hand."

"Stay where you are. The ladies won't want your great dirty boots in the dining room."

Nick eyed Harvey's well worn but clean boots. "I'll see the letter." He perused the page signed by his friend of twenty years and massaged his forehead. "Walk the horse. I might send her back."

Alfred frowned. "Who would send you a horse?"

"Tony." Nick quickly scanned the papers that came with the letter. "He says Blue Bobbin jumped into the wrong paddock and met with an unsuitable mare." He lifted his glass of wine and finished half.

"Bound to happen." Alfred reached for the salt. "A ruddy great stallion like that. He belongs to Tony Hawthorn," he explained to Sarah and Charlotte. "Bred by his father. Been dead eight or so years—his father not the horse. He made a tidy sum on the stallion at the racetrack, Tony that is, and he put him out to stud. That's, er..." Glancing at Sarah, he cleared his throat. "Used him for breeding purposes."

"And in the intervening years, Tony has made a fortune from him. I've made a guinea or two as well." Nick finished his wine and refilled his glass. "His progeny are the best blood stock in the country, except, Tony says, for the mare outside. Her sire had a pedigree a mile long, but her dam was a hack. Tony thought Charlotte might like the mare for a riding horse." His jaw clamped.

Sarah gasped. "A horse. Charlotte, you've always wanted a horse of your own."

Charlotte sat unmoving. "Yes, I *have* always wanted a horse of my own. I happened to mention that once in conversation with Mr. Hawthorn."

"He is calling this a wedding present." Nick watched her with narrowed eyes, hoping she would have the good taste to reject the gift. Hawthorn ought to know better. His delightful wife would surely be hurt if she knew he was handing out gifts of livestock instead of leaving well enough alone.

"Is a horse a common wedding present?"

"Would you have preferred rubies?"

"I would rather have a horse than anything else in the world."

"And so, we will accept the gift, although you can hardly expect to ride."

Her eyebrows drawn, Charlotte met his gaze. "If you won't let me ride, I see no point in having a horse."

Nick, shrugging, turned to the coachman. "Stable the mare with the others."

At that moment, the fruit arrived. Cousin Sarah decided to out-stare her plate.

Nick glanced at her. "Not to your taste?"

She gave him a placating smile. "I'm sure it will be delicious."

Nick wondered why he had bothered. He didn't care whether she ate or not. Nor could he maintain interest in a conversation with his wife that appeared to be going nowhere. He quaffed his wine, made his apologies, then left, arriving at his club in the city center some half hour later.

Dixon, the owner, greeted him. "Lookin' for a meal or a bout, sir?"

"More like a fight," Nick said, still annoyed that he had been forced to accept Tony's reprehensible gift.

Dixon inclined his head and indicated the large gymnasium sited down a flight of stairs. Most of the light came from the high windows, leaving the walls lined with punching bags. A few were being treated to a pounding. Two boxing rings filled the center of the area. Currently, both rings were being used, and Dixon's bruisers were either idling or skipping the ropes to warm up for a bout with any likely club member. "You ain't been here for some weeks. How's your condition?" Ben, his usual sparring partner, asked.

"Middling."

The man grinned. "Best you work off your choler with a bag rather than me, then, Mr. Alden."

Nick nodded curtly and left for the dressing room where he stripped down to his smalls. When he returned to the main area, he bandaged his fists and worked up a sweat. He needed a drink but, apparently, Dixon had decided to serve only watered ale today. Nick downed two, which barely moistened his throat. Still irritable, he aimed a high hard punch at his bag, which was grabbed by two large hands.

A head appeared to one side—a head filled with carroty hair and brighter sideburns surrounding a strong-boned face usually described as interesting. "Work, you fairy. Stop playing at boxing."

Nick aimed a punch close to Luke Worthing's nose. "What did you call me?"

"Daisy. Sprite. Girly-boy." Luke, a friend since schooldays, dropped his hold on the bag. "Bastard."

"Your fortnight in the country didn't do much to improve your vocabulary." Nick shot a dismissive glance at Luke's hardy body. "Do a round with me. Though, perhaps you'd rather join me upstairs for a drink. A good sustaining bottle or two will solve more problems than a pounding."

Before Nick could take a step, Luke grasped his upper arm and swung him around. Encouraged by the color of his hair, Luke had a quick temper. "Not *my* problems. I don't drink to forget. I remember. And I remember exactly what you said on your wedding day, you bastard," he said, his voice oiled with anger. "You'd *known her for a couple of months.* Why in hell did I never know that?"

Nick shrugged.

Luke moved a step back, legs apart, his big hands clenched on his hips. "You made a fool of me," he said through his teeth. "She never even let me put my hand on hers."

"Apparently, one man at a time is enough for her."

"Apparently, when she no longer wanted to *know you*, you decided to force her."

"Do you want everyone to hear you?" Nick held Luke's gaze.

Luke snorted. "I can't imagine why you saw the need to mishandle her. The fact that you've consumed most of the grape-stock in the colony would excuse you to others, but not to me. Your behavior was disgraceful."

"The dear creature forgave me. Accept it."

"Whenever you appear, the dear creature sees nothing but a face that sends angels into spasms of jealousy." Luke half turned, a disgusted expression on his own face. "I hope you've saved her reputation by this marriage."

"Unless you've been gossiping, I presume so."

"Gossiping about what?" Luke's mouth clamped.

"Exactly." Nick unwound the bandages on his fists.

"I should have broken your damned nose that night instead of slinking off." Luke clenched his hands at his side. "But she already has enough people talking about her. Even now I can't believe she'd been conducting a secret relationship with a soak like you."

Nick raised his eyebrows. "Believe what you like. It makes no difference to me. Now, I'm off to find a bottle. I haven't seen a tall enough glass today."

Luke jammed his hands into his pockets, hunching. "Do you plan to play the faithful husband?"

"I don't intend to embarrass her."

"I ought to beat you to pulp."

Nick twisted his mouth. "Wait until I'm falling-down drunk, and you might have a better chance."

He left his friend staring daggers after him and strolled upstairs for more convivial company. Charlotte couldn't have forced him to marry her, despite deliberately involving him in a compromising situation. He didn't believe in honor or duty.

He did, however, believe in justice. His family deserved an heir. His great-grandfather in England had been an only child, as had his grandfather and his father. Nick, as well, was an only child, not that his mother hadn't tried to rectify this situation. She had conceived four babies after him. All had died before birth. His mother had died with the last.

If Nick turned up his toes without issue, his father's great effort in making his fortune in the colony of South Australia would be entirely wasted. The least Nick could do was continue the family line, though with a twist. Charlotte was already carrying an heir, but not of Nick's faulty seed.

The gift of the horse and the attached story of the wandering stallion had finally confirmed Nick's reluctant suspicion that the next Alden heir had been bred by hardier stock, that of Tony Hawthorn.

Meet the Author

From art student to stylist, to nurse and midwife, Virginia Taylor's life has been one illogical step to the next, each one leading to the final goal of being an author. When she can tear herself away from the computer and the waiting blank page, she immerses herself in arts and crafts, gardening, or, of course, cooking. You can visit her website at www.virginia-taylor. com, and tweet her @authorvtaylor.